Acclaim for Craig Nova's

C R U I S E R S

"Subtle, understated, and humane. . . . The tension build[s] to a thrillerlike assault. . . . Nova never diminishes his psychological insights by making them explicit. . . . He blasts apart [clichés with] the intelligence of his characterizations and the sheer, unforced eloquence of his prose."
—*The Washington Post Book World*

"An absolutely riveting, page-turning drama."
—Chris Bohjalian, author of *Before You Know Kindness*

"[An] ambitious, multilayered novel. . . . The bare-bones plot unfolds almost imperceptibly, interweaving the two men's workaday lives in brief, charged vignettes. . . . Nova displays an uncanny flair for evoking his characters' innermost fears and desires through sensuous details—from the rank ferment of kitchen garbage to an autumn fox hunt among sumac with leaves 'the color of the reddest lipstick.' Grade: A."
—*Entertainment Weekly*

"*Cruisers* just made me hold my breath. It's so intense, it blew me away. . . . Just fabulous."
—Ann Beattie

"Fast pacing and high tension. . . . Yet [Nova's] empathetic sense of what makes people tick guarantees an extraordinary depth."   —*Newsday*

"Thrilling, intense. . . . A high-speed chase through a psychological landscape that is by turns menacing, violent, and inexplicably tender. . . . Craig Nova is a great writer and this is his best book yet. I couldn't put it down."
—Valerie Martin, author of *Property*

"Nova is one of the finest stylists working today, and it's hard to think of many contemporary writers who could match the simple elegance and economy of his prose. He consistently exhibits an amazing figurative sensibility, and there's not an excess or egregious word in the book. . . . Nova's language [is] precise, lucid and loaded."   —*Las Vegas Mercury*

C R A I G   N O V A

CRUISERS

Craig Nova is the award-winning author of
eleven novels. His writing has appeared in
Esquire, *The Paris Review*, *The New York Times
Magazine*, *Men's Journal*, and other publica-
tions. He lives in Putney, Vermont.

CRUISERS

A NOVEL

CRAIG NOVA

VINTAGE CONTEMPORARIES
Vintage Books
A Division of Random House, Inc.
New York

FIRST VINTAGE CONTEMPORARIES EDITION, JULY 2005

Copyright © 2004 by Craig Nova

All rights reserved. Published in the United States by Vintage Books, a division of
Random House, Inc., New York, and in Canada by Random House of Canada
Limited, Toronto. Originally published in hardcover in the United States by Shaye
Areheart Books, an imprint of Crown Publishing Group, a division of
Random House, Inc., New York, in 2004.

Vintage and colophon are registered trademarks and Vintage Contemporaries is a
trademark of Random House, Inc.

The Library of Congress has cataloged the Shaye Areheart edition as follows:
Nova, Craig.
Cruisers: a novel / Craig Nova.—1st ed.
1. Murder victims' families—Fiction. 2. Fugitives from justice—Fiction.
3. Middle-aged men—Fiction. 4. Traffic police—Fiction. 5. Murderers—Fiction.
I. Title.
PS3564.O86C78 2004
813'.54—dc22
2004002494

Vintage ISBN: 1-4000-3069-2

Book design by Lynne Amft

www.vintagebooks.com

Printed in the United States of America
10 9 8 7 6 5 4 3 2 1

For Eric Albright

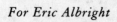

N O T E

All characters in this book are figments of the author's imagination, and none of them represent, partially or completely, any human being, living or dead. While this book was inspired by a real event, it does not purport to be, and is not, a representation of anything that did happen. No real member of any law enforcement agency is portrayed here, although the author would like to express his admiration and respect for the bravery of the men involved in the incident that inspired this book.

—CN

"Whatever is not conscious will be experienced as fate."
— CARL JUNG

CRUISERS

RUSSELL BOYD

THE CRUISER MOVED FROM THE DARK ONTO THE highway in a fluid rush, but inside, Russell Boyd felt the acceleration as a hard and yet pleasurable bump. The engine whined as he went through the gears, and at a hundred and ten miles an hour the lines on the road began to blur. In the turns, Boyd accelerated, and this pushed the rear end of the cruiser down so that it hugged the highway. In the certainty of speed, which was at once reassuring and still exciting, he had a thrill that was like seeing the purple approach of a storm. And where pursuit was concerned, Russell liked the flowing attraction toward those lights up ahead, just as he was aware, in the moment, of how he and the driver of the other car were bound together by speed. It pulled them together with a constant attraction, like gravity. And as the speedometer swept upward, Russell tried to relax, to take it easy, and to make sure he didn't miss much.

He went after an Audi with just two seats, and when he came up behind it, he keyed the mike and asked the dispatcher for a check of the license plate. Who owned the car, priors, outstanding warrants, unpaid fines. The dispatcher couldn't say who was in the car. Boyd turned on the blue lights, and the Audi pulled over, the driver making a signal when he did so.

Boyd angled the cruiser's nose turned toward the passing traffic, and he turned the wheels, too, so that if the cruiser got rear-ended, it wouldn't hit him as he stood next to the Audi. Then he opened the door and swung into the shudder of air that was left by a passing car. The anxious trembling of wind was enhanced by the throbbing of blue light, and Boyd hesitated, taking a moment to look around. Some nights when it was cold he saw the indifferent stars, which were the color of the blue haze beneath the lights from a Sunoco gas station. When he was scared, which was the next step up from being alert, the haze appeared to him like ground mist spilling into an open grave. This didn't last long, and he was glad when dread receded into the part of the mind where shadows blended with only half-formed apprehensions.

There were other times, though, when everything was going as it should, when the speed had its effect on him, like music, and then the haze beneath the lights of a gas station appeared to him like the steam when Zofia was in the shower and the liquid sheen of water ran down her hips and legs. Boyd couldn't quite recall her as well as he wanted, not photographically, but he was reassured by something else, which was the seep and itch of desire. But even so, he still wanted to be precise about what happened the instant she came into a room in the evening when he had been waiting for her. It was as though the room was suddenly filled with . . . he wasn't sure what to call it. He knew she changed the room, but he couldn't say more than that. And even though he wasn't sure what the precise word was, he knew that when Zofia came into the room, her hair moving into the light of a lamp, he instantly existed in a state of pleasurable alertness. Then she'd drop her papers, her teacher's roll book, kick off her shoes, drop her skirt, and stand there looking at him. "I'm going to take a shower," she would say. "Want to come with me?"

Now he looked for a detail about the Audi that would tell him something, a smell, a broken light, the way the car sat on its springs. Was it carrying something heavy? Was the license plate clean while the rest of the car was dirty? Were the people in the car passing anything between them? Were they red-eyed and slurring on alcohol or something else? Were their pupils like pinholes? He stood there in the blue light and put his hand on his pistol, which was made out of stainless steel to protect it from the corrosiveness of road salt. Then he took his hand away, not wanting the cheap reassurance of the thing. Reassurance came, as it always did, from the way he spoke, and in trying to make sure he gave people a way out.

"Hi, how are you tonight?" he said to the driver. His voice was one cut above neutral, more friendly than not. "Do you know why I stopped you?"

The woman in the passenger seat put one hand to her head, as though the man she was with had made her so angry it had given her a headache. Boyd saw her dark hair and black coat and felt again that sense of entering someone's private place. People built up history in a car, one word or act at a time, just as they consumed liquor in it or flirted and had sex or where, from time to time, a long-hidden betrayal was discovered, just as the implications of it were made clear, too. ("Do you really want to know? Do you?

Are you sure? Well, I didn't do it with him, but I wanted to . . .") The driver passed over his license and the registration.

Boyd went back to the cruiser and wrote out the ticket, which was for eighty-five in a sixty-five. It could have been eighty-nine or even ninety, but Boyd gave him a break. Then he got out and started back toward the Audi, and though his business was done, he still thought that the most dangerous time was when you thought everything you saw was one thing, but really it was another, and that the people in the car weren't quiet because of an old disagreement but because there was a bag of something in the back they shouldn't have, or maybe some other ugly thing Boyd couldn't think of but would recognize when he saw it.

Boyd passed the ticket over, and as the driver took it the woman said, "Take me home."

"Home?" the driver said.

"Yeah," she said, "My house. You know, where my husband lives."

"I thought we had been through all that," he said.

"Be careful when you pull back on here," Boyd said. "People get going fast in this section."

"You hear me?" she said.

"Yeah," the driver said.

"I want to get back before he finds the note," she said. "Before my husband finds it."

"He's probably read it," said the driver.

"Look," she said. "There's nothing more to say."

"All right," the driver said.

"I just want to go home. I've been thinking."

"It isn't because I got a speeding ticket, is it?" he said.

"Oh, shut up," she said. "He's listening."

Boyd wasn't really listening so much as looking at the other cars as they went by, all of them trailing something, which he apprehended as the small essence that every fast-moving thing leaves behind. Then he turned and walked back to the cruiser, where he waited for the Audi to move into the slow lane, its tail light blinking with a sad urgency. He saw the woman in the front seat put her hand to her head one more time. Then Boyd got back onto the highway and smoked it up to a hundred, a hundred and ten. At the next turnaround he crossed over to the southbound lane and went back to the place where he had waited before, which was screened by a grove of poplar, even though at night, at this hour, he didn't need cover. The engine ticked with heat, and in the hush of the radio, the dim lights from the dash, he thought about Zofia. The darkness around him wasn't so grim, or when it was, he was helped by the memory of sheets of moisture as they ran down her legs.

One evening she stood in the bedroom, toweling her hair. She said, "You know, a friend of mine was pregnant, and when she was big, she couldn't shave her legs. Her husband had to do it for her. She said it was the most exciting thing. You know, lying there, feeling the tug of the razor as it went down her calf, seeing his head bent over her as he went about it. Careful about cutting her."

Russell had met her a month before in the parking lot of the post office in the mill town along the Connecticut River in southern Vermont where he lived. The town was built against a hillside, and while it still had businesses like Crystal Oil and Ice, there was also a Thai restaurant and a Korean one, not to mention two vegetarian outfits, a French bakery, and dress stores that sold skirts for more than a lot of people in town made in a week. It had a food co-op, too, which sold organic spinach and granola. The town had the usual problems, drugs and suicide, an ugly murder every two years, shoplifting, drunken fights, the odd stabbing, an occasional bank robbery by someone under the age of twenty-five.

Zofia had been changing a tire on her car, and when he had come up to her, she had been straining to loosen a lug nut. Her arms trembled with the effort, and when he said, "Would you like a hand?" she said, "No. It's all right. Thanks."

While she was still straining, he put his hand next to hers on the lug wrench. When he pulled up, the nut gave with a squeak and with something that both of them felt in their hands, which was a soft release. Most of the work had been done, and all it took was a little more pressure. She looked up, still feeling that soft, giving release. Then she went on to the next one, which she strained against, too.

"Well?" she said. "Aren't you going to help with this one?"

He helped her get the tire over the bolts and to tighten the nuts down, and then she stood there, looking at him.

"What do you do, you know, when you're not helping people change tires?"

"I'm a cop," he said.

"Oh," she said. "Like with a gun?"

"Yeah," he said.

"Have you shot anyone?" she said.

He didn't want to talk about this, since it was a matter, as far as he was concerned, of infinite bad luck.

"No," he said. "What about you?"

"No," she said, laughing. "I haven't shot anyone. At least not yet. I'm a teacher."

Now at two in the morning, in the turnout between the northbound and southbound traffic, he listened to the subdued crackling of the radio, the dispatcher's voice at once dispassionate and concerned, and he saw the green and orange of the gas gauge, the promise of the tach, its needle lying there like some sleeping thing, the red digital readout of the radar. The cars approached from the south, their lights appearing yellow, although here and there he saw the new silver-blue varieties.

The luminescence from the headlights moved through the car in sheets, and with them, welded by an invisible seam, were the shadows. They swept through the front seat, the light and darkness combined like the surface of the moon. These moments in the car often led him to brood about other things, too, such as the sudden, unexpected sound of gunfire, the flashes all mixed up with the surprise of them.

Boyd knew that in going up to cars in the dark, and in other things he had to do, such as approaching houses where there was trouble, or answering calls when things went wrong, he would come across someone who was a perfect expression of malice, and every now and then it occurred to him that his entire life was dedicated to finding the person he was most afraid of. That was the trouble with those hours when he was alone: the night was filled with so many possibilities, not only those on the highway, but his own brooding conclusions about how things really were.

So he sat there waiting for the noise of the radar, the little squeak, squeak, which went off from time to time. Ninety-one, maybe eighty-nine, somewhere in there. Then he started the engine and felt the hard bump of acceleration. Mostly, though, he had time to think of Zofia as she came into a room, her hips moving in that languid sway. She lived in a small house at the end of a drive that wound through some scrubby poplar mixed with a couple of birch trees.

In the midst of the shift, the blue throb from the top of the cruiser, the spotlight, the gauges on the dashboard, the needles as orange as the tip of a soldering iron, the toaster-filament color of the radar, all seemed unnaturally bright. Every object was covered with a haunting glitter, which was a matter of fear melding with light. But as the night ended, as he turned off the highway and went toward Zofia's house, the bright light, the reds, blues, and yellows as garish as neon, began to fade. By dawn, everything was washed out. The trees, the road, the houses, even the most brightly painted cars, looked as though seen through fog. As the fatigue came on like a drug, he wondered what he would do if he had to live without those intense lights, so perfectly enhanced by his own excitement. He suspected that during the day he was only a ghost of himself and that the time he really lived for was when the sun went down, as though he was a creature of the dark, kept alive on adrenaline and speed.

He used his key to open the door. The shadows of the house were silent and reassuring, not black so much as like dark gray silk. When he went through them, they left him with the sense of being caressed by the place where she lived. Upstairs, he heard the creak of the floor as she got out of bed and went into the bathroom. He came up the stairs and saw her as she put her full lips under the faucet to get a drink. When she was done, she touched her lips with the back of her hand, and came out to see him, looking him over and then pulling the Velcro straps of his body armor, which made a lingering ripping sound.

"I always like that sound. It means you're home," she said.

She went back into the bathroom, brushed her teeth and then came into the bedroom, the shadows falling across her like more pieces of dark silk. He lifted the body armor off like a turtle shell. She sat down on the bed next to him, her lips still wet, and giggled.

"I was thinking of the time you told me about when you went into a bar and a woman groped you. . . ." she said, with a sultry lilt in her voice. "Who would grope a cop?"

"That wasn't me. That was a friend," he said.

"Oh," she said. "Well. I could imagine it happening to you."

She moved closer and the shadows swept across her like a dress that fell from her shoulder.

"I worry sometimes," she said. "But you'll always come back, won't you?"

He listened to the hush of the sheet as she moved, the sound of her breath as the first sunlight came into the room. She stretched. He strained to hear the little clomping sound she made at the end of a yawn.

The coffeemaker downstairs had a timer and, like magic, it made a throaty hush and gurgle. She sat on the side of the bed, her hair in a mess. The atmosphere in the room was that mixture of possibility and puzzlement with which people often start a day.

Then she got up and ran the shower. Through the door he glanced at the sheath of water as it went down her back in a rush, something like the fluid shimmer on the blacktop in the heat of August. The steam rose to the ceiling of the bathroom and curled into the bedroom, and then he heard the water stop and the glass door of the shower thump as she opened it and stepped out. She was still wet when she came into the bedroom and sat down next to him. When she moved closer, she left the round, damp shape of her rear end on the sheets. It reminded him of the swelling of an instrument, like a cello.

"Sometimes I worry that you're going to touch me and I'm going to explode, just lift off into bits of light, flecks of it that just . . . I don't know. Shimmer. Like I'm made of sequins."

"Me too," he said.

"Oh, that's my charmer," she said. "I bet you say that to all the girls."

She stretched out with the luminescence of dawn on her wet skin. He put his lips into the drops of water on her neck and felt the tickle of her wet hair. In her damp skin, in the perfume of soap, in the slippery and surprising heat of the moment, everything about the night, every fragment of doubt and uncertainty, disappeared into excitement which seemed to him, at this moment, to be the center of the otherwise cool and domestic house, so perfectly anchored by the aroma of coffee and the lingering steam from the shower.

She looked right into his eyes and said, "It makes it more interesting, doesn't it, when we do this after having been a little worried all night." Her alarm clock, which she hadn't turned off, began to buzz, and he put his hands over her ears to shield her from it, but then she turned and hit the button and said, "Well, we'll settle this later."

He watched as she got dressed, which she did with an efficiency that amazed him: At first she stood there naked, her skin damp from the shower, and almost instantly she was wearing her stockings, her skirt, her blue shirt, her beige jacket. When she was about to go, she said, "And when I get back, I'd like you to give me the answer to a question. You won't mind, will you?"

"No," he said.

"Maybe you can tell me why you do this. Why do you go out there at night?"

He shrugged. Whenever he was asked this question, he thought about two things, a night at a hunting camp, and a black snake. But how could he begin to explain them? She waited. The digital clock flipped over with a little flash, the numbers the same color as the readout on the radar at night. It made him think about the shadows seeping through the cruiser.

"O.K.," he said. "I'll tell you."

"You don't sound too sure," she said.

"It's hard to explain," he said.

"What isn't?" she said. "I'm not easily shocked."

"Are you sure about that?" he said.

"Yes," she said. "I am."

"Well . . ." He shrugged again. "All right."

She stopped at the door on her way out.

"Don't say you weren't warned," he said.

THE DOOR clicked behind Zofia and then the house was quiet again, just as it was when Russell first came in from a night on the highway. Usually this was when he went to sleep, but now, instead, he lay awake in the shadows of the bedroom.

In addition to their year-round home, Russell's family had owned a hunting camp in central Vermont. Whenever he approached the camp, at sixteen and seventeen, he always felt the quiet brooding that the place seemed to inspire, as though its presence was intimately related to mortality and the passage of time, of seasons that came and went. Russell always liked that moment when he first saw the house, since he felt the effect of time in a way that could be appreciated without any of the pain.

The camp had five hundred acres of maple and birch, a few stands of pine and spruce. In the pine groves the red needles had been collecting for years, and walking through them was like wading through shallow water, the needles making a pattern around the ankles just like the last rush of a wave at the beach.

The camp itself was a house made of stones. It was deserted aside from the week in the fall when his family came to hunt, although every now and then desperate young men and women broke in to use one of the beds. When seen from the outside, the house was nothing more than cemented cobbles with a pitched roof. In the front were two windows and a heavy wooden door, its grain rough to the touch. Inside, a loft had been built upstairs behind the chimney, which was also made of cobbles, although some of them were as large as footballs.

Russell had started going there to hunt when he was fourteen, and the first few times he had just tried to be careful, to handle his rifle properly, and to stay out of the way. The hunt that he remembered, as he sat in the shadows of Zofia's bedroom, was one he had gone to when he was sixteen. The hunts were organized by his grandfather, a small-town lawyer who took pride in telling the truth as nearly as he could, and was never surprised by the difficulties the people in town brought to his law office. Russell's grandfather had blue eyes and gray hair. Often, when Russell thought of him, he remembered his grandfather sitting in his law office, where the old man leaned back in his oak chair with slats in the back, like a piece of furniture in a courtroom, and considered the problems clients brought his way. Russell's father was a logger, who died when Russell was in his twenties, leaving two skidders and a logging truck and a bulldozer, all of which were owned by the bank.

Still, on the night Russell thought about from time to time, both his grandfather and his father had still been alive. Russell had come into the house and put his rifle, a flat-shooting 7mm Mauser, into the rack at the side of the room. The older men sat around the table in the corner, talking about deer and telling stories and jokes. At about ten o'clock they began to think about sleeping so they could get up before first light and cook the slabs of ham they had brought along, browning them and letting them sizzle while they fried some eggs. Russell began to look around, trying to decide where he would sleep, but his grandfather said, "Russell. Come here. Sit down."

He poured Russell a drink of bourbon in a water glass and put it down in front of him.

"I've been thinking," said his grandfather. He went on looking at Russell. "You're growing up."

"Not yet," said Russell.

"Oh, don't be too sure," said his grandfather. "Anyway, I've got something to tell you."

"You mean you're going to give me advice?" said Russell.

"He knows about girls," said his father.

"Does he?" said his grandfather. "Well, I'm glad to hear that. I wish I did."

One of the other men heard this and laughed. "Isn't that the truth?" he said.

"You could call it advice," said Russell's grandfather. "Or maybe it's just a warning." Russell's grandfather's chin was pitted as he sat there, thinking it over. "There are things hidden by ordinary life. I don't know what to call them. Things you can suggest, but you can't really describe. You know, those possibilities down there in the muck that make you squirm. At 3 A.M. You might get a glimpse every now and then but mostly you have the good sense to look away. And with good reason. Who wants the terror of it?"

"I guess," said Russell.

"Oh, no," said the grandfather. "There's no guessing. Not in the midst of it! Don't you see?"

Russell shook his head. "No," he said.

"Hmpf," said his grandfather. "I want to tell you something you won't forget."

"You mean like in books?" said Russell.

"Well, they're all right, as far as they go. They hint at it, but they never tell you," said Russell's grandfather.

"Why don't you ask him if he wants to know?" said Russell's father.

"Oh, he wants to know. It's knowledge that youth wants, isn't it?" said Russell's grandfather.

"I don't know," said Russell. "I guess."

"Why, sure you do," said Russell's grandfather. "Sure you do. That's the way things are. No one's going to change that."

Russell's grandfather looked at his own son. Russell's father shrugged.

Russell's grandfather had a sip of his drink. The men on the other side of the room milled around in the pointless manner of men, alone, when they are getting ready to go to bed. The movement was more like a dog that turns around three times, chasing its tail, before flopping into a corner to sleep. A log collapsed in the fire with an ashy sigh, the sound itself suggesting a delicate invocation of defeat and finality, or maybe Russell perceived it that way because of the emotional pressure in the room, which he imagined came from the moment just before a secret was revealed. Later, Russell wondered if the stars would have changed in the way the room did if he had heard this secret outside. But then he thought, of course, they did change. They had something new in them, as far as Russell was concerned, after his grandfather bumbled through what he had to say.

"I bet you think I'm going to tell you a war story," said Russell's grandfather.

Russell nodded. Yes, he thought, that's right. Thank God. It is just another one of those stories that get told in places like this, and that the old man has had too much to drink.

"I guess," said Russell.

"Hmpf," said his grandfather.

The coals in the fireplace looked like red and silver foil that had been balled up and thrown into the fire.

"Maybe we should just go to sleep," said Russell's father.

"I'm getting old," said Russell's grandfather. "Who knows how many chances I'll have?"

"I know a lot of it already," said Russell.

"Do you?"

Yes, thought Russell. He knew his grandfather had been a prisoner of war in Germany in World War II. He had heard the stories of the Red Cross boxes in which there had been raisins, and how the men had used the raisins to make beer. Russell had heard stories of how the men had tried to tunnel out of the camp, the fact that Russell's grandfather had been a spy, and that when he heard useful information, he had a code to include it in letters he wrote home. He knew all that.

Russell's grandfather looked around the room and then back at Russell and said that it wasn't the years of starving that needed to be mentioned, or forced marches and the rest of the stuff that you read about or saw in movies. That was the least of it. No. The unfathomable element, the essence that you wanted to be careful about, was something else altogether. And what was this thing that no one should ever forget, that was dangerous not to know, the very heart of what everyone should be afraid of? No. Not afraid of. Horrified by. What could that be? said Russell's grandfather.

"You've had too much to drink," said Russell's father.

"Of course," said Russell's grandfather. "But what difference does that make?" He turned to Russell and said, "Take a sip of your bourbon."

Then his grandfather sat there, rolling one shoulder, as though whatever he was trying to convey could be felt on his back, and it itched and tormented him. But, he seemed to be saying, wasn't that quiet torment the nature of really knowing something? And if you knew it, didn't it change you, and make you want to be precise in what you said and did, and wasn't that what determined how you spent your time? Wasn't that knowledge what was behind being a small-town lawyer and never saying a word that wasn't true and never being surprised by the problems that came his way?

"It was at the end," said Russell's grandfather.

"What was the end?" said Russell.

"Why, that was when the Russians came."

His grandfather wanted to be precise about this. But how can you be precise about that moment when everything is changing, and when no one knows what the next moment will bring? And yet, in the midst of it, nothing seemed to be happening at all, as though everything was still: the entire landscape seemed to have stopped. It appeared in shades of gray on gray, the fenceposts to which the gray wire was affixed, the mud, the stumps around the perimeter of the camp, the huts, made of rough-cut lumber that had weathered to a gray like a dirty towel, all of it, even the slender shape of smoke that rose from a fire behind the huts, seemed to be hardly moving. And so, in the midst of it, in Russell's grandfather's apprehension of something coming his way, he was also profoundly bored. Nothing moved. Just that silver and gray light, that lazy smoke, the men who walked around, some of them with blankets over their shoulders. So, that was part of it, the fear so perfectly combined with boredom.

And there were practical considerations, too, said Russell's grandfather. This is where you can see the problem. Since the problem is always in what you do in the face of a moment like this. For instance, the guards were running away, and the prisoners could walk off, too, but then there was the chance of being shot on the road as an escapee. This was one of the things that the men considered as they stood there in that light, under their blankets, thinking about walking through the gates.

One of the guards stayed. He was a fat man who had eaten well during the war, or at least he had eaten a lot of potatoes and blood sausage. The other guards had slipped away, their shapes disappearing with what they could carry into the woods beyond the stumps that had been left where the trees had been cut down on the other side of the wire. Still, one of them thought better of it, and decided that the camp was probably a better place to be. Who knew what was out there on the roads?

So all of them, the prisoners and the one guard, were milling around in that slow-motion, aimless way, at once alert to malice and almost falling asleep, when they saw two Russians. The Russians were so thin they looked like a joke, like sticks on which someone had hung torn uniforms that were so dirty and ill-fitting as to leave one wondering just who the hell these people were. Deserters? Phantoms of an army that had been defeated by the years it had been fighting?

The two Russians picked their way through the stumps that were left after the trees around the camp had been cut down. They were weak and so dizzy that they took a convoluted path around the stumps, and even stopped from time to time to stare in the direction they were going. When they stood up, they did so with an exhausted effort that could be distinguished a hundred yards away. Then they started their slow, circuitous, inexorable locomotion toward the wire where the blinking Americans and British stood, holding their blankets. Somehow or other, in a way none of the men behind the wire could articulate, they were more strangely troubled by these stick figures, these exhausted phantoms, than when they had just been waiting. This was the thing, said Russell's grandfather, the unnameable sense of something you knew you should be afraid of. Still, it was hard to be certain whether there was anything here or not. The men in the camp were tired and hungry, sleepy and bored, and yet prone to exaggeration. Maybe that was all it was. Although, even then, Russell's grandfather said, we knew this was more of a desperate hope than anything else.

The guard who had stayed, though, wasn't having anything to do with hope, desperate or otherwise. He could feel it, too, and he was a lot less fuzzy-headed than the prisoners were. It was obvious to him, said Russell's grandfather as he took Russell's arm and pulled him close, into the hot, bourbon-scented breath. Russell leaned forward, close to the man's whitish stubble, grown for the hunt, and close enough, too, to look into the man's oil-colored pupils, which, while in some ways disgusting, were mesmerizing in their serpentine depth. He looked back at his grandfather, as though daring the old man. Go on, Russell seemed to be saying. What do you think I'm made out of? We've gone this far. There's no going back.

The guard watched those scarecrows approach. He turned and looked around and then back at the Russians as they tottered among the stumps. But there! said Russell's grandfather. That was the moment. The guard could tell by something, I don't know what, the colors, the stillness of the air, the exhaustion, but something tipped him off. He began to move, slow, cagey, as though going no place, just walking around, as he always did, but he was steadily working toward the gate, which was open about a foot. Then, when he got there, he slipped into the open.

And the prisoners went back to that dull waiting. The stillness of the smoke, the sluggishness of movement, as though nothing was happening and yet everything was changing. Russell's grandfather stepped closer to the wire in time to see the guard take a look over his shoulder at the Russians and begin to run. For an instant the entire landscape seemed changed, as though in this one action all the sluggishness and boredom were brushed aside and violated. One of the Russians swung his rifle around with a practiced, supremely confident if fatigued movement, done so many times as to be second nature, like a man chopping wood. He mounted it on his shoulder, flicked off the safety, and seemed to lead the running guard, who fell with a suddenness that seemed to put an end to the sense of freedom, of movement that could escape the thick, sluggish air, which more and more seemed filled with the smoke from a fire behind the bungalows. What could be burning? Camp records? Was another guard hiding back there and getting rid of the paper?

"So, that's it?" said Russell.

"No," said his grandfather. "Oh no."

He had leaned forward and whispered. This is between just the two of us, his grandfather seemed to be saying, and frankly, who else is important? No. There was more. The Russians began to move through the stumps, coming forward with that same fatigued if not exhausted gait. They stood next to the dead man. One spoke to the other and then they reached down and began taking off his clothes. Surely they could make use of the jacket and the rest, but then maybe it wasn't a good idea to wear the uniform of a German.

Russell's grandfather had taken hold of the wire. He watched while the other men turned away. The Russians built a fire. "Like that one!" said Russell's grandfather, pointing to the fireplace. They went about their business with a quiet, methodical air, which was probably more starvation and fatigue than anything else, the knife moving along the German's leg, to cut him up. Russell's grandfather said, "See?" Russell took a drink. We could see them, said Russell's grandfather, from a distance, around the fire, and then eating, too. They didn't look in our direction. It was the blankness and the businesslike air that was as bad as anything else. We watched the smoke of their fire rise, gray like everything else, as the Russians ate until they were filled. Then they pulled themselves up, discarding a bone, and went on walking, passing the stumps and moving into the edge of the woods, leaving us staring through the wire.

But that is what happens, said Russell's grandfather, when things come unglued. So, do you see the essential horror? It is ungraspable and yet so obvious, nameless as it makes its appearance, as though there is nothing you can do. And once it starts . . . He shrugged. There is nothing to do. How are you going to stop something like this? In the moment? Why, you aren't going to do a thing but stare and turn away.

Russell's grandfather finished his drink and said, "Don't you see? Tawdry, brutal, and yet indifferent. And dangerous? Oh, not by half. Now I'm going to sleep for a couple of hours before I go out and shoot a deer."

He stood up and looked around at the other men and said, "Has anyone seen that black snake this year? There's one that lives in here. Heh?"

In the morning it rained, and they all sat outside in the driving coldness of it, waiting, looking at the woods. Russell leaned against a tree, hearing the ticking as drops fell onto the leaves on the ground. The landscape appeared in shades of black and gray, in front of which there were slashes of silver rain.

It was impossible to say how this was related to what Russell did for a living, but that didn't mean there was nothing between the two. To explain the connection, Russell supposed it was like his appreciation of the scale of the stars and his delight in the sparkle of a single drop of water in a blade of grass after a rain: the two were completely separate, yet related. This relation between the enormous and the everyday, between the horrific and just living, had a moral quality, too, not a Bible-thumping rigidity, but Russell's awareness of how human beings faced the scale of what surrounded them, as ominous and indifferent as the stars, and how people appeared as sparks against the darkness. And there was one final element here, which was like a spark, too, and that was how his sense of isolation vanished in Zofia's touch, in her appearance in a room, with her sigh and yawn in the morning.

When people asked him why he'd become a trooper, he thought of how accurate his grandfather had been about this other world, this sudden, nameless gloom that Russell hated. This horror was everything that beguiled and injured, that was tawdry and remorseless, without concern for consequences, as though the future had been banished by vanity and ill will.

—— —— ——

HE WAS LOOKING for his tuning fork, which he used to set the radar, when Zofia came in at four o'clock in the afternoon. They had a cup of coffee in the kitchen and he told her about the hunting camp, the words coming out in a slow, steady way, like a man driving nails, and when he was done, she sat there, blinking, one hand to her face.

"I've got to get to work," he said. He kissed her on the cheek. "I'll wake you up in the morning, okay?"

"I meant to get here earlier," she said. "You know, to finish what we started this morning."

"It'll keep," he said.

"Yes," she said. "That's right, isn't it?"

She put her hand to her face again.

He leaned close to her and told her that he loved her, that she had changed him, and that everything was better now.

FRANK KOHLER

FRANK KOHLER KNEW HE WAS RUNNING OUT OF time. He sat at his kitchen table with the newspaper spread out so that he could see the ad. He put his head in his hands and then he looked out the window, where he could see the Vermont hillside. It was spring. Everything was a lizardlike green, and the hillside opposite the field below his house resembled an enormous alligator. The ad said, "Russian, European and Asian Women Looking for Husbands." Around the border of the ad were passport photos of women.

Kohler stood up and walked out of the kitchen and into his shop, where he had his workbench, his manuals for computers, software CDs, many of them out of date, motherboards, chips, modems, computer tools, old computer cases, and some machines, dinosaurs, which he kept for no good reason. He had noticed, now that he was thirty, that he didn't like to throw things away quite so much as he had a few years before. He opened the case of a machine and saw that it was filled with dust balls as thick as cotton candy. Often these machines weren't working because they needed to be cleaned. They were just filled with dust, blown in by the computer's fan: no one thought of how the need to keep the machine cool would lead naturally to this other problem. The sounds he made—the swish of canned air, a screwdriver against the head of a Phillips screw, the click of a keyboard, and the small, perfect sound of a cable going into a port—were reassuring, but even so he kept stopping. He looked at the kitchen. Finally he walked back and stood at the table again, where the advertisement lay in black and white, like danger and possibility perfectly mixed.

He was tempted. He was willing to admit that. How could he try to do otherwise when he looked at the maddeningly suggestive passport photos? They had a quality that was at once clinical and yet sultry. But he was worried that one of these women, or all of them, might be up to something, and while he was uncertain what this might be precisely, he suspected that it would have something to do with trying to get money from him. He guessed that wasn't so bad, really, in that he could just not send it. Of course, this was not much of a guarantee, since if someone was any good at being up to something, it would be more complicated than that. Say that he started to correspond with a woman who wrote back and said she liked animals and long walks in the country, and generally seemed to be sincere, and maybe she would even have problems, like an aunt or a sister, probably a sister, who had leukemia and was a financial drag on the entire family. But the way it would work was this: One day the phone would ring and it would be the woman, calling from Belgrade, and she would be in tears because she was being threatened by a gangster, and then the gangster would get on the phone and say that unless the woman got some money, and got it fast, why then . . . well, it wouldn't be too good for her. What then? Would Kohler be able to ignore such a threat? There was always the possibility that it could be true. Everyone heard the stories about Eastern European or Asian women, and what happened to them. One might take a job as a waitress, or that's what it was supposed to be, and the next thing she knows, she's working as a prostitute outside an army base in the Philippines.

He crumpled the paper and threw in it the trash and went back to his workshop, and when he couldn't stand the silence any longer, he turned on the radio and listened to NPR. There was a story about a blind Cuban musician who, now that he was dead, was finally getting recognition. Frank tried to do what was called an overlay with the machine he was working on, putting one operating system on top of another, but before he even knew what he was doing he had stood up, like an impulse incarnate, and went back to the kitchen. There he bent down and went through the coffee grinds and half-eaten toast in the trash can, the orange peels, canned spaghetti, and bacon grease until he found the paper. He spread it out on the table again, but now it was harder to read since the print on the back side of the sheet came through where the paper had gotten wet or greasy. But even this stink of garbage added to his sense of attraction, since somehow the smell of coffee grinds and bacon combined with the pictures of these women to suggest the domestic.

The ad had been put in the paper by a company named Matchmakers International, and when Frank got out his map of Boston, which is where the place was, he saw that it was located off the Commons, on the edge of the Combat Zone. Nothing conclusive, really, aside from the fact that

Matchmakers International existed in a transitional strip between the respectable and the tawdry. He decided that he'd have to go and take a look.

■ ■ ■

HE DISLIKED his anonymous, two-year-old lime green Chevrolet with its plastic seats and the trunk filled with computer parts. Everything about it seemed out of date, and the dullness of it added to his uneasiness. Rather than increasing his sense of fitting in, being anonymous only made him feel more excluded. And while he drove to Boston, he watched the cars in the opposite lane, as though considering each one. A Porsche, an Infiniti, a two-seater BMW . . .

There was no place to park on the street near the Commons, so he went into the underground garage, getting a ticket at the entrance and then spiraling down into the depths, where the cars were parked. The echoes of the place, the squeal of tires as he made a turn, the hurried movements of people, all left him with the desire to get away, back up to the light. He climbed the concrete stairwells, where everything was covered with an oily patina from the exhaust of the cars.

He emerged into the pale light of the afternoon in Boston. The warmth of the sun on his face reminded him of the time when he had been sixteen and had danced cheek to cheek with a young woman. Where they were pressed together he had felt the rising, seeping heat, which had bound them together like some maddeningly ephemeral substance. He opened his eyes now and regretted the disappearance of such innocent promise, but what good did thinking about it do? It just left him teary and angry. He looked around to get his bearings and started walking toward the Combat Zone.

The building was on the edge of Chinatown. The sign above the glass-and-aluminum door was next to one in Chinese, but the script of Matchmakers International's logo was like a wedding invitation, curly black letters against a white background, although the background was as yellowed as a wedding dress that has been in a trunk for fifty years. Frank stood under the sign, thinking it over, and then went up to the Chinese grocery on the corner and bought a cup of coffee in a Styrofoam cup. It burned his lips.

A bride in a white dress with a small bouquet in her hand went up to the front door of Matchmakers International. She had the high cheekbones of Eastern Europe—Poland or Yugoslavia, Kohler guessed. She was flushed with excitement and from the schnapps that the best man, who wore brown trousers and a green jacket, kept offering to her. The groom, in a black suit, smiled shyly, and from time to time the best man spoke Polish or Hungarian, and then all of them laughed, bound together by the old, incomprehensible words. They passed the bottle around again and went up the stairs.

"Wait until they see!" said the bride.

They disappeared inside and then Kohler walked up and down the block, looking at the pigeons which suddenly flew into the air, in a flock, at once forlorn and orderly. He went to an alley to wait until the wedding party left, and while he stood there two Chinese men in bloody aprons smoked cigarettes without saying a word. Finally, from the alley, Kohler saw that the couple and the best man had finished paying their respects to the place where the bride and groom must have met. The three of them started walking toward the subway.

Perhaps, he thought, the matchmaker would offer him some method of sorting out people who were up to something from ordinary women who, like Kohler, just wanted to get married. He threw the empty cup into a Dumpster and went up to the door. The building smelled of bacon and grilled cheese sandwiches cooked on a hot plate. The stairs went straight up to the first landing and then straight up again, each step covered with a black plastic tread.

Matchmakers International reminded Kohler of the front office of a discount dentist. A room about ten by fifteen, some chairs that looked like they came from a small airport, and a short Formica counter with a plastic flower in a cheap vase. Next to the counter there was an interior door. The receptionist wore a red jacket and a black skirt, and her lips were made up with bright lipstick. Kohler walked up to the counter with the advertisement in his hand, and when the receptionist asked him what he wanted, he pushed it forward.

"This . . ." he said. "I saw it in the paper."

"Well, sit down, Mr. . . . ." said the receptionist.

"Kohler," he said. "Frank Kohler."

"Well, sit down," she said. "I'll see if Mrs. Blanchett can see you."

Kohler sat down, ramrod-straight, his hands on his knees. On the walls were pictures of Rome, Paris, Tokyo, all evoking an air of romance, and while it was hard for Kohler to say where the romance came from, it was still there, as thick as perfume. He wished he had gotten his hair cut. But, he thought, at least no one is going to see the Chevy.

The phone rang. In the hall he heard a heavy tread. Kohler put a hand up to a birthmark he had on his neck. At night, when he couldn't sleep in his house in Vermont and he lay there, hearing the coyotes yapping, he imagined a woman, in new stockings and a nice dress, looking at this mark and kissing it, slowly and wetly, and then saying, "I want to kiss you where you have been hurt." Then he would try to imagine the lingering dampness on it, the faint, almost imperceptible odor of lipstick and saliva. As he sat in the Matchmakers office, this memory and the desire of it made him realize how futile his attempts were. No one was ever going to do that. He looked around the room, and had begun to stand up and go for the door, when the receptionist came back and said, "Mrs. Blanchett will see you."

Kohler went in. The room was larger than the reception area, but not by much. It had a desk, which was covered with wood veneer. There was a bookshelf, and on the ceiling a large fluorescent light. Mrs. Blanchett was a woman in her early sixties, dressed in black, wearing pearls. She stood up and shook Frank's hand. He looked around, as though to make sure he knew where the door was.

She said that she had been a matchmaker for thirty years and that an arranged marriage could be better than any other kind, since often when people fell in love and decided to get married, they made bad decisions. She told him that people needed someone to look into practical matters such as the ability to care for someone or keep house or pay the bills, or plan for the future.

"Don't you agree?" she said.

"Yes," said Kohler. "I do."

"Well," said Mrs. Blanchett. "I'm glad." She stood up. "Come on."

She opened a door he had thought was a closet, and there, in a small room was a television and a VCR with a chair in front of them. She told Kohler to sit down, and then she put a tape into the machine. He guessed if the office had once been a cheap dentist's office, this is where they must have kept the drugs.

"I'll be right back," she said, giving him the remote control. "If you want to rewind the tape, use this. This is the stop button. And the play." She left the room and Kohler saw his reflection in the screen of the television set.

Frank had a couple of chocolate kisses in his pocket, and now he took them out and undid them slowly, balling up the silver paper and throwing these things, which weren't too much bigger than BBs, into a wastebasket in the corner. He turned the VCR on and let the chocolate melt in his mouth. On the videotape, the women from Asia said they believed in families and wanted to have children, that they loved America and wanted to meet an American man. They all seemed to be reading from the same cue card.

There was a jump cut and a new woman appeared. She had blue eyes and black hair, and she was tall, which seemed suited to her perfect posture and her obvious dignity. She said she was from Ukraine. She spoke directly to the camera. She had a lovely smile, beautiful white teeth, but Kohler kept thinking, Why is she sitting there in front of this cheap video camera? Why does she need to find someone this way? Then he thought that these judgments about how people met were impossibly provincial and what he was seeing in this dignified and beautiful woman was just how desperate things were in the former Soviet Union. It seemed to him that he changed a little bit when he was watching her, and that the small difference was at once pleasant and exciting. He stopped the tape so that it froze on the woman.

Mrs. Blanchett came back and she said, "Well, I see you are interested in a Russian woman."

"She seems nice," said Kohler.

"Well, why don't you find out?" said Mrs. Blanchett. "Why don't you have her write you a letter? Would you like that?"

They went back to her office, and Mrs. Blanchett asked him some questions: Where did he live? How much money did he make a year? Did he own his house? He answered as clearly as he could.

"What kind of car do you drive?" she said.

"A Chevrolet," he said.

"How many miles does it have on it?" she asked.

He shrugged.

"Seventy-five thousand," he said.

She nodded. Did this count for him or against him?

"Are your parents living?" she asked.

"No," said Kohler.

"What did your mother die of?" asked Mrs. Blanchett.

"She was murdered," said Kohler.

Mrs. Blanchett glanced up. Kohler looked around the office, at the books on the shelf behind her, the light slanting in from the window, and in the staleness of the place and in that dusty light he thought, Why did she have to ask? Look how we feel now.

"I'm so sorry to hear that," she said. "Did they catch the man who did it?"

"No," said Kohler. "The police didn't have much to go on."

"Where did it happen?" said Mrs. Blanchett.

"Northampton. That's where I grew up."

"In Massachusetts?" she said.

"Yes," said Kohler.

"Well, I'm sorry," said Mrs. Blanchett. "I really am."

Underneath her makeup and her theatricality, she seemed to have had her heart broken at one time, and now, when she heard about his mother, she naturally spoke with a soft, empathetic voice. It reassured him. He got out his checkbook and wrote out the deposit that was needed before he could receive a letter from the woman in the tape. Her name was Katryna Kolymov.

"You'll be hearing from her soon," said Mrs. Blanchett. "Katryna is a new listing. Just this week." She put his check and the form she had filled out into a file, and let the cover of it fall shut. "If it doesn't work out, there are other possibilities."

Outside, it was getting dark. He walked down to a church and went in. The overhead lights, which were bare bulbs in fixtures that must have come from a local hardware store, gave the place a functional air, like a machine shop. He took a pew near the rear of the church, and as he sat on the hard wood of the seat, he imagined Katryna, the Russian woman, in this light with the pews all around them, the shape of her lips, the color of them, too, if she was wearing the cherry-red lipstick she had on in the tape. He imagined the cool touch of her fingers, the smell of her hair, like incense from those Russian churches, the rustling and the definite sense of another human being right next to him. He prayed for her understanding, and for his ability to understand her. He trembled with the effort. He put his hands together to pray for her health and her happiness. Then he thought, You fool. You utter fool. Why are you doing this?

He heard the cars in the street, the flapping of the wings of pigeons as they rose, and in the distance the yapping of dogs on the Commons.

When he left the church, the signs in the Combat Zone had come on with a cheap promise. Frank walked along, going slowly, looking over his shoulder now and then, staggering a little as though he had had too much to drink. He didn't know why he was looking for trouble, but he was. He passed alleys where young men smoked, their cigarettes showing as crimson points. Maybe, he thought, if he had a chance he'd let them see how things were.

He slowed down when he passed an alley. A man in a down coat that was patched with duct tape flicked his cigarette into the street, exhaled a cloud of smoke, and fell in behind Frank. The lights above the stores were covered with soot, which cast muted shadows on the sidewalk, and as Frank went through them, they appeared to him like phantoms, just dreams and half-formed impulses. Still, Frank knew what he was looking for in the aroma of fried noodles, in this half-light, and the attitude of men in the shadows who hunted for an easy mark. He'd turn on them with all the fury of . . . Then he stopped. All the fury of what? He looked at the shadows on the sidewalk, like old stains that never quite wore off.

One of the shoes worn by the man behind Frank had a sole that had come loose, and it flapped on the sidewalk. The shoe must have come from Guatemala or San Salvador, where they didn't even have any good glue. Then Frank slowed even more, giving the man time to catch up, and when the man was about two feet away, Frank stepped into an alley that was lined with trash cans and a bunch of cardboard boxes that had been cut into flat sections.

The man followed, and after he turned the corner, he found Frank. They stood opposite one another for about thirty seconds, the man thinking things over, looking into Frank's eyes, which were bright with the luminescence of a yellow sign for a Chinese take-out restaurant. The man glanced into the street, and then back again, going through the possibilities.

"Do you have business with me?" said Frank.

The man hesitated, one hand in his pocket.

"No," he said after a minute. "I guess I don't."

"Too bad," said Frank. He waited a moment more. "You're sure?"

"Yes," said the man. "Yeah. I'm sure."

"Then get out of here," said Frank.

The man stood there for a moment, and then backed up, into the light.

"I didn't mean nothing," said the man.

"I did," said Frank.

The man took a paring knife out of his pocket, the handle of which he had wrapped with adhesive tape for a better grip.

"Don't come after me," said the man. "I'm warning you."

The man turned and went back out, into the light, the sole of his shoe making that steady flap, flap, flap. Frank waited until the sound disappeared into the honking of horns, the distant rumble of trucks and cars, and the buzz of old neon. Then he started back toward the Commons, mystified that he had taken this chance, but still certain about what he had wanted. But even so, he was desperate to find a way out of this. He knew he needed to calm down, to relax, to see things from the right perspective. Maybe he should go home and read.

Kohler read Greek and Roman history, although he had to do so in translation, which gave him the sensation of being remote from what he was fascinated by. Maybe there was something in Caesar, or in Xenophon, Tacitus, or Seneca. He would reread *The Peloponnesian War*. Surely he would discover something useful.

Then he returned to the entrance of the parking garage and descended into the underworld, where the cars were lined up like tombstones. Halfway down the stairs, he stopped and put the back of his head against the concrete wall to feel the cool, reassuring surface.

— — —

HE HAD MISSED the rush-hour traffic, and on the way home it was late enough that he didn't have to drive into the setting sun at the end of Route 2. He noticed, too, that the Chevrolet didn't have 75,000 miles on it, but 87,000. Then he thought about his mother.

Frank Kohler had been twelve years old when the police came to the door to tell him that his mother, Jerri Kohler, was missing. He was in the living room, in the small house in Northampton, Mass., looking at the TV, which had rabbit ears that were covered with aluminum foil. He had squeezed the foil down until it looked like a silver cocoon on the antenna, a metal pod that was going to give birth to mechanical insects. The policemen stood on the front porch and then knocked, one of them putting his hands to the side of his face to cut down the glare on the panes of glass in the door.

Frank had made himself some macaroni and cheese, and he came to the door with the bowl in his hand, the spoon held in his fist, like a wrench. The policemen told him that his mother was missing, which Frank knew, although usually, when she disappeared, the police didn't find out about it. The police knew because her boyfriend had reported it. So he had two things to worry about: how to stop the police from interfering with his usual life, and then the other, more important matter, which was where his mother had gone this time.

The police asked if she had packed a bag, been upset, made phone calls, or told him of any plans, and they wondered, too, if she had met anyone new recently. Frank stood at the door with his bowl and shook his head, but of course she had done all of these things. She was always making plans, meeting new men, often in bars but sometimes through ads in the *Advocate,* which was the local paper. It was difficult to describe his mother's plans, her hopes to meet the right man, or a lot of other things about her: her bad luck and her resilience, too, in facing up to it. Frank knew that she loved him, and that she wanted the best for him. Recently she had even bought him a computer, which had been repossessed, but what he remembered about this, and used as a kind of psychological charm, was his mother's generous impulse. They had opened the boxes together, his mother sitting on the sofa with a rum and Coke and Frank setting the machine up on the coffee table. When they turned the power on for the first time, Jerri said, "Frank, that's the sound of the future. Hear it, darling?"

"She didn't pack a bag," said Frank to the police. "Not that I know of. She wasn't planning on anything, like a trip."

He put the bowl down on a table by the door.

"I guess I better call my uncle," said Frank. "He'll come over."

"Will he?" said one of the policemen. He looked around the living room with the TV on a Goodwill table, the sofa with some stains on it, and the bare floor.

Frank nodded.

"Sure," he said.

"Do you know her boyfriend?" asked the other policeman.

"You mean Joe?" said Frank.

"No," said the policeman. "I mean Bob."

Frank shrugged.

"I guess so," he said.

"What did you think of him?"

"I don't know," said Frank. "Kind of usual."

"You're sure about your uncle?" said the other policeman.

"He'll come," said Frank. "I just have to call him. He doesn't live far away."

The policemen stood by the door and the subdued sound of the television blended with the cars on the interstate, which was about a quarter of a mile away. Then they turned and went down the broken concrete walk, between two bare patches of dirt. Frank closed the door and went back to sitting in front of the TV, although he didn't finish the macaroni and cheese. He wished the computer were still here and that his mother would come home soon, as she always had in the past. He missed her touch, even her wobbly gait and the smell of the perfume her boyfriends gave her. Her absence was so enormous as to color everything, the sounds in the house, the way his skin felt, the taste of the food he made, the noise of the cars on the interstate.

Once she had disappeared in the middle of winter, and while he was waiting for her to come home, it had snowed. The street at the back of the house was a long, straight one so the snowplow could get going fast, and when it did, at three or four in the morning, the house shook with a deep, appalling rumble. There was the sound, too, of the blade as it bounced on the pavement. When he heard that rumbling onrush, he looked out the window and saw the sparks from the scraping of the blade on the pavement. The plow looked like it was part machine and part monster, a combination of flesh and steel that made those shooting stars and left the smell of burned metal. Then the rumble diminished, becoming more and more distant and leaving him with the realization that while the sound had disappeared and the house had stopped shaking, he hadn't.

Jerri's boyfriend, that is Bob, not Joe, sold insurance and had left his wife, but this was the kind of man Jerri often had. The men saw her as a way station, just sweet enough and dependable enough and good looking enough to spend some time with while they tried to figure out what they should really be doing. They all had names like Joe, Mike, Mick, Jack, Bob, Jim. When she met a new man, Frank asked if it was a new Bob Jack, and she would just smile. Sometimes Frank saw her sitting in her room, by herself, next to the nightstand where she always kept a glass of water that had a bunch of small air bubbles in it. She never drank it. She just wanted it there in case she needed it. Even then Frank knew that she didn't want a glass of water, she wanted someone to comfort her, but she was stuck with that stale water.

She sat and looked into those bubbles, as though she could see something in them, a clue that would be valuable, but mostly when he asked if she had found someone new, she looked away and said, "Frank, close the door, will you?" Sometimes after she said this, Frank went in and sat next to her, looking at her fishnet stockings and smelling her perfume, which was expensive, although it had been given to her when she and Frank had really needed something to eat.

There was no one, though, as happy and filled with hope as Jerri when she had met someone who looked like he was going to work out. Then she would take Frank out to a diner in town, out by the highway, and talk about how they were going to live in a three-bedroom apartment or maybe a house with two stories, and Frank could get a computer and a motorcycle. She had a small tattoo, which she had gotten when she had been going out with a man who rode a motorcycle, a Norton with a black tank and chrome that was as shiny as a mirror. When she was sure that she was onto something good, she'd pull up her sleeve and show it to him, as though to say she had made mistakes in the past, but now everything, even the tattoo, was going to look different. Frank let himself be convinced, since she seemed so happy, and he didn't feel bad afterwards, either, when the new man turned out to be like the others, since that moment of hope had been so wonderful as to seem not delusional, but just premature.

One of these men gave Frank a pair of pliers. Another gave him a condom in a foil pack. One of them sold Frank a broken watch for a dollar.

And one of the Bob Jacks had given Frank twenty dollars to hide in the closet in his mother's bedroom. Frank had taken the money and gotten into the closet innocently enough, and when he looked out, amid the odor of wool and the mixture of scents his mother had worn, and feeling the tickle of the stockings that were hung on the door, he saw her kneeling in front of the man who had given him the money. As Frank peered out, his face hot with confusion, the man winked at him. Frank closed the door softly and sat back, under the coats, his hands trembling as he reached up to cover his ears.

Another of these men had seen a black eye that Frank had gotten at school, and he took Frank outside, in the backyard, which was under a billboard that could be seen on the interstate and which advertised a steakhouse, and up in the air, visible from the highway, there was a slab of rare steak, about six feet thick. Below the sign, Jerri's boyfriend told him that he should never be afraid in a fight, and that if he was going to fight, he had to win. Use a two-by-four, a pipe, a rock, the man said, hit them hard and don't stop. Break a bone. Or a nose. Don't be a pussy. Don't be afraid to put them in the hospital. Don't fight to fight. Fight to win. It's not about honor. It's about scaring the shit out of people.

— — —

AFTER SCHOOL, Frank sat in the kitchen, hearing the throb of the cheap icebox while he waited for Jerri to come home. He opened a can of tomato soup and had it with a pat of margarine in the middle, eating it with his spoon and making patterns out of the melting margarine. The clink of the spoon against the bowl made his mother's absence more real. He also noticed that the house was mustier now that Jerri was gone. When she was home, he hadn't minded so much. He often thought this smell was a sign of how he and his mother weren't like other people. Still, Frank craved those occasions when they splurged on dinner or when she overcharged her credit card. She told him then that they were going to make up for what they had missed, and even when it didn't work out, he was glad to be with her. She was what he had, and when they were inside the house, with her scratching his head while she drank her rum and Coke, everything was fine.

Jerri's brother came into the kitchen and said that the police had come to see him. It would probably be best, he said, if Frank came home with him for the time being. Frank went into his bedroom and put a couple of pairs of underwear and a couple of T-shirts into a brown paper bag, and then the two of them went over to the uncle's house, walking along the river, where they appeared like two black silhouettes, one tall and heavy, the other smaller and thin, carrying a black lump, against that yellow sky. Even the air seemed different now, a little sick making and with a slight emotional tug, too, as when you first notice a chill in the early days of fall.

His uncle's house was next to a bridge that went over the river, and at night Frank could hear the cars' tires on it. On nice days, he liked to stand in the middle and look down and think that there were fish in the river, silver ones the size of a wheelbarrow, or maybe a sturgeon as big as a Volkswagen, all going upstream to a secret place where they would spawn. He stood there and imagined that he could feel the fish swim along underneath him, the creatures so big and perfect that they—instead of the traffic—made the bridge hum.

Frank sat on the single bed in his uncle's house. On the other side of the door and through the wall he heard the TV his uncle was watching, which was tuned to a football game. Some shows, according to his uncle, were one six-pack long, but a football game took two.

Frank didn't see God as a person, as a man or a woman, but as a bright presence, or just a feeling that might help you. He asked for help now. Then he felt ashamed for praying, because he didn't know how to do it, really. He felt this mystification again, years later, when he slept with a woman for the first time. Had he done it right? When he prayed, he saw the glass of water on the nightstand next to his bed. Bubbles had formed overnight. Sometimes when he was close to those lead-colored bubbles he saw his face in them, distorted as in a fish-eye lens. He had never felt so close to his mother as when he looked at the bubbles, and had never missed her so much, either. When he prayed for an answer, he heard the sound of the TV through the wall.

After school he stood on the bridge and noticed dogs nosing around a trunk that someone had left in the mud at the edge of the river. The bridge had struts, rivets, a cross-hatching of supports, and a curve that went over the top, from one side to the other. Frank knew there was a powerful and unseen principle of engineering at work here, like other principles he didn't understand, such as the cumulative effect of each new day that his mother was gone and how each additional one changed his perspective. He didn't like the change, since it felt like falling and left him trying to hang on to something, but no matter how often he tried to catch a root or branch at the edge of the cliff, this sense of free fall was what remained. The horror of it, though, was its quality of slow motion. He had all the time in the world, but nothing to do with it.

The next afternoon the police had parked their cars at the end of the bridge, but the people in uniform were by the water, stepping around that black trunk in the mud. Frank came along from school and went out into the middle of the bridge and watched them, some in blue uniforms and two in bright yellow slickers. The box was locked, and now they broke it open with a hammer and a screwdriver, and then they lifted the lid. A woman cop who was there stepped back and put her hand to her mouth. A police photographer obviously wanted to have the camera between himself and the black chest in the mud, and he started taking pictures. The dogs were on the bridge, too, looking down at that trunk, the kind that you would take on a sea voyage.

Frank started walking toward the end of the bridge, where there were a couple of policemen watching what was happening at the side of the river. When one of them tried to grab him, Frank dodged to the side and went straight down the bank, giving in to the steep grade of it, not trying to brake himself at all, just running. When the policemen by the trunk tried to stop him, he went between their legs, moving with the quick agility of a child. Then, as he glanced inside at what was left of Jerri, a policeman pulled him away. The others closed ranks around the trunk, like a curtain swinging shut in a theater.

A policeman brought Frank up the bank and they sat on a bench outside an ice-cream place that had plywood in the windows and a sign that needed paint. It read THE REAL SCOOP.

"Is that her?" Frank said. He didn't care that his voice was quavering.

The cop looked around, but didn't answer, and Frank didn't say anything more, although for an instant he wondered if this man had been touching her, too, and then he thought, What difference would that make? Everyone was always touching her.

"I'm just sorry," said the policeman.

At night, Frank tried to sleep, and his uncle brought him a cup of warm milk. He had put some bourbon in it, but Frank couldn't drink it. After a while Frank pretended to go to sleep so that his uncle would leave, and then he sat in the dark, thinking about what he had seen. He realized she was gone, and that the darkness around him wasn't going to change the way it did when she showed up at the front door. Frank tried to grasp the scale of that darkness, which was everywhere, even oozing down to the river. It was the last sign he had of Jerri, as though she had left this enormous emptiness behind and while he was appalled that this was the only way he could feel her presence, it was what he had, and even though he was too frightened to cry, he still clung to the darkness, like the memory of a goodnight kiss, or her grand way of signing her name to a credit card chit she was never going to be able to pay. He tried to make sense of how much he had loved her, no matter what she had been, and to decide what good it had been to care so much about someone who could vanish and leave him with this loss mixed with knowledge of the malignant. He seemed to teeter on the edge of letting go, of almost crying, but the hot throb of it scared him. He suspected it was better to keep things under wraps, since crying was like stepping into a current that was too deep and too fast. He felt closer to her by having that sense of pain, and he didn't want anything to relieve it, since if it was gone, it would be like losing his last real memory of her.

He had lived with his uncle after that, going to school, walking back and forth across that bridge every morning and every evening of the academic year. His uncle had a job driving a street sweeper in the summer and a snowplow in the winter. They lived close to the garage where the plows were parked, and on a snowy night Frank heard the engines of the plows start. They made a noise like something grinding in the depths of the earth, and then the trucks groaned as they emerged from the garage, where the blue smoke hung.

It was late when he got back to Vermont, and he parked in front of his house and listened to the coyotes as they wailed on the ridge about a mile away. Frank leaned forward, against the wheel of his car, and realized that he was no longer waiting for some unknown event to take place. That was over. Something definite was coming his way now. And as he sat in the car, hearing the howling of those coyotes on the ridge, the night seemed more opaque than ever. There wasn't a star out. When he glanced up, in absolute darkness, there was nothing to see. So he sat there trembling, hearing his heart beat and listening to the sound of those wild dogs.

RUSSELL BOYD

NO ONE HUNTED FOXES ANYMORE, AT LEAST WHERE
Russell and Zofia lived, and instead they had what was called a drag hunt.
This was done by having someone, who was known as a "fox," lay down
scent ahead of the hounds and riders. When Russell was transferred from
the north to the town where he now lived, he took a job as the fox for a local
hunt club. He did this in the fall when the ground froze and the leaves
turned red and yellow and when the riverbottom was filled with mist in the
morning. Now, in October, which was just after he and Zofia had decided
he should move in with her, the ground froze at night, and in the morning
there was ice on the windshield.

As he worked on the windshield of the car, he thought of the difference
between himself and the people who organized the hunt. After he had put
down the scent and been chased by the horses and riders, he would be
invited to a picnic. This was usually held in a field where people had parked
their horse trailers and cars. At the picnic, the women glanced at him with
a kind of elegant hunger. He would smile and be polite, and then Virginia
Lowary, whose husband was president of the hunt, would put forty dollars
into the pocket of his warm-up jacket. Not quite tipping him, but the gesture reminded him of the distance between them. She was a slender woman
of forty, with red hair and freckles, and when she did this, her fingers lingered in his pocket as she pushed the crisp bills into it. Russell liked being a
fox, and he decided that he was going to leave it at that.

"Until next week," she said.

Russell had brought his scents to Zofia's house, the small bottles filled
with a yellowish fluid that reminded him of lacquer that you would put on
a violin. He had his roll of Geological Survey maps, too, for the different sections of land where the hounds were run. He showed Zofia the contour lines
and those little watery drawings that were supposed to represent a swamp.
The hunt Russell liked best was in the riverbottom, alongside the Connecticut: it had open places and fields, and there were game trails in the wild

cranberry and brush, as well as stagnant pools left by rain and the times when the river was high. The brush, the deadfalls, the treelines at the sides of the fields were places a fox would love.

Russell told Zofia he had seen a fox at the side of the road, just at dusk. It had stood with its head back, tense, trying to smell what was on the wind. The fox was alert to the smallest details of the landscape, since even the most insignificant thing might reveal danger, if you just knew how to see it. With an air of wariness and dignity, the fox turned his head toward Russell, who looked back, the two of them seeming attached by this gaze, which, when the fox disappeared into a field, broke as delicately as a filament of spiderweb.

"Can I come along?" Zofia asked. "You know, just to see."

"It's a long run," said Russell.

"I like to run," she said.

So, they went together on the morning of the first hunt. The hounds were put into a harvested cornfield in which only lines of stubble remained. The field was in a riverbottom, and on three sides of it were acres of brush that were slowly growing up into woods. The river ran along the fourth side in a wide, undulant channel, which at this time of the year, in a light fog, was as silver as a mirror.

Russell dragged a piece of fox-scented fur along the walls, at the edge of the fields, over deadwood and along the edges of swamps, and he did so in a large, S-shaped pattern that would allow the riders and hounds the greatest amount of chase in the acreage they had to hunt. Sometimes when he came to the end of a loop and turned back, he could get very close to the horses and hounds. Often there was just a screen of sumac and maple saplings between Russell and the riders.

The fog was just lifting. Zofia appeared in a nimbus of light when the sun was just behind her, and when she came close to him, he could smell the perfume of her hair. Her forehead was silver with moisture, and as they ran, she said, "Let's go. I don't want them to catch us. You didn't tell me it was so exciting." Then they ran along the swamp maples, which were as bright as lipstick.

Beyond the wall of brush, the hounds began to howl. Russell stopped. At these moments the cross-hatching of poplar, the stagnant ponds at the edge of a swamp, marked here and there with the birth of a mosquito, were bathed in silvery light, and then the vista throbbed with luminescence, with an intensity bound up with the warmth of the run and the pleasure of feeling right at the center of the smoky landscape.

Zofia ran up to him and he felt the heat of her skin. Then she leaned forward, her hands on her knees, her head down. He glanced at the whorls of her hair along her neck and her shirt where it was stuck to her back. Zofia stood up, too winded to speak, but she made a gesture, an imploring movement, as though to say that she thought they should keep going. But even so she reached up and kissed him, using her tongue, still breathing hard and pushing her pelvis against him. In the heat between them, with the sweat of their running, she looked up and stared right at him with just enough of a smile to make an invitation. He thought, She isn't serious. Not really. Not here. But then she hung against him, taking pleasure in the frank, daring seduction. She put her lips against his ear and said, "It's so exciting. Can you feel it?"

All around them was the rank odor of fall, which came from the frozen ground thawing, the harsh rotting smell coming up from the soil with all the promise of a distant spring. Then they looked through the screen of brush, where the horses were coming closer, pursuing them, and this added an intensity to the way Russell saw the brush and wild cranberry, the edges of the swamp, the sumac that was turning as red as a candy apple.

"Come on," said Zofia. She pulled him into the brush, which was like disordered rolls of barbed wire, seemingly impregnable until you got into it and saw those places where you could get down low so as to avoid the worst of it. Then she stopped him again, the two of them next to each other, looking back. She was breathing hard, looking from the landscape back to his eyes, where she lingered for a moment. Then she put her hand on his shoulder, tugging him, pulling him toward her. "What do you think?" she said. "Would you dare? I mean right here."

They stood on one side of a screen of brush, and a horse went by on the other side. Its shape wasn't clear, although it was still a definite presence, a combination of sleek black neck and flank that was defined by an onward rush and the sound of its hooves. There was a white horse, too. Zofia looked at them and then turned, bumping into him, her lips touching his neck as she tried to turn, her sweat and his mixing together in the sound of the baying dogs and the distant shouts of the hunters.

"Come on," she whispered. "Come on."

They went along the windbreak, through the clutter of the wild cran-berry, and toward the flat surface of the river. She pulled him toward it, being careful about the brush so that it wouldn't swing back at him, and then they came out on the bank, where they stood in the black soil. Zofia reached down into the water and made a cup of her hand, scooping the water over her face. Their reflections disappeared in the neatly undulant water, the waves as precise as an illustration of a mathematical principle. Zofia stood up and took his hand, then kissed him again. She was wearing Spandex run-ning shorts, which she pushed down and stepped out of, her skin white against the silver water, on which the crimson leaves were reflected. Then she tugged at his shorts, still hearing the jingling tack and the horses, the shouts of the riders, the baying of the hounds, and as he knelt there, seeing the water over her back, as she looked over her shoulder, smiling at him, still making this into a variety of fun, shoving back against him with a sudden impulse, he thought that the certainty of the moment, the alertness of it and the sudden warmth of her, the sense of heat and friendly sweat overcame everything else. It was this sense of alertness, without any other considera-tion, that was overwhelming. It was a contradiction: getting away from the heat and the buzzing insects, the colors of the leaves and yet never having been closer to them. They both breathed hard from the running, and from this too. The warm press of it, the heat of it, the frank impulse, right here, in the smile and shove, in the pink flesh, in the glistening of light on wet skin, in every attribute, in the odor there by the river, they both felt the pleasur-able sense of existing outside everything else and yet they seemed to float in it. It was naughty and it was fun: but it was flirting with a kind of gravity, too, which they understood through a specific thrill and a slippery itch. "Oh, fuck," she said, "don't you ever lie to me. Ever. Oh, fuck."

He found that they were just kneeling there on the gray soil at the side of the river. They pulled their shorts on and stood there, looking at each other, hearing the hounds. Zofia reached down and down and splashed water on her face, and then made a cup of her hands and dribbled water over his hands and arms, and said, "Doesn't that feel cool and nice?" She ran the water over his sweaty forehead and face, and then she whispered, "I've never done anything like that. Ever. I didn't know that people . . ." Then she put her head back and laughed, making a frank, keenly pleasurable sound.

"Do you think they saw?" she said, putting a hand to her face and blush-
ing.

"Let's hope not," he said.

"Oh, god," she said. "How are we going to face them if they did?"

Then they turned and ran back, stumbling around the deadfalls, the
long black trunks hidden in the brush.

Finally they came out where the hunt had started, the horse trailers
arranged haphazardly, and where there was a table set up with sandwiches
and drinks and beer. Zofia came up to the table, still trembling a little with
the chase, and when the woman who was behind the table offered her a bottle of beer, she took it and drank with her head back, the long bubbles rising in the neck.

"Oh," said Zofia to Russell, the beer on her breath. "I'm so itchy. Let's
go home. Did you get bitten by something back in there?"

They had to wait awhile, though. The riders came back, some in
clumps, some alone, some looking exasperated and a little ashamed. They
all wanted a drink. The entire group existed in the odor of wool clothing,
bourbon, and perfume. Virginia Lowary stood in front of Russell in her
jodhpurs and black boots and jacket and said to him, "Here's your money."
The landscape was made up of the smoke-colored bark, the bright red of
swamp maples and the streaks of yellow from the poplar.

FRANK KOHLER

KOHLER SAW A WOMAN IN TOWN WEARING BLACK lipstick, and at night he lay awake considering the shades of black, from absolute midnight to charcoal, and how in certain contexts these hues had the effect of revealing a previously hidden power. He considered women's shiny black underwear, or the effect of black fishnet stockings, the mesh masking yet revealing the promise of the skin underneath. What was it in this blackness? At night he closed his eyes to see it better.

Part of the mystery was the way black took light, as on the surface of a black silk skirt over which the light flowed like a silver liquid. And another element was black hair against white skin, or a woman's lips as she wore black lipstick: What was it they promised? At first he thought it was just a sensual tug, but then it occurred to him that black silk over a woman's hips was made more intense by other qualities, such as life disguising itself as attractiveness to hide its real power. He guessed this mixture of fun and power could be seen in a black latex skirt, tight and shiny, or sheer black nylons, the skin beneath them glowing with life. Black nail polish. Black eyes.

Still, he wanted to know what the nature of this opaque shade was, this color that suggested the most private of connections, which took place in a realm that people couldn't see but by which they were so controlled. Kohler thought that the depths of the earth, where the black oil waits, was where the powerful aspect of this color was most perfectly distilled, most obvious, under pressure, sleek and wet and compelling. Or maybe it was in the shadows under those dark skirts, in the hint of black lipstick, in the wink of a black eye.

Kohler decided he needed a new car. A black one. Something sleek and powerful.

He had avoided Northampton for years, even looking away from the signs on the highway for its exits when he had to drive by, but now he decided that this was where he should go to buy the car. It was about an hour from where he lived, and he drove his sedate Chevrolet, so much like what a computer repairman would own, down I-91. As he got closer, he saw the exit and beyond it the modern clutter that surrounded most towns, although from a distance it was indistinct, signs, traffic lights, the claustrophobically familiar logos that suggested he was at home, although he knew he wasn't. He stopped at the first signal and thought, Why have I come here? This is stupid.

He went through the intersection toward the car lots, and then pulled into a gas station. He sat there, away from the islands, and imagined that he looked teary and stupid. These moments had become constant now, and he was mystified by their sudden arrival. They were like hearing a piece of music that was associated with an exquisite tenderness. At these moments, in which everything was imbued with a sad intensity, Kohler was desperate to forgive everyone, and the warmth of this forgiveness, the joy of it, perfectly covered up his deep and nameless turmoil, like a blanket laid over a child having a nightmare. Everything was turned upside down, and where he should have been scared and angry, he was filled with love. Or this was one half of the equation. The second half was what he had felt in Boston, in the Combat Zone.

In his car, he put out his hand, as though he could touch the Russian woman in the videotape. Then, as the sensation faded, he was left with a desire for an unknown and yet still beguiling presence, large and golden, like the edge of a cloud from which beaconlike rays of roseate light cut right into him. Soon, though, he found himself just sitting in this deserted gas station, on the edge of these fucking tears, as he called them. And on the verge of panic, too, because he didn't know where they were coming from. In his fearful trembling he found himself asking if he could be smart enough now to see what was happening.

Well, one thing is for sure, he thought. I need a car.

The clutter of dealerships looked like chance itself. A new Toyota franchise was built in an empty space next to an old Nissan lot, which was next to one for Chevrolet, each new showroom adding to a general sense of disorder.

The first place he stopped was the GM lot, where he walked among the cars that were all pointed the same way, the prices painted on their windshields with a big brush dipped in white stuff, starch, he guessed, and over-

head, like military flags of a low-rent country, the triangular plastic pen-
nants made a fatigued and anxious flutter.

The car he liked was a sleek model with no chrome that looked as if it
were made out of the same material as a stealth bomber. He slowly walked
around the car, looking at the magnesium wheels, the double exhaust ports,
the black leather seats. Stick shift with a chrome lever and a black ball. He
felt the underlying, mysterious power of the color.

"It's a beauty, isn't it?" the salesman said.

He came up behind Kohler and stood in the sun, smiling a little. He was
blond, overweight, tall, balding, so that his scalp was shiny under his hair.
He put out his hand. Kohler shook it and introduced himself. The salesman
said his name was Billy.

"Oh, yeah," Billy said, "it's a beauty. "Are you interested just for pleasure, or are you a collector?"

"Pleasure," Kohler said, already feeling the pleasure, too, like a bug
squirming in a chrysalis.

"Would you like to take it for a little ride?" Billy said.

"Yes," Kohler said.

"Well, Frank, you wait here a moment and I'll fix you up. I'll get the
keys and a license plate. Can I have your driver's license? I'll just make a
Xerox of it."

Billy took the license and walked along those orderly rows of shiny cars.
On the sidewalk, about ten feet away, pigeons were picking at crumbs, a bit
of something thrown out of a window, a hot dog or hamburger bun. Their
heads went up and down mechanically. Kohler looked at the clouds and the
low hills in the distance and felt it begin again. He could apprehend the
presence of an extraordinary gentleness, so maddeningly remote, so hard to
get a grip on. At these moments he felt himself so close to the beautiful and
omnipresent that . . . he didn't know what, really. Then it ended, just like
that, and he found himself in front of that black car while those pigeons
walked back and forth in the remains of junk food.

"Here you go," said the salesman.

"What's your name again?" Kohler asked.

"Billy," the salesman said, giving him an odd look.

He put the dealer's plate on the back, low down on the bumper, but not
right on the car, since it was fiberglass and the magnet wouldn't hold there.

Then the salesman dropped the keys into Kohler's hand with a salacious touch. Everyone knew what a car like this was all about. The interior was hot from being shut up there in the sunlight, and the leather seat creaked as Kohler got in.

The engine erupted with a snarl. Oil pressure came up. Alternator started charging. The digital tach throbbed. The salesman got in and put on his seatbelt.

"Never can be too careful," he said. "You want to put yours on?"

"Sure," said Kohler. "Thanks. It's funny how a car like this can make sense of things."

"Five-speed," he said. "Reverse is back here." The salesman looked straight ahead. "Yes, a car like this is a great cathedral."

Kohler backed up. The pigeons fluttered into the air. The flags overhead made a little popping sound. The salesman looked both ways at the exit of the lot and turned to Kohler with that pale, uncertain smile.

"O.K.," he said. "Good to go."

They drove along the strip to the ramp that led up to the highway, and by the top of it Kohler was doing seventy-five miles an hour, but not a steady seventy-five so much as a rising one. All the gauges were LCDs, and so there wasn't any speedometer needle, just a series of quickly changing and ascending numbers. The car was filled with the grinding sound of the motor that moved the seat as Kohler adjusted it.

"This section is patrolled pretty heavily," Billy said. "You know what I'm saying?"

At this speed the other cars appeared like pylons in an obstacle course, slipping away as Kohler drove around them. Some of them, driven by people who glanced into their rearview mirrors, just got out of the way.

"What kind of mileage does it get?" said Kohler.

"Mileage?" Billy licked his lips. "Well, it's fuel-injected and its got three hundred and eighty-five horsepower."

"So, it's lousy?" said Kohler.

"No. I wouldn't say that. It isn't bad so much as an indication of other things."

He looked a little sick, but even so he went on trying to sell a car at close to a hundred miles an hour. Kohler glanced over at him, inspired and yet strangely irritated by the man's dedication.

"No," Billy said. "It's just a reflection of the horsepower. You could go out and get a Volkswagen and it would get great mileage, but what about pickup?" He swallowed. "All leather interior. Tinted glass."

"I was thinking about storage space," Kohler said.

"Well, it's not a truck."

"Let's say you went deer hunting. How do you get a .30-06 in and out?"

"Through the hatchback," he said. "This is the exit to take if you want to get back to the dealership."

A sign at the side of the road read NEXT EXIT 10 MILES.

"Do you want to pay cash, or do you want to finance?"

"Cash," Kohler said.

"Oh," Billy said. "You know something? It's got a radar detector. Why don't we just turn it on?"

He reached down to a switch on the dashboard and turned it on. The thing beeped. Then the pale yellow, green, and red lights flashed, one after another. Up there over a hundred, Kohler noticed that the steering required more concentration. It was exciting to see the cars up ahead move over and then disappear as though something were sucking them backward.

"Yeah," Kohler said. "Cash. I was thinking maybe we could do a little something with that price."

"Well, make me an offer," he said.

"Knock two thousand off."

Up ahead there was nothing but the white lines and the median, where the grass had just been mowed. It had been done badly, and the windrows of uncut grass gave the entire thing a striped appearance. At this speed, Kohler had a sudden and unexpected apprehension of freedom, as though you could only feel it at a hundred and ten, which made him suppose it was a dangerous thing to have, but then what freedom doesn't have a little danger built in? Or a lot?

"So, what about that price?"

Billy licked his lips. Looked at the radar detector. Kohler supposed the salesman was trying to make the sale before the radar detector went off. Everything went by in a blur, at least close to the car, but farther away it was just those rounded hills, some houses that looked out of place and awkward in fields that had once been farmed.

"Okay," Billy said. "Two thousand."

The radar detector made a little squeak.

"That means you should slow down," he said.

"Good, good," said Kohler. "Glad to see the detector works all right."

"I guess you aren't married," Billy said.

"How can you tell?"

"No married man drives a car that fast," he said. "And certainly not one with kids."

"No, I'm not married," Kohler said. "I'm almost engaged, though."

"Your wife will slow you down," Billy said. "That's a promise you can take to the bank."

In the office of the dealership they came down to cases, which is to say trying to decide how they were going to find a source for that two thousand dollars. Kohler kept glancing at that black car out there, sitting in its own black shadow, like a piece of dark silk. Billy looked at Kohler's Chevy, and they worked the deal out so that they split the difference—that is, Billy didn't give Kohler the entire two thousand, but just one, since he offered Kohler a thousand less than the Chevrolet was worth.

"Okay," Kohler said. "You've got yourself a deal."

Kohler gave him a check on the account where he had been saving for years now. Billy got out the temporary plate, a cheesy paper one. He put it in the license holder. Kohler signed over the title to his Chevy and Billy dropped the keys to the black car into his hand.

"Be careful," he said.

Kohler idled along, passing the car dealerships with their small plastic flags as though for a nation of a million defeats. Even then he knew right where he was going, as though the place were tugging on him. Maybe, he thought, the car will give me something extra to help confront the place. The memories of it were like recalling a shimmering mass of clouds in the distance, which at first appeared to be a rainstorm, but turned out to be hungry locusts with rainbow-tinted wings. He drove by the house where he had last lived with his mother, and looked in the dim windows. The house had been repainted in a color that looked as if the paint had been bought because it had been on sale, just like when he had lived there. Yellow-green. Then he stopped and got out.

The small yard in front still had the same bare dirt with a path of cracked and buckled concrete leading to the door, and during the day, the place was still in the shadow of the billboard that was near the interstate. The house was dark, and he guessed it was all right to walk up to the window to look inside. He cupped his hands around his eyes. Inside, he saw the same dim light of his childhood, which had a humming resonance to it, as though the things that had happened here were encoded not in memory so much as in a variety of vibration. Then he saw a television set in the corner that had aluminum foil on the antenna, just as his own had, years before. He recognized this with a shock, as though a familiar face had appeared at the window. But he didn't jump back in surprise. Instead, he closed his eyes and leaned his forehead against the cool, peeling sash. When he opened his eyes, he saw the reflection of the black car. At least, he knew, he could get away.

He guessed it was on the strength of this that he got in and started driving straight to the place he had been thinking of in the beginning.

The bridge had been painted, and now the girders, cross-braces, and rivets were all a municipal green. The bridge had a sidewalk on it that was made of wire mesh, through which you could see the slick movement of the river down below. The bank had been cleaned up, too. Just that fine sand, marked with parallel ridges where the water had been before receding. No junk in the woods, no trash, no beer cans and bottles, the way it had been years ago. Kohler stopped in the middle of the bridge, and the cars went by with an airy rush and the steel shook beneath the black car, as though even the metal had to vibrate with the impact of what had happened here.

There was a roll of Tums on the seat, which Kohler had taken out of his pocket, and now he unrolled the silver paper and put a couple into his mouth. He wanted to be precise about what had lifted from that trunk and filled the air, the spirit of the event, the moral haze of it. When he had gotten down there and before he had been dragged away, one of the cops who had taken a look, staggered back. He said, "They cut her up like that? Like that?" And another one said, "To get her in, I guess. What's that kid doing here?"

Kohler put another Tums into his mouth and chewed, looking down. Then he glanced at the hood of the car. No chrome. Nothing bright, as if it were absorbing light.

He felt the impulse to keep moving, but didn't know where to go. The downtown section was older, not like the strip where the car lots were, but more like a mill town that had experienced an inevitable decline. Now, though, it was being pulled out of this deterioration by coffee shops and sushi bars, dress stores and art galleries, vegetarian restaurants right next to bars for workingmen. On the street, the smell of incense mixed with baking pizza.

It hadn't been this way when Kohler lived here. Then it had just been run-down, the stores boarded up, with men leaning against the old brick, drinking beer out of paper bags. The town looked better, but something of the old days still lurked behind the incense and the sushi.

Kohler went into a diner for a cup of coffee, but there were ten different kinds, and for a while he just looked at the menu that was written in colored chalk on a blackboard. The waitress who came up to him had red hair and a tattoo, a vine with barbed wire, that went around the biceps of one arm. He said, "A cappuccino," as though he did this every morning. Kohler picked up the local newspaper on the counter and flipped through it, glancing at the articles about political corruption mixed in with reviews of transsexual rock bands. In the back were personal ads.

He read the kinky ones from people who were "D and D," which meant drug- and disease-free. Then he turned to the ads from women looking for men.

"Find something?" the waitress asked.

"Maybe."

"Yeah," she said. "That's the trouble. You never know."

"Boy, is that right," he said.

"Well, good luck," she said.

He finished his coffee, and when he got to the cash register the waitress said, "Are you going to call her?"

"No," he said. "I think I'm onto something already."

"Good. Good," she said. "I'll send positive thoughts your way."

In the street he looked at the distant hills that had been worn down by the glacier, and in the afternoon light, so soothing and pink, he stood there, blinking, looking north. He thought, I need gas. An oil change. Maybe a car wash. To bring out that color.

RUSSELL BOYD

JACKSONS FALLS IS A MEDIUM-SIZED TOWN THAT sits on a bluff above the Connecticut River. It was a beautiful town a hundred years ago, when the mills were productive and people had money to spend, but all that is left of the flush times is a collection of elegant houses that are now divided into apartments. These buildings have an air of the tattered and weather-worn, like a regimental flag that has been through one battle too many. And below the elegant houses, closer to the river where the mills used to be, there are some brick buildings, functional four-story structures that are streaked around the windows by a hundred years of rain. The streets in front of them always have a chill, even in May, as though winter lingers here and the shadows are impervious to the green-and-pink-tinted spring light. This chill is more spiritual, Russell supposed, than actual. Or maybe another way to put it is that the people in these brick buildings, down by the river, usually had more trouble than they could handle.

Russell often got partial information, just bits and pieces that were not true, or had been true. He perceived the unknown, in these moments, as having a tactile quality. The air had a slight buzz. It was what he felt when he was working days and got a call about a man in Jacksons Falls who was arguing with a woman in one of those buildings that always seemed to have an air of winter about it. A neighbor had gotten tired of hearing the never-ending arguments and had called the police. The man in the apartment had his girlfriend with him, along with her child. At least that's what the neighbor said. When the girlfriend tried to leave, the man in the apartment had stopped her. She started crying and this made her baby cry, and to be heard, the man had to yell over both of them. There was a possibility that the man in the apartment, whose name was Sam or Sammy, had a "funny" gun, something from Eastern Europe, or so the neighbor thought. In Jacksons Falls, Russell drove through the short main street, past the movie theater and a couple of abandoned storefronts, and then stopped in front of a building which had that lingering chill. When he opened the front door, it was like walking into a shadow.

He wasn't sure why he didn't like this particular call, and his very uneasiness made him uneasy, which was a spiral that led him around and around until he found himself guessing that what he didn't like was being inside, confined between walls, which meant that he was already penned up and limited by someone who was about to make a mistake. When he found himself worrying about uncertainty, which was what he was doing now, he shrugged and tried to tell himself that this was always what it was like when he was in the middle of it. Later he could say he had been having doubts. In the middle he just saw that the light was getting brighter, and felt an airy sensation in his chest. Then he wiped his hands on his pants and went into the building. At least he wasn't alone, since he had seen another cruiser parked in the street, number 602, driven by a friend of his.

Russell let the door close behind him. The hall downstairs was painted a shiny green, and the light fixture at the end of it, back near the stairwell, left the paint with a silvery film. Even from here, Russell could hear the argument, which was on the third floor. He went to the back of the building and up the marble staircase, veined like blue cheese, and climbed up to the third floor, where Tony Deutsche, the other trooper on this call, was waiting. Deutsche was a heavy-set man with a shaved head. People often thought of him as being slow, but this was because he took his time to think about a question before answering it. In fact, Deutsche was one of the few people Russell would have easily gone to for advice. Russell said, "What's going on?"

Deutsche shrugged. "I just got here."

The apartment door was about twenty feet from the landing where Russell and Deutsche stood. The sound of the argument was at once staccato and piercing, like a television heard through a wall, and as Russell tried to hear, he couldn't make out the words, just the irritating cadence. Then Russell and Deutsche went down the hall until they came to the apartment door. The argument was louder here.

Russell looked around the hall and smelled unwashed clothing mixed with another odor, which he guessed came from someone pissing on the stairs. As he stood with Deutsche next to the door, which was covered with chipped paint, the voices inside the apartment suddenly stopped. For an instant Russell had the sensation that there was someone on the other side of the door, head cocked, listening in the same way he was. He wanted to say that there was something wrong here, but he didn't know what it was, and since this was so, it was a good idea to say nothing. Still, he kept looking for a detail, a sound, or an object that would explain his sense of uneasiness.

Deutsche tapped on the door. A man opened it. He was holding an automatic weapon, a short-barreled thing with a pistol grip and a stainless-steel receiver and barrel. From the back of the apartment, the girlfriend said, "Sammy. Sammy. What are you doing?"

"You want to know?" said Sammy. "Do you? I'll show you."

He shot the Eastern European machine pistol at the ceiling. It was loud enough to make Russell think that he was being slapped and that the walls, too, were reverberating with a hard smack. Sammy glared at Russell and Deutsche and slammed the door, making more plaster fall out of the ceiling. Upstairs another door was slammed shut and then someone flushed a toilet and Russell heard the water whine in the pipes. The floor of the hall was covered with plaster that had fallen out of the ceiling, and when Russell and Tony retreated to the landing, they left black outlines of footsteps where he and Tony had walked away from the apartment door. The outlines of shoes in the dust looked like diagrams for dancing lessons, that is, if the dance was one that went straight from one place to another.

"Where's Peterson?" said Russell.

"What? I can't fucking hear," Deutsche said.

"Where's Peterson—you know, the guy who negotiates with these assholes!" said Russell.

"I don't know," said Deutsche. It was hard to say if he had heard or if he was referring to a more general doubt.

"There's something about this one I don't like."

"Like what?" said Deutsche.

"I don't know," said Russell.

"Well, you don't know and I don't know," said Deutsche. "Where does that get us?"

Russell looked at the hall floor with those shapes of footsteps in the dust, which seemed eerie, as though they had been left by a ghost.

"Either he's going to come out of there, or we're going to have to go in," said Deutsche.

"We could wait for Peterson," said Russell.

"And let that asshole kill the woman and the kid?" said Deutsche.

Then they went back to the door. Inside, the girlfriend was crying, and when she wasn't gasping she kept saying, "This has gotten totally out of control. Totally. Why don't we get some counseling?" Sammy said, "Some what? Why don't you practice being quiet? Counseling? Christ. I'll counsel you. You want counseling. You want it?" From the sound of their voices, they seemed to be in the back bedroom, and the woman's voice faded more as she tried to soothe the child, and when she couldn't do anything with the crying baby, Sammy threatened to kill her and the child and anyone else who came near the place, or anyone who was handy. When the woman yelled at him, the words were muffled, but the meaning was clear.

Deutsche and Russell got the man to crack open the door so they could talk to him. Everything is O.K., it's all a misunderstanding. Everyone is reasonable. Nothing has to go wrong. Deutsche had a nice, calm voice, but the more calm and reasonable he was, the more Sammy got excited. Russell guessed this was because Sammy had been hearing calm, solicitous voices telling him things he didn't want to hear all his life. Russell asked if there was any alcohol in the apartment or drugs or anything like that, and when he asked, he did so with simple, ordinary words, just trying to find a common language that he and the man shared. The man looked at Russell with a blank, flat expression that showed no awareness of where he was or what he was doing, at once so scared and disoriented that there was no way to reach him.

The kid started crying again. The girlfriend sounded as though she was getting worn down, too, and that she didn't have the strength just to sit there, to be quiet and let things play out. Instead, she got more and more vocal and this made Sammy say, "Will you shut the fuck up? What do I have to do to shut you up? Is that what you want? You want me to shut you up?" Her kid started to scream, and this did to her what her screaming did to Sammy. She told him that he was terrifying her child.

"Are you saying that the crying baby is my fault?" he said.

"The baby is scared," she said.

"Oh, yeah?" he said. "Well, it better get over it."

Deutsche began to shout, too, but Russell reached over and took his arm and pulled him back down the hall. He didn't want it to come to the point where they were all screaming, the voices rising higher and higher until everyone went right over the top. Russell sat down on the top step, eyes closed, concentrating. Then Deutsche said to him, "What do you think?"

"This is getting out of control!" the woman screamed. "Why can't you just stop?"

"The guy just keeps going up and up. Like a hot-air balloon," said Deutsche.

From inside the apartment the voices started again, just as if they were having an argument on a Saturday night, loud, insistent, almost funny. Almost. The man in there shot the machine pistol again, and the woman screamed, "What is wrong with you? What the fuck is wrong with you?"

"You want to see?" Sammy said. He said it over and over again, "You want to see? You want to fucking see?" The exasperation behind this question got bigger and filled the room and the hall, too, with Sammy's disappointments, his anger, his failings, his confusion. Russell disliked the confusion more than anything else, since it allowed Sammy to think he was someone to clear matters up, but in fact he was only digging a deeper hole.

The kid went on screaming in a repetitive two-tone shriek that had a grating edge to it.

"All right," said Russell.

"All right, what?" said Deutsche.

"You know," said Russell. He gestured to the door.

They moved through the dust from the ceiling, which they could smell, almost like wet plaster. Tony tapped on the door.

"Open up for a minute," he said.

The man opened the door, but he had the chain on it. The kid's crying was instantly louder. Sammy's face looked as if he had a bad fever. Everything about his appearance, the unshaved sweatiness, the tired and yet manic look in his eyes, showed that the way he handled being afraid was to be stupid. He was mesmerized by the power of stupidity, by the scale of the mess it makes, but messy or not, it was what he had. He was sweating there, his face looking slick and damp, and while he was trying to swagger and to convince everyone to do exactly what he wanted, he also showed that he wasn't in control of anything.

The light in the hall changed, or so it seemed to Russell. It became brighter and darker at the same time. The places where the light fell seemed so clear, so illuminated as to look silver, but the shadows were even darker, more obscuring, and tainted, too, with that cloying odor of urine.

Inside the apartment, Sammy shouted over his shoulder at his girl-friend, "Didn't I tell you? Didn't I tell you?" And she screamed back, "What, what did you tell me?" Their voices went up and up, their exhaustion and disorientation leaving them incapable of seeing anything outside of the small space, surrounded by opaque walls, where they stood. This was it, they seemed to be saying. This was what they had always been waiting for, and now it was here. "That fucking kid," said the man. "That fucking kid. You can't even shut it up. Shut it up."

"I can't," she said. "It's a baby. Babies cry. Don't you know that? Do I have to tell you?"

"What did I say?" he said.

"Nothing," she said. "When you talk, all that comes out is nothing. Just noise."

Deutsche motioned to Russell, who nodded. All right.

Sammy turned toward the woman they couldn't see, made a gesture toward her, and Deutch put his shoulder against the door and broke the cheesy night chain, which looked as though it was made out of metal, but was plastic coated with shiny stuff to look like stainless steel. The door swung open.

An unhappy party had been going on in the apartment. The floor was covered with bottles and a couple of bags from McDonald's, a stuffed animal that was stained and had a leg ripped off, a sink with a dripping faucet. It felt like a collection of broken things, as at the collision of two cars. The baby cried and the woman turned her slack, tired face toward Russell. The man, the woman, the baby, and Deutsche all waited to see what was going to happen.

The man swung the barrel of the automatic weapon at Deutsche and pulled the trigger. Just a click. Russell strained to hear it. Then he thought, Thank God. Thank God. The baby screamed, its mouth open, pink gums and lips showing, and the woman just stood there and stared. Russell noticed that the ugly gun was turning in the air, like a baton, and then the man grabbed it by the barrel so he could swing it like a club, and as he hit Deutsche in the jaw, Deutsche shot the man in the chest.

DOWNSTAIRS, RUSSELL stood around in those blue shadows and felt that chill. Other policemen arrived and began to do their work upstairs, snapping pictures, talking to the neighbors, and taking charge of the dead man's pistol. While Russell waited, he thought about that lingering chill. Part of it, of course, came from the accumulation of winters here, and the severity of them, too. Warm air came up from the coast and hit the cold air from Canada, and in this collision the wind with the grains of ice in it really would take your skin off, if you gave it the chance. And beneath it all, Russell detected a sense of the inevitable, too, which could be seen in what happened to those signs on the highway north of White River Junction. They had been green and cream-colored just a year or two ago, but now they were a pale, snake-belly white, as though the ice had sandblasted them until they looked like signs in a desert. The shadows downstairs between the buildings had this sense of a slow, steady attrition. And as Russell stood considering the winters, he still couldn't shake the atmosphere of the apartment upstairs. It clung to him like the odor of smoke.

When he finally left, after the reports were written and a statement signed, he drove to Zofia's house. He knew there would be an investigation by the head of the internal affairs section, whom everyone referred to as the Prince of Darkness. He'd look for a way to blame Deutsche and Russell. But it was a clear case of self-defense. It would be all right. Or at least Russell hoped it would. But when he considered an investigation and remembered what had happened, he was left with a new feeling, which was a perfect symbiosis of fear and exasperation.

The leaves of the poplar trees were silver and pale green, the two colors shimmering in the afternoon breeze. Dust swept up behind Russell's car, and when he went up to the door of the house, it blew over him like a storm in a dry, lonely place.

Zofia was in the kitchen. He stood just inside the door and realized that something had changed, and when he looked at her, blinking in the sudden realization of it, she said, "Hey. What's going on?"

He sat down at the kitchen table and looked at her as she put a pan on the stove and turned on the gas with a *whooff!* So, what had changed? Even here the shadows were portentous, as though something were lurking just beyond the light. Zofia put oil in the pan and some chopped garlic, which began to sizzle.

"What's wrong?" she said without looking at him.

Out the window he saw those silver leaves, trembling in the breeze, and beyond them the last purple sky of evening, with just one or two stars coming out, like holes punched in blue paper.

"We had some trouble today," he said.

Even now, what happened didn't lend itself to being summed up, but he tried to come up with the words that would convey that apartment, the bottles on the floor, the crying baby, the blood-wet floor, where people had walked and left shapes, like hieroglyphs, of blackish water.

"I thought I was going to get shot," said Russell. "And then I thought Tony was going to get shot, too."

"You mean the cop with the shaved head?" said Zofia.

"Yeah," said Russell. "Yeah. Him."

She turned off the pan as she reached for two glasses and poured a little brandy into each one, and then sat down at the kitchen table.

"How often does that happen?" she said.

"Not very often," he said.

"Really?" she said. "Are you telling me the truth?"

"I think so," he said.

"You think so?"

He nodded.

"Or is it more that you hope so?" she said.

"Both could be true," he said. "They aren't contradictory, are they?"

She shook her head. No, they could both be true.

"I don't know if I'm ready for this," she said.

"It's all right," he said. "It's fine."

"Is it?" she said.

"Yeah," he said. "Sure."

He was still sweating.

"There's more to it than just that," he said. He picked up her hand. "You don't mind, do you?"

"No," she said. "I want you to touch me."

"I wasn't scared of getting killed, because the thing I thought of was that I might lose you."

She took a swallow of her drink. Then she put her head down on her arm.

"Do you really mean that?" she said, her voice muffled by her arm and the surface of the table.

"Oh," he said, "I mean it."

She looked from one of his eyes to the other, trying to see if he was sincere. It was obvious that she wanted to look right through the pupils, to an interior that was inexhaustible in its possibilities, at once unknowable and still somehow trustworthy. It was this opaque depth that was at the heart of what she would have to believe in.

"It's not that mysterious," he said.

"There's where you're wrong," she said.

She got up and turned the stove back on.

"But do you understand what I'm saying?" he said.

She nodded, looking down at the pan.

"I know what you meant," she said.

His ears were still ringing from the noise earlier in the afternoon. The sound changed a little when he moved his head one way and another, and in the midst of this sound he thought about how he had begun. In the beginning, when he had first started on the road, he had approached a car without thinking as much as he should have, and then when an older trooper began to give him some hints, Russell went up to a car with a list of things to consider: How did it sit on its springs? Was it carrying something in the trunk? Had any of it been repainted? Had some new hiding place been built in? Was the license plate clean when the car was dirty (which meant the plate could have been stolen)? And, of course, there were other matters, of increasing seriousness, such as how the people in a car moved, or how Russell should behave when he had asked a driver to step out of the car, not to mention other things that he knew to be true, such as the fact that couriers often traveled in pairs, so that if the first car, carrying something it shouldn't, was stopped, the driver of the second car could kill the trooper who made the stop. All of these things and many others went through his mind as he stepped out into the greasy wind at night, but after a while, much to his amazement, he started looking at the cars he stopped as he had in the begin-ning, just as cars, but somehow it was different. The same, but different.

With Zofia, he wanted to know what pleased her and flattered her, what made her unexpectedly angry or unexpectedly sweet, what she wanted to do, not only at work, but desires that she couldn't really articulate or only dreamed about, like going to Rome or taking a bicycle trip to France, or going to Finland, where they would take a sauna and then roll in the snow. He wanted to be aware of how he could hurt her without meaning to, or to realize that while she had seemed unreasonable, she was actually thinking about something from a point of view he had never considered. And, after having gone through these and too many other small details to list (as many or more as he had to contend with when he was on the road, trying to do the right thing and to stay alive, too), he would be able to look at her again, just as he had in the beginning, and it would be the same, but different. He could imagine the moment when this happened. She would have her hair in a bandana, wearing jeans and a T-shirt, as she went around her house pick-ing things up to put in the washer, where she would stand and smell her underarm and strip off her T-shirt and throw that in, too, and stand there in the piles of clean sheets and towels, which were scented with soap. She might look at him then, her stomach in neat segments when she bent over to pick up a towel.

AT THIS TIME of the year, Tony Deutsche's mother cooked a dinner for his friends. She was a woman in her late sixties who wore simple, some-what severe clothes, a gray skirt and a green sweater that buttoned up the front, for instance, and good, serviceable shoes that she could use to walk out to the barn. The dinner was a warmup for Thanksgiving, and she made a turkey, which she cooked in a bag. This year, after going into that apartment in Jacksons Falls, Tony asked if Russell and Zofia wanted to come.

Tony's mother and father lived in a house that had once been part of a dairy farm, but there wasn't much left aside from a barn that was falling down around abandoned stanchions. A sugar house across the street had partially burned down and was falling in, too. The place wasn't dreary so much as used up, as though you could still feel the effort that it had taken to live on a dairy farm.

Tony had his jaw wired. During the afternoon, when the turkey was cooking and the house was filled with the smell of it, Tony's mother kept looking at his jaw, as though the injury were somehow connected to her, too, and that what had been done to him had also been done to her. Then she looked away and went about her business, rolling out dough for a pie, and making a filling. She turned to Zofia and said, "You know the secret to making a really great apple pie? Put in some pears. That's the trick." Then she glanced again at her son's jaw.

"You'd think they would be more careful," she whispered to Zofia.

"I think they were being careful," said Zofia, quietly.

"Not careful enough," said Mrs. Deutsche. She bit her lip and then went back to rolling out the dough with hard, quick movements.

"I understand," said Zofia.

Mrs. Deutsche went on rolling out the dough, glancing up at Zofia once and then going back to work. The dough was on a piece of marble, which was white with dark swirls in it, and when Mrs. Deutsche was done, she said, "That's too bad."

Before dinner, Tony sat in the living room with Russell, Zofia, and a couple of troopers. They talked of a naked man who had painted himself all over in red and blue, and a woman who gave birth to a baby in the backseat of a cruiser. No one wanted to mention the moment when Russell and Tony thought something had come to an end, but in fact had just begun. They could say the guy was an asshole and that he deserved it, but they craved a more substantial answer than that. But what was it? Everyone knew that it was better not to go on about something you couldn't resolve. It was better to hope that you wouldn't have such bad luck again.

Tony talked like a man in a dentist's chair. Dinner was served. Tony's father, a bald man in a pink shirt and blue jeans, who wore green rubber boots as though he still had cows to milk, carved the turkey with a neat economy, as though he were being filmed for a manual about how to carve a turkey. Everyone sat around the table with plates of turkey and stuffing with mashed potatoes and gravy, carrots, cranberry sauce. Tony looked down at his and, after a moment, got up and went into the kitchen, from which the others heard a glassy clink and then the sound of the blender. In a minute he came back, his dinner turned into a drinkable gruel. He had a straw with him to put into the glass, and he took a sip through it.

"You know something?" he mumbled. "I'm glad I killed that sucker."

On the way home, in Zofia's car, in the green light from the dashboard, she reached over and took Russell's hand. Then she sat there, obviously hoping that she wasn't going to cry, putting her other hand to her face and breathing slowly.

"What do you suppose the chances are that you are going to have that kind of trouble again?" she said.

"Oh," he said, "I don't think it's very likely."

FRANK KOHLER

KOHLER TOOK THE ENVELOPE FROM THE MAILBOX by the road and turned toward the house. The label on it showed the silhouette of a man and a woman dancing, the woman looking up, one of her hands on the man's shoulder, her eyes set on his. The envelope was thin. He ran his fingers along it, squeezing it to feel the letter that was inside. He stood there looking at the graying siding of his house, which appeared to him like a jungle station on the Amazon that one sees, all of a sudden, after coming around a bend in the river. In the silence and isolation of here, he could sense a barely subdued threat that he supposed was the essence of living in an isolated place. Then he felt the envelope again.

In the kitchen he cleaned the table and made tea, and while he sat there with a starkly fragrant cup of it in front of him, he stared at the letter, which he'd propped up against a pepper shaker. It was a blue envelope, addressed with real ink, and had *Par Avion* printed on it with wings on each side of the words. He opened it with a sharpened paring knife, thinking for a moment of the man he had confronted in the Combat Zone. As he reached inside the slit envelope with two fingers, he thought, You fool, you fool.

Her letter was on paper she had ripped out of a spiral notebook, which somehow made him feel a little closer to her, as though poverty or at least thriftiness constituted a universal language. She had the neatest handwriting he had ever seen, made up of perfect letters that looked as though they had been printed by a machine. He put his nose to the paper and smelled it. She hadn't put any perfume on the letter, but it nevertheless had the fragrance of a distant place.

She said that she was writing to introduce herself. Now that the moment had come, she was at a loss. What could she say, in a letter, that would give him an idea of who she really was? And what, after all, would she like to be admired for? Don't we want to be admired for those qualities that can't be seen, but that exist like a fragrance? And there is a mystery here, too, she wrote, in that she was easily affected by other people, and in their presence she became someone who was a little different from when she was alone. And so, to describe herself as she would be with Kohler, actually meeting him, she was at a disadvantage, because without being with him, she was a little less certain of who she would become. Well, this was scarcely a good introduction, she wrote.

He tasted the bitter tea. He felt, too, a small, intimate pleasure in the fact that he had come enough into her life to make her think about how she would change in his presence. And, of course, he wondered if this would happen to him, too. He looked around the kitchen and tried to see if there was any small difference in himself that came from holding her letter and reading it.

After a minute, he thought, Yes, there is. A small thrill of excitement ran through him that was like having a little trouble breathing. He was alert to the small effect that two people had on one another, in the words they spoke, which made for a private language, in the jokes and small understanding that came from a mutual pool of experience. The details were small, but the import of them was large. It was what people had. It was how they understood and loved one another. This awareness, he realized, was a gift that he had from just reading a letter from her.

She said that she lived in Moscow. She liked to go out at night along the Arbat, which was a long mall where there were restaurants and stores, although there wasn't much to buy. There weren't any pet stores in the Soviet era, and now, when people wanted to buy a dog, they had to find one at a street vendor. Did he like dogs? she asked. She had always wanted a dog. A black one with a shiny coat.

She wondered, too, where he lived and what it was like in Vermont. Could he tell her something about himself? What films did he like? She had learned some of her English, the "idiomatic" English, from the movies.

There was something else she wanted to mention. Russia couldn't even take care of the women whose husbands had died in the Second World War. You saw them sitting in the subway, begging. That incapacity and the desperation that went with it were precisely what she wanted to get away from. She wanted to live beyond the gray concrete flats of Moscow.

And, she wanted Kohler to know, she wasn't interested in just being a housewife. That was what happened to so many Russian women, no matter what the theory had been under the Soviets, may they rot wherever they are. No. She wanted a job, and she had a very good idea about what she wanted. She had always liked trains and she wanted to be a conductor. Everything about it appealed to her, the color of the uniform, navy blue with brass buttons, the hat with a shiny black visor, the black belt and the pouch that hung from it with blank tickets, and, strangely enough, she said, the thing that she thought of all the time, like a dream, was the paper punch. She liked the idea of standing there, her legs braced against the swaying of the train, with her punch in one hand and the ticket in the other, and the sound, too, the click, click, click of her work when she put holes in the ticket. She even had a small fantasy, she said, about standing on the platform between two cars, where she would empty the punch and take all those small bits of paper, like confetti, and toss them into the passing dark. They would explode there like snow. Well, she said, now I have trusted you.

She included a picture, a snapshot that showed her standing on an avenue in Moscow, and in the background Kohler saw a large building. She described the building as being an example of "Vampire Architecture," which was the stuff that was built in the 1950s. She was thin, her thick hair blowing in the breeze, her eyes blue, her skin pale. He put the picture up against the cup of tea.

At night, in bed, he heard the coyotes yapping, their cries at once alarming and compelling, as though they were scared and yet filled with longing. From his bedroom upstairs he felt that picture, which was still down in the kitchen, pulling on him like the moon. So he went down there and sat at the table and put his head in his hands and thought, What is my favorite movie? He imagined the explosion of that star-shaped confetti as she threw it into the night. He could almost smell the diesel oil.

In town, he went into the stationery store and found a paper punch in a leather pouch, and his need for privacy about it was so great that he slipped it into his pocket and walked out without paying. At home, when he got a letter from her, or when he had a cup of tea (as though it had come from a samovar), he took the punch out and made that click, click, click. The sound was all mixed up with other small noises, like the undoing of a snap on her clothes, the click of her heels on the floor, the clasp of her handbag as she closed it, the crackle in her hair when she brushed it, the pop of static electricity from her finger in the winter when she reached for a doorknob.

He tried, too, to see clearly. He thought of the house where he had grown up, and those years after his mother had been found by the river. He had been able to survive by being careful about what he let himself feel and what he let himself remember. For instance, he had been careful not to think about the money that had been given to him by one of his mother's boyfriends to hide in the closet and watch as she went about doing what the man wanted. Kohler remembered the claustrophobia of that closet, the tickle of the stockings that hung against his face, the sense of being unable to do anything but sit there with his eyes closed. It was as though everything about the world that he couldn't get control of had been in that closet with him. Since then he had tried to be careful and precise. He had done what he could. Now, when he looked at the picture of the Russian woman, he thought she would help him.

He got up and went to the gun cabinet in the kitchen and took out a 6.5mm Mannlicher, an Austrian deer rifle. It was perfectly machined and engineered, the bolt having a flat tab and the magazine set up as a grooved cylinder that took each one of the brass-and-copper hulls. Open sights. He never liked the notion of a scope. Not with sights like these. He stood there, smelling the oil and feeling the weight of the thing, which he put away before going upstairs.

RUSSELL BOYD

THEY ALREADY HAD ONE BOY IN THE BACKSEAT OF the car, and the second one ran out of his house, letting the door slam shut behind him. He was about ten, a little slack-jawed and wet-lipped, and he wore glasses that made his eyes seem large and runny, like a broken egg yolk. He ran with his head down, as though trying to slam his way through an invisible wall. Zofia had already gotten out of the car and opened the back door so that the boy, Jack, could get in. Russell drove. Zofia had packed a lunch of egg salad sandwiches, which was in a basket in the trunk.

Jack climbed in next to the other boy in the backseat, and both of them seemed to exude an expectation so keen as to be physical. The other boy, Marshall, had red hair and freckles, and a habit of moving his head in time to his walking. Both of them were kids from Zofia's special education class.

Zofia got into the front seat, next to Russell, and said, "Okay, where are we going?"

"I know a place," he said.

"You hear that, boys?" Zofia said, turning to the boys in the backseat, "My friend here says he knows a place to catch fish."

In the rearview mirror, Russell looked at the two ten-year-olds. A foam cup of worms was on the backseat, next to them, and they kept looking down at it as though it were a keg of gunpowder.

"Sometimes there are fish," he said. "I can't promise."

"Some fisherman," said Zofia.

"What's his name?" Marshall asked, gesturing toward the front seat.

"Russell," said Zofia.

"Is Russell a teacher?" said Marshall.

"No," she said. "Not a teacher."

"Well, if he isn't a teacher, what is he?" said Marshall.

"He's just a friend," said Zofia. "He helps people."

"Oh," he said.

"I'm a cop," said Russell.

"Have you got a gun?" said Jack.

"Sure," he said.

"Wow," said Jack. "Wait until I tell everyone . . ."

Jack looked out the window. Marshall put his mouth up against the glass and mouthed one word, "Pow!"

"Are we going to kill them?" Marshall said.

"Kill what?" said Zofia.

"The fish," he said.

"If you want to take them home," Russell said. "We have to kill them."

"I want to take them home," said Jack. "Are you going to shoot them?"

"No," Russell said. "Maybe I'll hit them on a rock."

"Oh," said Jack. He went back to staring out the window. "I'd like it better if you shot them."

"I don't think it's a good idea," Russell said.

"Pow," Marshall said. "Pow. Pow. Pow. Blood and guts."

"That's enough," said Zofia.

They drove along the river, in which, here and there, a tree trunk floated. The sky was reflected there, with big clouds showing in the water. Russell parked and they piled out of the car. Zofia carried the basket with sandwiches in clear wrap, and Russell took the fishing rods and the foam cup with the peat inside.

"Have you caught a fish?" Jack asked.

"Yes," Russell said. "I have."

"Was it nice?"

Zofia stopped and turned back now.

"Was it nice?" she repeated.

"Yes. It was very nice," he said.

"How do you know you've got one?" Jack said

"It tugs," Russell said.

They went farther up, to a sandy section where another brook ran in. The fish in the main stream would like it here because they could hang back in the slow water and wait for food to come to them out of the feeder. The boys and Russell sat down with Zofia while Russell got the monofilament out of the reel and through the eyes of the rod and tied on a hook. He used a clinch knot, and the boys watched as he wrapped the monofilament around itself and pulled it tight so it looked like a little noose.

It hadn't seemed like a long way to walk when they started, but now Russell realized they were pretty far from the main road. He looked around at the isolation of the place, and for a moment he was glad that they had gotten away from the traffic, the noise, the greasy exhaust of passing cars. He finished the first hook as he felt a shadow sweep over him and the boys. He looked up at the bank above the stream, where the sun came through the trees.

A man stood on the bank, his arms crossed, his shape like a target cut out of black metal. His lack of motion seemed like an accusation that ran down the bank like a shadow. Russell went back to looping the monofilament around itself five times, as he always did, but as he felt the slick leader under his fingers, he found himself glancing up the bank.

"Who's that?" said Zofia.

"I don't know," said Russell. He pulled the knot tight.

The man started walking down the bank, his feet making a shushing sound in the leaves, and in each gesture, in each movement, he was able to convey disapproval and something else, too, which Russell tried to name, but couldn't. He was surprised by this since he had had a lot of experience with people who were at once vague and still dangerous. The man came out of the sun, ominous in his blunt locomotion, in his directness that verged on a state of mind carefully subdued, but not fully controlled.

"My name is Kohler," said the man.

"My name is Boyd," said Russell.

"What are you doing here?" said Kohler.

"I thought we'd catch a couple of fish," said Russell.

Kohler put his head back, as though he had smelled something he didn't like.

"This land is mine," said Kohler. "I pay the taxes on it."

"It's not posted," said Russell.

"Come on, boys," said Zofia. "Let's go over by the water."

Jack stood absolutely still, as though this were a way of being invisible. Kohler stared at the boy for a moment, seemingly recognizing something in the way the boy refused to move: the memory, if there was anything specific, didn't seem to do him any good.

"They tear down my signs," said Kohler.

He went along the bank until he came to a ring of stones that someone had used to make a fire, and in the middle, in the ashes, Kohler reached down and picked up a piece of paper, the edges of it burned. He held it up like an accusation.

"See," he said. "Here. They use my signs to start fires to cook the fish they catch."

He held out the piece of paper, which could have been anything, a piece of a donut box or the packaging of an ice cream bar. Russell looked at it and then at Kohler.

"I'm sorry we bothered you," said Russell. "We had no intention of doing that."

"Show him your gun," said Marshall.

"What?" said Kohler.

"I haven't got a gun," said Russell.

"You said you had a gun," said Marshall.

"Come on, boys," said Zofia.

"I'd like to ask for your permission to fish for an hour," said Russell. "Is that all right?"

Kohler made that same backward jerk of his head, as though the wind had brought him something else he didn't like. Then he looked around, at the two boys and Zofia. He didn't say anything. Instead he turned and went along the river, looking here and there for the signs that had been ripped down. Then he started to climb the bank.

"It'll be all right," said Russell.

"Well, I don't know," said Zofia.

Kohler stopped at the top of the bank and turned. He crossed his arms again, his shape perfectly centered in the sun so that he stood in an umbra of platinum light. He looked at the four of them, and in particular he lingered over the boys. It was as though he hadn't seen a child for a long time. Then he started moving along the bank, back and forth, his entire gait feral and loping. He went about forty yards and was about to turn into the woods, but stopped, drawn back to the four people who stood by the side of the stream. His sudden halt, his intense considering of the circumstances here, his brooding in the sunlight changed the sound down by the stream. Not louder, exactly, but more silvery, more as though it were being played through a tinny loudspeaker. The worms writhed like snakes, and Russell hooked them under the yellowish band in the middle of each one.

"Look," said Russell to Zofia, "I asked for his permission. We'll just fish for a little and then go."

The boys and Russell moved along the stream until they came to a pool, where they threw the worms in and just like that, bang, Jack caught an ugly fish, a bass or something Russell had never seen before, not a trout, but a fish with odd-looking scales that were colored like an oil slick. The boy pulled it onto the bank and they all stood there staring at it. Russell glanced up the bank. He couldn't see anyone there.

"Do you want to keep it?" Russell asked.

"Yes," he said.

"Okay," Russell said, and killed the fish. "Well, let's go catch another one."

"See," Zofia said. "I told you Russell knew where there were fish."

It took a little while but they caught a fish for Marshall, a rainbow trout this time, heavy in the shoulders, fat with green coloring on the back in which there were black spots. A streak of pink on the side. Marshall looked at it and trembled, hands outstretched, wanting to touch it but afraid to do so, too. A long, spreading stain ran down from the crotch of his blue jeans into each leg. All of them stood in the warm smell of urine. Then he looked up at Russell with his face compressed, as though it were drawn on a sponge and someone had crumpled it up.

Russell took his hand, while with the other he held the fish.

"Sorry," said Marshall. "I'm sorry."

He said this through his crying. But he still wanted the fish, which he tried to grasp even though his crying made him jab at it with both hands.

"Please don't be mad," said Marshall.

Kohler was back at the top of the bank, arms crossed, still considering the people who were on his land. His stance, with the sun behind him, seemed as motionless as a statue, and as utterly impervious. He seemed to stand there like a post that had been driven into the ground, and it was this unyielding quality, the frank, unnecessary insistence that left Russell looking from the child who had wet his pants, back up the bank at the man whose land this was. Marshall went on crying for a moment, and this repeated and gasping sound had an effect on Kohler. He was almost vibrant, like a bird dog that was pointing a bird. Then he raised one arm in half a gesture, as though compelled to make a sign, but seemed to realize halfway through it that no one would understand anyway. His passionate attraction to the sound of the crying boy appeared to color the shadow that fell from the bank in a long, broken pattern, like a carpet going down a flight of stairs.

"Ignore him," said Russell.

"I don't know," said Zofia. "I just don't know."

"Is it cold yet, or is it still warm?" Russell asked Marshall.

"It's getting cold," he said. "How do you know it's getting cold?"

"I can remember," Russell said. He turned to Zofia. "Don't you have extra clothes in the car?"

Zofia glanced up the bank.

"Yes," she said. "But maybe we should all go back to the car. We can change there."

"Let's have our lunch and then go," said Russell. "Screw him."

"You used a swear word," said Jack.

"It's not a swear word," said Marshall. He sniffled. "'Fuck' is a swear word."

"That's enough," said Zofia. She sighed. "All right."

She started walking along the stream to the car, but after ten yards or so she turned and looked back. The boys began to compare the fish, but they kept coming up against the fact that one was ugly and the other so pretty.

"One's bigger," said Russell. "The other's a rainbow. That's makes them the same."

"Mine's meaner," said Jack. "See, it would eat anything."

"Sure. It's ugly. It has to be," said Marshall. "It's yours."

"You wet your pants," said Jack. "Wait until I tell."

"You told before," said Marshall. "You always tell."

Russell turned toward the bank. Kohler started walking through the dead leaves, which made little waves around his feet. As he came, Russell thought, It's the crying. There's something about the crying. Above Kohler the tree trunks rose to the light, and the straggly upward grasp of them reminded Russell of hands in the midst of a desperate prayer.

"He's coming again," said Jack.

"What are we going to do?" said Marshall.

"Nothing," said Russell. "It'll be fine."

The boys froze. Kohler walked with a long-legged, distance-consuming gait, as though he knew every piece of dead wood here so well that he didn't pause when he came up to one, but just stepped over it without breaking stride. Russell turned to face him.

Kohler stood opposite Marshall. There was a lingering essence that came from the boy having cried here, a slight change in atmosphere like a drop in temperature. Kohler lifted his hand again, as though offering something, but he stopped in the middle so that whatever he had intended was only half-realized and nonsensical. Then he sat down on a piece of dead-wood so that his face was on the same level as Marshall's.

"Don't cry. It doesn't do any good," said Kohler.

"Look," said Russell. "We don't want any trouble."

Kohler went on staring at Marshall. Then he blinked and swallowed.

"I didn't mean to scare you," he said. "I just get tired of people coming in here. See?"

"Yes," said Marshall.

"You know why crying doesn't do any good?" said Kohler. "It makes you lonely. And what good is that?"

Kohler blinked again.

"Ah, shit," he said. "Goddamn it. You want to know what does some good? If someone gives you a hard time, hit them. Don't fight to fight. Fight to win."

"That's enough," said Russell.

Marshall started to cry again.

"You're scaring him," said Russell. "Stop it."

Kohler turned to Marshall.

"Hey, hey," he said. "It's okay. I don't mean anything. Forget about me. That's a nice fish. What kind is it?"

"A bass," said Marshall, blubbering.

"No kidding, a bass. Do you have a lunch?"

Marshall nodded.

"What kind of lunch?" asked Kohler.

"Egg salad sandwiches," said Jack.

"Have your sandwiches here," said Kohler.

"Okay," said Russell. He stepped closer to Kohler. "We'll do that."

Kohler seemed to recede back into that stance of complete, statue-like immobility, which, in its stillness, in its complete quietness, was more threatening than if he had moved, since everything about him suggested a building up of pressure rather than a release, an increasing intensity that only appeared calm in his own contemplation of it. Russell stood about a foot from him, their faces close together.

"I'm sorry," said Kohler. "I'm not myself recently."

Then he turned on his heel and covered the land by the stream in that same long-legged gait, stepping over the deadwood with a fluid ease and then going up the bank.

Zofia came along the stream now, her pink blouse the same shade as the leaves of the sugar maples, so much so that she seemed to emerge from them. She had a black plastic sack with her, and she took Marshall to one side, helping him strip off the wet pants and underwear. His feet were covered with leaves, but he shoved them into the dry jeans as quickly as he could, to get away from being naked. Then he picked up his shoes. Before he put them on, Russell brushed the forest litter, the moth and beetle colored twigs and leaves off the boy's webbed feet. The deformity of them made Russell instinctively turn and look up the bank again, but Kohler was gone.

Then they sat down on a blanket that Zofia had spread out. She had sweet pickles and chips along with the sandwiches. They ate quietly, waiting for Kohler to come back, but he had vanished into the woods at the top of the bank. Russell shrugged and tried to forget him and then looked at the dead fish, the ugly one green and shiny, like it was smeared with petroleum, the other sparkling and perfectly shaped.

"Who do you think that was?" Zofia said.

"I don't know," he said. "Just some guy. You see them all the time."

"Do you?" said Zofia.

FRANK KOHLER

WHEN THE BARBER WAS DONE, THE EFFECT WASN'T
quite what Frank had wanted. He felt the buzz of his hair on his fingertips,
which was a lot like the lingering sensation left by the barber's electric
shears. He guessed that he would go without shaving for three or four days
and get a pair of dark glasses, the black wraparound kind. Then he would
get a dark jacket and charcoal pants, and maybe a black shirt, too. He didn't
think a white tie was a good thing, but he considered it. To get the look of
a Russian gangster, he would buy a black shirt and wear it open at the neck.

In the morning before he went to meet the plane in Boston, he stood in
front of the mirror. The stubble on his face made him look a little more
bumlike than menacing, but the effect was more evocative when he put on
his black shirt and black coat. He had supposed that Katryna would be reassured by someone who looked like a gangster, since in Russia such people
had money. Was this right? He didn't have the least idea. His hands shook
when he thought about making a mistake. He was certain about one thing,
but he wasn't sure whether it helped in this case: Russians were reassured
by the ominous, or maybe they had just gotten used to it.

He gagged and brought up a little blood, and then he washed out his
mouth. As he trembled at the sink, squeezing the sides of it, he tried to dis-
tract himself by imagining the sound of the airplane on which Katryna was
flying, the rush of the air outside it, just as he tried to have a notion of the
distance to Moscow. For instance, how far east of Germany was it? Could
she sleep on the plane, and if she did, what did she dream of? Working as a
conductor? Her uniform? The bits of paper that she would throw into the
air like confetti? He imagined the sense of the airplane's passage through the
cold air as being indistinguishable from the buzz of the clippers at the barber's. His dread, his fear, his ridiculous hope all blended into one sensation,
a unified apprehension that left him wishing he had taken his chance when
he had it with that asshole in the Combat Zone.

He concentrated on the noise of wind around the eaves, the toilet upstairs that ran a little bit, the pitch of it like the most diminutive cry. He opened the icebox and took out the flowers that he had there, the roses dark and almost black on the inside where the petals disappeared into the center of the flower. The cold air held the wonderful smell of the flowers, and Kohler hesitated with his face close to the cool opening of the refrigerator. Then he took them into the bedroom, where he turned back the covers and looked at the new sheets. The petals of the roses came off in bunches, and he spread them there on the sheet. They looked like drops of red paint on a white floor. He spread them around and stood back. Then he sat on the foot of the bed for a while, looking out the window.

The black car left him with a vague sense that it was too blunt, too vulgar where delicacy might be required. But what car would suggest delicacy? His old Chevrolet? That was like failed sensibility itself, an automobile driven by a bookkeeper with no sense of humor. The new car still conveyed a sense of strength, and the color added that same mystery of blackness and hinted at the endless erotic power of the unknown. At least with mystery you always had the chance that you were onto the right thing.

He sat behind the wheel with the door open, one foot on the gravel of his driveway. His uneasiness existed here with such intensity that it was like being in a bell jar that was made of the clear substance of his anxiety. Then he slammed the door, started the engine, and wheeled down the drive to the main road. He thought of the rooms where he had grown up, the atmosphere that he seemed to carry wherever he went, like his own private genie that just wouldn't go back into the bottle. Then he just listened to the sound of the engine and looked at the gauges from time to time, tach steady, oil pressure good, temperature a little warm.

Kohler had hired the immigration lawyer that Mrs. Blanchett had suggested, a man with a Southern accent and blond hair that wasn't turning white so much as just fading and leaving the yellow of it looking nicotine-stained. He had arranged the wedding by proxy. In addition to his normal fee, the lawyer had charged Kohler close to a thousand dollars for bribes in Moscow, although there was no way to get a receipt for a bribe, and this left Kohler feeling that he had been screwed somehow. Anyway, they were married.

In the tunnel on the way to the airport in Boston, the tile on the ceiling looked icy from the headlights of the cars. The tunnel went under the river, and while Kohler only saw the tiled walls and the oily asphalt ahead of him, he still was aware of the weight of the river. The cars ahead of him stopped and he sat there, tapping the steering wheel. He glanced up at the ceiling and imagined the green-gray water, tainted with oil and whatever else had been thrown into the harbor.

Kohler pulled into the airport's parking lot, where there was a machine with an arm painted with slashes of black and white. He rolled down the window and pushed a knob on the parking machine. The ticket, which stuck out of a slot like a small paper tongue, was cheap and gray. Kohler guessed it was like the stuff the Soviets used for forms. Or toilet paper. He had never seen any, but he was pretty sure it was rank and ridiculous, but then Frank thought, Great, here I am thinking about Soviet toilet paper. What the fuck is wrong with me? He glanced at himself in the rearview mirror, his face nearly hidden by the band of his dark glasses.

Frank pulled out the ticket, but the arm didn't move. He waited. Then he tried to take another ticket, but when he pushed the knob, nothing came out of the machine. There were now two cars behind him, and then a third pulled in. Kohler got out and stood next to the machine and hit it with the heel of his palm. The machine was red and covered with grime that must have come from the jet fuel, and so the effect was like a Coke machine in a coal town, cheerful, but defeated by the circumstances of where it was. The car directly behind Kohler's was filled with people from India or Pakistan who spoke to one another with irritated voices. Then they stared at him, and as they did he noticed that one of them was wearing a pair of dark glasses just like his.

The driver made a gesture of dismissal. A woman in traditional dress sat in the backseat, and with her there were a couple of kids, one of them playing a Gameboy. The driver, who wore a turban, honked the horn. He pointed at the machine that produced the tickets and then at Kohler, as though he was too stupid to take a ticket. Overhead, a jet whined, the pitch of it changing as it came in lower, the noise having an urgency to it. British Air. Kohler stood there watching it go past. This was the airline that Katryna was on.

The sky was clear but still tinted by the reddish smoke of the jet engines, so that everything looked like the highway at rush hour, and in that tint Kohler turned to face the car behind his. The driver started yelling, although it was in a language Kohler couldn't understand, and when he got closer, the driver put his turbaned head out of the car and gesticulated. The woman in the back glared. Kohler could smell a spice, something in their cooking that clung to their clothes, saffron, perhaps, or garlic or ginger. Couldn't they see his haircut and his dark glasses? Why were they making noise?

"Back up," Kohler said.

"Back up? Back up!" said the driver. "I have to meet a plane. Twelve-forty-five. Twelve-forty-five!"

The woman in the back jabbered at the man in the passenger seat. The kid in the back kept on with his Gameboy.

"Air India!" said the driver.

"It's broken, kaput!" Kohler said.

"Don't threaten me," said the driver. He put a hand under his neck and made a quick cutting motion, as though slitting a throat.

"The machine is broken," Kohler repeated.

"You said you were going to break his head," said the man in the passenger seat.

"No," Kohler said.

The planes continued to go over. There were even more cars behind the Pakistanis' now, and the drivers were honking their horns. The sound of it, Kohler supposed, was like a traffic jam in India, or someplace where there was no order at all. Just everyone grasping for what they could get, driven by horrible necessity. The smell of kerosene was suddenly very strong in the air.

The man on the passenger side of the car got out and went over to the machine and pressed a button and a ticket came out. The arm rose.

"Here," he said. He pushed the ticket at Kohler.

The driver made a gesture of contempt.

"Twelve-forty-five!" he said. "Flight number three-nineteen!"

The black door of Kohler's car was still open, and he got in and put the thing into gear, making the tires chirp as he pulled away and seeing in the rearview mirror that the Pakistanis were gesticulating and speaking to one another. They made a point of turning into the row beyond the one where he parked, as though this gave them a small moral superiority. Kohler turned off the engine and sat there. He ran his hand through his haircut. Why hadn't they been impressed? For all they knew, he could have been a thug. In fact, when he thought about it, he had contempt for their lack of perception. They had gotten off easy.

Then he counted, one, two, three, four, five. What was that smell? Coriander? Cilantro? He got out and locked the door after slamming it shut. The Pakistanis made their way through the parking lot toward the International Arrivals Building. They walked with a quick, hurrying gait, which gave them the appearance of being on a conveyor belt. One of them looked back at Kohler, and then said something to the man with the turban, who kept staring straight ahead.

Then all of them came up to the International Arrivals Building, which was an ugly structure of glass and aluminum. A metal awning stuck out in front. The doors were double glass ones, smeared with a million handprints, and on each side of the entrance the police had put up barriers, so that there was a path in the middle, right in front of the doors, but on both sides there were crowds of Indians and Pakistanis, all of them speaking languages he didn't know. About ten feet away, the family that had been behind him at the parking lot entrance lined up. The child was still playing his Gameboy. People came through the glass doors, carrying boxes tied with string, or new suitcases, and all of them had one of two expressions, a starstruck wonderment, as though they had just stepped off a flying saucer, or they just looked tired.

Kohler said to a man next to him, "Do you know what flight this is?" but the man just shook his head. Either he didn't know or he didn't speak English. When the child with the Gameboy stepped away from his mother, toward Kohler, his mother grabbed him with a jerk that made him start to cry, and then the man with the turban glared at Kohler. What was he doing to his son? The other man, with dark glasses, made a gesture with his arm, like the gate of the parking machine, going up and down. The woman shrugged. Kohler wished, on the verge of prayer, that he hadn't put those petals on the sheets.

Katryna was taller than he thought she'd be. She came out of the door, dragging one bag and carrying another, exhausted, just looking around with that bewildered wonderment. Kohler stepped out to her, brushing by the man with the turban.

"Hey, hey," said the Pakistani.

"Do you see that!" said the man with the dark glasses.

"You think because I am an immigrant you can treat me that way?"

Katryna looked at Kohler and then searched the crowd. He walked directly up to her, then he tipped his dark glasses down his nose so that she could see his eyes.

"You! You!" said the Pakistani.

"Is there something wrong?" said Katryna.

"I'm talking to you," said the Pakistani.

"Look," said Kohler. "Be polite."

"Polite! Polite!" said the Pakistani. "You can't even get in the parking lot." He turned to his family and nodded. See?

"I told you," said Kohler.

The Pakistani said something in the language that Kohler couldn't understand, and as Kohler was about to take a step toward the man, Katryna put her arms around him, her slender figure coming up against him, her hair smelling of Russia. The man with the turban stopped gesticulating, shrugged, and got back on the curb. The family formed a row, all staring at Kohler and Katryna. Then they looked at one another and shrugged. The child went back to his Gameboy.

"Welcome to the U.S.A.," said Kohler.

She was sweating, and she put her hand to her head. The Pakistanis glared. Kohler turned to them and said, "Do you have something to say?"

"Me?" said the one with dark glasses. "What do I have to say to you?"

The man with the turban moved closer, although he still stood on the curb.

"We know how to deal with you," said the man.

"Would you like to try?" said Kohler.

"What?" said the man with the dark glasses. "What did he say?"

"Let's go over there," said Kohler. He gestured to a concrete barrier.

Katryna tried to follow the English spoken by the Pakistanis, and while she obviously had trouble with the specific words, she had a good idea that something was wrong. She looked around, as though hoping to see a policeman, but all she saw was that red-tinted air. A line of perspiration, like a small clear mustache, was on her upper lip, and she was breathing through her mouth as though she was nauseated and trying to resist it. It had been a long trip, and the air here was rank with jet fuel. It was obviously hotter than she had thought it would be, and her sweater was too heavy. The fumes from the taxicabs in front of the building rose with an undulating move-ment. She gave them a queasy look and then glanced at Kohler. She swal-lowed again.

"You think you can push me around because I am an immigrant?" said the man with the turban.

"Over there," said Kohler. He made a gesture with his head.

The man with the turban glanced around. He stepped off the curb.

"Oh, look. There," said the woman in the traditional dress. She pointed at a man with a new suitcase who had just come through the door. Then all of them shrieked with pleasure and moved toward the edge of the police barricade, leaving Kohler next to the curb. The man with the turban glanced back, though, and then gave Kohler the finger.

"Asshole," said Kohler.

"What?" said Katryna.

He picked up Katryna's bags and they started working their way through the crowd toward the parking lot, Katryna wobbling a little on her new high-heeled shoes. The asphalt had cracks in it through which grass grew, and the surface of the parking lot glittered with broken glass. The shards cast colored light on the ground, and the accumulation of reds and blues, yellows and sparkling silver left Kohler hesitant. The elemen-tal colors, as though a secret were being revealed, left Kohler surprised and frankly alarmed, since as the fragments of light pierced him, each one at once festive and thoroughly mysterious, he was aware of that maddening, gentle, and yet universal presence which he had so often felt without warning recently. It was the hint of power that got to him, as though there was a love so inexhaustible that he would find himself weeping uncon-trollably at the least sign of it, which is what that shattered light seemed to be—a sign, a hint, a promise that he wasn't quite able to understand. Maybe that was his problem: he was trying too hard. Maybe he should just let himself go. Then, in that turmoil which seemed decorated by those flecks of light, he thought, Please. No fucking tears. Not now. His sense of fragility, which he detested, or his closeness to that abyss of sparkling light was all the worse because the Pakistani had flipped him the bird. Now, of course, he didn't want to see the man in the turban. He just wanted to get away, as though flight would save him from making a fool of himself in front of Katryna.

On Storrow Drive they went by the river, where sailboats gently moved along on their own blurry reflections. Katryna stared at them with disbelief, since it was incredible that anything as peaceful and serene as this could exist while she had been rushed so violently from one place to another.

"Would you like a cup of coffee or something?" he said.

She was still sweating. Yes, maybe something to eat would help to settle her stomach. He pulled off the highway and turned the car into the parking lot of a Burger King, the asphalt here as sparkling with broken glass as it had been at the airport. They went in through the front door and stood in line while the clerk, in a uniform, gave them a cup of coffee and a hamburger, french fries, and a Coke. Kohler was sweating too, now, with the effort to be cool. Maybe it was a mistake to come in here with so many things to worry about, the money, the change, the order, finding a place to sit, trying to smile, making sure they had napkins and a little thing like a tongue depressor to stir the coffee.

He led them to a table that was screwed to the floor, but they could look out the window at the sky, with its big rags of clouds. Katryna unwrapped her sandwich and looked at it. Kohler smelled his coffee. She tried to take a bite of the sandwich, but instead her eyes filled. Kohler took a sip of his coffee, and then ran one hand through the buzz cut of his hair.

"It's the excitement," she said. "I'm trembling. Look."

She put out her hand. The fingers were shaking.

She put the back of her hand to the side of her face. Kohler looked out the window and saw that there was broken glass on the sidewalk here, too, and the light hit it in the same way as at the airport. A beautiful accumulation of reds, blues, yellows. He swallowed the hot coffee, resisting that moment which promised so much but delivered so little. It was like listening to choral music sung in a monastery. He bit his lip. Then he exhaled. She held her sandwich and looked around, obviously trying to decide how to handle this. He thought that if he was quick about it, he could get into the bedroom and clean up those rose petals before she saw them. She wiped her eyes with a paper napkin and blew her noise. Well, he thought, at least they hadn't got lost at the airport, or had to page one another. They had met right where they said they would. She had seemed to like the car, and had even put a hand on the black leather, as if it were a skirt or a belt she had always wanted. She looked good against that background of darkness, like a diamond on a piece of black satin. He noticed she had stopped sweating and didn't appear to be sick anymore. She carefully wrapped up the sandwich.

"I'll eat it later," she said, and put it in her handbag.

RUSSELL BOYD

RUSSELL PULLED IN BEHIND THE CRUISER AT THE side of the road. The blue luminescence from the flashing lights swept over the woods and made them appear and disappear. The trunks looked smoky and blue for an instant before they vanished into the night, only to reappear when the blue lights of the cruiser hit them. It was early November and cold. The exhaust of the cruiser ahead of Russell's rose like a white feather boa, and then Nowatarski, a trooper from Russell's barracks, stepped through it like someone appearing out of the fog. He hesitated there, the boa of exhaust beginning to wrap itself around him. Then he came up to Russell's window.

"How's it going?" said Russell.

Nowatarski was over six feet tall, heavy, with a short haircut.

"I want you to see something," he said.

Nowatarski looked back at those trees. The exhaust from his car was caught in that blue throb, too, and this made everything seem at once hyper-real and yet ethereal.

"Have you got your flashlight?" said Nowatarski.

Russell reached into his glove compartment, and as he glanced down he felt a little separate from the green phosphorescence of the gauges, the shot-gun that sat in a rack behind his head, the papers and clipboard, the pen, his leather gloves that he had left on the seat when he was drinking a cup of coffee. The night seemed to be distilled into a substance that was thicker than usual, harder to walk through, more filled with unpleasant possibilities. Russell called the dispatcher and told her where he was.

The body was next to a barbed-wire fence at the back of the mowed part of the shoulder of the road. The frost wasn't hard, not way below freezing, but the ground was still firm. The woman was naked, without any marks (aside from stretch marks on her abdomen; she'd been pregnant at some time). It seemed obvious that she had been dumped there after being killed somewhere else. No clothes, no blood, no sign of a struggle, none of the trash that a murder makes. The woman's nipples were torn. Russell looked around at the woods, and then at the woman again, before he was able to comprehend what had happened. Her nipples had been pierced, but in order to make it harder to identify her, her killer had ripped out the rings she had worn.

"How did you find her?" Russell said.

"Some guy had a flat tire. After he changed it, he came back here to take a leak."

"I'd like to cover her up," Russell said.

"Yeah," he said. "Everyone will be here soon. After they've had a look, we can get a blanket from the car."

"Doesn't look like she's been here very long," Russell said.

"Hard to say," Nowatarski said.

There was nothing to do but wait, and yet just standing there was like falling. He kept wanting to put his hand out to catch something, but the entire prospect was only made up of the blue, throbbing trunks of trees and blades of grass. And yet, in Russell's disorientation, in the serpentine movement of the exhaust from the cars, he recognized something. It occurred to him, too, that while it might have been hard to prove, his grandfather had loved him. It was an odd kind of love, but nevertheless Russell understood that love had been behind his grandfather's impulse to convey what it had been like to stand behind the wire and watch those Russians do their work. Something similar seemed to hang in the air here, too, just as it had when his grandfather had stared into that dull and yet horrifying afternoon. As Russell waited, he tried to decide just what it was he was trying to hang on to, his grandfather's love or the certainty of what things are like when they go wrong. Whichever one, he was still left with the elusive sense of needing to get his hooks into what was going on here, or, better yet, needing to stop it. That was the hard part: he knew it was too late for anything like that. But, he thought, isn't that what my grandfather was trying to tell me? That there are times when you are left with utter disbelief and with the certainty of just how ineffectual you can be? And then what do you do? Russell blinked and looked around.

"Maybe we could put a roadblock in here and ask people who go by if they saw anything," Russell said. "A car, someone walking on the side of the road."

"That's probably where we'll start," Nowatarski said. "Have you had your lunch break?"

"No," Russell said.

"Are you going to the pizza place at Exit One?" he asked.

"I don't know," Russell said.

Above those blue, throbbing trees, the stars were purple. Even now, though, they were still beautiful, and as Russell looked at them he guessed that if you could see beauty when you were standing at the side of the road like this, then it must be real, not sentimental or an acquired taste. Then Russell and Nowatarski walked back to the side of the road, where the van and another cruiser pulled up.

JUST BEFORE DAWN, Russell came up to Zofia's house and let himself in. There was still time before she had to get up, and he wanted to let her sleep a little while longer. He took off the body armor with a tear of Velcro and reached up to the shelf where they kept the coffee. He could see the first light outside beyond the trees, the sky pink and yellow. Then he stood with both hands on the counter, pressing down. Every noise he made in the kitchen was louder than it should have been, the clicking of the cupboard, the plastic snap as he opened the coffeemaker, so much so that he just hesitated, waiting there. What, after all, could he do? He was aware that he was trying to avoid a detail that left him speechless, and if he could just forget about it, or put it off until later, he wouldn't have to admit to that hungover feeling which he couldn't shake. He took the scoop from the drawer, doing so as quietly as he could, and started measuring the spoonfuls of coffee into the brown paper filter. One, two, three, four. He closed the machine and hit the button, which made a red light come on. He thought of those pierced, torn nipples. Then he went back to standing at the counter, looking out the window. What was it that surrounded him there? What sensation bled off into the house? He wanted the house to be warm and comforting, and he strained to smell the first warm aroma of coffee, but the place resisted him. It still was empty and cold.

He went upstairs, carrying the body armor, and stood in the hall. He could tell that Zofia was awake. It was as though when she opened her eyes, the room had a small charge that wasn't there when she was sleeping. He went in and sat down on the bed, putting the armor on the chair by her dressing table. She was on her back, looking at the ceiling.

"You're late," she said. It was both a statement and an implied question.

"Yeah," he said. "The coffee will be ready in a minute. You'll be able to smell it."

They heard the gurgle of the machine downstairs. He put the pistol on the nightstand and lay down next to her in his clothes. He was careful not to touch her, or to intrude on that moment when she was waking up and getting ready to face the rest of the day, the kids at school, the people she had to keep happy, parents, the principal. He thought that the best way to get what he needed, or to let the house warm up, was to make no noise and to lie next to her, doing nothing at all. Slowly the memory of that blue light, those frozen eyelashes, that distilled darkness began to recede. Then Zofia threw back the covers and walked across the floor.

In the sound of her splashing and brushing, in the smell of the coffee coming from downstairs, he wanted to be precise, and he supposed his revulsion at what he had found in that blue light was not only a reflection of his sense of an unnecessary and stupid travesty, but it was powered, too, by his own sense of mortality. What did you do in the face of that? You had to be sure you were never maudlin, that you looked at things clearly. Well, surely he had done that tonight.

She came back into the room and sat down next to him, toothpaste on her breath.

"You know what I would like to do?" he asked.

"What's that?" she said.

"I would like to spend the morning here with you," he said. "The light would come in and touch your skin. We'd sit here, feeling it creep up over us like a warm caress."

"And what would I do about work today?"

"I don't know," he said. "Or maybe we could do something else. We could go up to a pond I know, a quarry, where we could swim naked. It would be so cold, and then we could dry in the sunlight. The shock of it would take our breath away."

"Ummmmm," she said.

"Or maybe we could plan a garden for the spring," he said.

"What would you like to plant?" she said.

"I don't know what they're called," he said. "Tall blue flowers."

"Delphinium," she said.

He knew he would say this at night, when he was thinking of her. Delphinium.

"Delphinium," he said, the buzz of the final *m* on his lips as he put them against her neck.

"And peonies," she said, "big pink ones."

"Yes," he said. "That sounds nice."

"All right," she said.

"All right what?" he said.

"I'll call in," she said, glancing at the clock on the bed, the color of the numerals on it the same color as the readout on the radar. "If I call early enough they can get a substitute." As she called, he closed his eyes and tried, for an instant, to make the memory of that blue, throbbing light disappear, or change into the deep blue of the delphinium. It wouldn't last long, but it was a place to start. She hung up and said, "So, what happened last night?"

FRANK KOHLER

KOHLER LIKED DRIVING THE CAR WITH KATRYNA asleep against the door, which he was able to lock by pushing a button. It was a small thing, that *thunk* of the locking of the door, but it was the sound of taking care of someone. She woke up when he stopped in front of their house, and she looked at the weathered siding and the tin roof, her eyes sweeping over the house with the deliberate cadence of a beacon from a lighthouse. They brought Katryna's bags in and put them on the living room floor.

In the kitchen she opened and closed the cupboards, glancing at the dishes and glasses, and then she stood at the stove and looked at the pots that hung above it. Her finger went back and forth over the black handle of the teakettle, and after a moment, as though looking for a way to be reassured, she went to one of her bags and searched for the tea she had brought from Russia.

"I got a new teapot," said Kohler.

It was blue, and he took it from the shelf and held it with both hands. Then he left it on the counter and filled the kettle, after letting the water run clear, and put it on the stove with a clatter. The flames came on.

"Strange how long it takes water to boil," he said.

She stood there by the window, looking out to where the field ran up against the wall of the woods. Then the kettle began to boil. She put the tea into the pot and poured in the water, a little wisp of steam coming up out of it, and when she swirled the water around in the pot she didn't put it down, but stood there, holding it by the handle, under her breasts.

He put new cups on the table. He knew from her letters that she liked to have tea in the afternoon, how it was a small thing she depended on, and he had written back to say that in the Russian novels he was reading they were always putting the samovar on, which he imagined as a variety of Russian Buddha. She poured the tea and they sat down.

"It's like Russia here," she said.

"I thought you'd like it," he said.

She said nothing.

"What did you eat on the plane?" he asked.

Her eyes were as blue as those pictures you see in magazines of the ocean in the Caribbean. Bright. Piercing. Her skin was white and soft-looking, as though she had never been in the sun.

"It was wrapped in plastic," she said. "Chicken. Broccoli. I don't know."

She sipped her tea and closed her eyes. The spoons and cups clinked when they picked them up and put them down. She turned to look out the window again.

Kohler stood up and left the kitchen, passing her bags on the floor and going into the bedroom, where he started sweeping the rose petals out of the bed into his hand, like crumbs off a table, and then he brought the trashcan from the corner of the room so he could get rid of all of the petals, brushing them off the new sheets with a steady, efficient motion, like using a brush to clean a workshop counter, and in the middle of it, when he was reaching over the bed for the petals near the pillows, he heard her come into the room. She stood in the doorway, her arms crossed, and looked at the bed. He put the trashcan back in the corner.

They moved the bags in and put them on the bed, where the odor of roses lingered. Then she started putting her things into the drawers of the dresser he had cleaned out for her and which he had lined with new paper, putting thumbtacks into the corners. Red ones that looked nice on the white paper. Or they had looked nice. Now they looked like something a hick would do. She put her cotton underwear into the drawer along with a couple of pairs of stockings, which were rolled up into neat balls. Three or four blouses, a couple of slips, a scarf, a couple of sweaters, an apron. A couple of dresses, two skirts, a few pairs of shoes. A nightgown. That was it. There was a wonderful fragrance of her that came from her suitcase.

He sat on the bed, watching Katryna put her clothes away, unsnapping and unzipping the compartments of her old leather case.

"I wanted it to be nice," he said.

"I know," she said.

She turned away from him and took off her blouse and skirt and her small, funny-looking brassiere.

"I can still smell the roses," she said.

"You don't mind?" he said.

"No," she said. "It's all right." She bit her lip. "I want it to be nice, too."

With a practiced gesture, as though she had done this many times, she unzipped his pants, and then he felt the warm, hot touch of her mouth and tongue. He could smell the inside of her suitcase and those roses. Holding him with one hand she stood up and then he did, too, so she could get under the sheets. Everything about him, as far as he was concerned, was stupid and too large, and when he got under the covers, he was amazed by the smooth warmth of her, and how she took hold of him with complete certainty and skill. He thought of the nights he had been alone with the coyotes making that keening sound, that yapping for something that could never really be expressed.

She looked right at him as though she didn't know what to say, or as if mystified as to how she had ever ended up here. Then she curled up next to him and he could feel her breathing. He lay there on his back, trying to concentrate on the smoothness of her hip and thigh. Then he realized she was asleep. The small sound of her breathing came as a surprise in a room that had been so quiet.

RUSSELL BOYD

"I'VE GOT SOMETHING I'D LIKE TO TELL YOU," Zofia said. They were in her car, on their way to town. Russell noticed a slight change in the way they spoke to each other when they sat side by side and looked straight ahead, rather than at each other. It was like speaking from behind a screen or whispering to each other in the dark.

"What's that?" he said.

"Well, I want to tell you about desire. About really wanting something. Have you ever really wanted something?"

"What do you think?" he said.

"Say it," she said.

"I've really wanted something," he said.

"Me too," she said. "Me too. You're not going to believe this. But I want to tell you about a hair dryer."

"A hair dryer?" he said.

"Wait," she said. "You'll see."

She told him that when she was about twelve, she had wanted a hair dryer with a sack that you put over your head. The sack had a tube, like one from a vacuum cleaner, that blew hot air into it. She said that it was hard to describe how much she wanted this dryer, and when she thought about it, she probably had never wanted anything else as badly. She had wanted it much more than the way an adult wants something, and she guessed this was because it wasn't just the stupid hair dryer, but that the dryer was part of an entire vision, of being an adult, of doing her hair so that boys would look at her, of romance.

Zofia's mother, whose name was Lillian, spent a lot of time over her appearance, dying her hair, squeezing into a girdle, wearing shoes that were too small and that made her feet hurt. She liked to be noticed and, more important, she wanted to be loved. Lillian took it personally, as though she were being denied something that was hers, when she saw an affectionate gesture or a loving impulse directed toward someone else. At such moments it was obvious that Lillian felt cheated.

One Christmas, Zofia's aunt had lost her job, and she was barely able to meet her expenses. Zofia had always liked this woman, whose name was Blanche. Blanche wore her hair all piled up on her head and she always wore clingy skirts and shiny blouses, the kind you would see in an old black and white movie. She wore perfume and powder. Her hips swayed a little when she walked, and her nylons had seams that went right down the backs of her legs.

Blanche asked Lillian if she could borrow the money to buy Zofia a present, and Lillian agreed. Then Lillian took Zofia aside and told her about it. She did this to make sure that Zofia understood where the present came from, and to guarantee that if there was any good feeling on Christmas, Lillian would be the recipient of it. Zofia was too young to understand these things, and all she knew for sure was that she wanted the hair dryer.

They had a beautiful tree and Lillian, Zofia's father, Hank, Blanche, and Zofia were there sitting around it on Christmas morning. Zofia's sister, Marta, was there, too. They opened books and socks and a sweater, but Zofia kept looking for the hair dryer. She was about to cry when Blanche gave her a present. Zofia unwrapped it and found the hair dryer, and she was so glad to have it that she turned to her mother and said, "Oh, thank you." And Lillian said, giving her a stern look, "Don't thank me. Thank your aunt." Zofia didn't know anything but the desire to tell the truth, and then she was so excited that she was completely frank and without the least guile. How could she be expected to be so devious, so grown up and suspicious of the truth? She said to Blanche, "Thank you. Even though I know Mom gave you the money for it."

They all sat there. Blanche looked at Lillian. Lillian looked back. Zofia's father sat looking from one to another. Zofia put down the hair dryer as though it had just burned her hand. After a while Zofia's father said he thought it would be a good idea if they went out to find a place that was open where they could have a drink, and so they all piled into the car, Zofia and Marta in the back, and drove around until they found a bar that was open on Christmas, and the three of them, Lillian, Zofia's father, and Blanche went in and drank while Zofia and Marta sat in the car.

Marta was only seven. After an hour she started to cry. She was convinced that Lillian and her father had sold them to the Chinese or the Mexicans or a tribe that didn't even have a name. Zofia told her that the Chinese or the Mexicans wouldn't want them, but that didn't seem to do much good.

"You see?" said Zofia to Russell. "You see what I am trying to tell you? You want something so badly and then . . ."

Zofia said that she could still feel the heaving of her sister in the backseat of the car, just as she apprehended the approach of sadness that there was no word for: that something was changed forever and that there wasn't a thing she could do.

"That damn hair dryer," said Zofia. "That goddamned thing."

Marta wore white socks and black patent leather shoes with one strap that went over the top of each foot and had a silver buckle. "Zofia," she said "Zofia?"

"Don't worry," Zofia said.

"I can't help it," her sister said.

"Sure you can," Zofia said.

Marta's nose was running.

"I don't have a handkerchief," Marta said. "What am I going to do?"

Zofia looked around in the car, but there was nothing. Not even a piece of newspaper.

"Use your skirt," she said.

"It's my Christmas dress," Marta said.

"I don't know what else you can do," Zofia said.

Marta picked up the hem of her dress and blew her nose on it and then started crying again, all the harder, since she had gotten her good dress dirty and she still didn't understand anything aside from the fact that something had happened and she couldn't help it.

A large, dark-skinned man walked down the street. A Mexican with a mustache that he wore with pride. It was not the mustache of a gringo. He was wearing khaki clothes, the sleeves of the shirt frayed and the pants stained. He had a bottle in a bag, what was called a sneaky pete, and took a sip while he walked, which was like being able to pat your head and rub your stomach at the same time, and as Marta saw him, she took in a little air. She trembled on the seat next to Zofia.

"I told you they sold us," she said.

"No, no, no," said Zofia. "That's just a guy drunk on Christmas. He's not coming for you."

Marta trembled on the seat. She put her head in her hands, but then she looked up, eyes wide open, face tear-stained. The Mexican looked in through the window. Marta's trembling took on a new intensity, like a moth that was shivering as it got ready to fly. Then she put her hands over her face and put her head down, toward her lap, rocking back and forth. The Mexican hammered on the window with his flat, open hand, and when it hit the glass, Zofia saw the white of his palm and the lines in it, like in a leaf. He leaned on the car a little, trying to get his balance, and when he did so, she felt the thing rock back and forth on its springs. The man spoke Spanish, his breath making a white mist on the window.

"Go away," Zofia said.

"She's here," said the Mexican in halting English. He put his hand on his chest. "Today. She is here."

"Go away," Zofia said.

"Tell her," he said.

"You promised me," said Marta. "You said they hadn't done anything. That they hadn't sold us."

"It's all right," Zofia said to her.

The Mexican took another drink out of his bottle.

"She's here," he said. "She's mine. She's pretty."

Bonita.

There was nothing in the car, no tire iron, no bottle, nothing at all.

"I won't let anything happen," Zofia said.

"You're too young," Marta said. "What can you do?"

"She is my present," said the Mexican.

"Go away," Zofia said.

Zofia made shooing motions with her hand. The Mexican took another drink and hit the window of the car. Marta started to rock from side to side, as though she could get away by just moving and that made the Mexican angry. He glared and then looked around until he saw a brick, which he walked over to and picked up. The thing was the color of paprika. He rapped the window with it.

"You think I can't get you?" he said.

"Go away. Go away." Zofia said.

The Mexican stood back, looking at them. Then he tipped up the bottle, shrugged, and dropped the brick. As he walked away, Marta kept rocking back and forth, crying so hard that Zofia put her arm around her, and after a long while Marta stopped. The girl still turned around from time to time to make sure the man with the mustache wasn't coming back. As she rocked inside her sister's arms, she said as a mindless eruption, as an impulse to relive a perfectly understood but yet inarticulate fact, "Zofia, Zofia, Zofia . . ."

"You know what scares me about the hunt?" said Zofia. "The horses. The flowing approach of them. Like they are going to get us. Like they are things I can't control. So, do you see? I need to know what I'm getting into. You're not going to leave me, are you? You're not going to appear one way and then turn out to be another, are you?"

"No," he said.

"Look at me," she said. "Say it."

Russell thought of the end of the last hunt, when her sweat had blended with the smell of the leaves, just as he tried to recall the tint of the air, a pink that held them suspended in the heat of the late morning, and at that moment, her lips seemed to disappear into the soft pink glow from the pools of maple leaves and that aureate light of the sun where it hung in the mist.

"You can trust me," he said.

FRANK KOHLER

KOHLER COOKED BACON FOR BREAKFAST, THE SLICES of it making a snapping noise in the skillet that was like the sound of electric sparks. The odor of it seeped into every corner of the house, and when Katryna smelled it, she went into the bedroom to get away, but even there the smell hung around her like a cloud. In the beginning, she assumed that this was just part of getting used to America: this house had odors that were so unfamiliar as to make her queasy. Even in Kohler's shop, where he kept his small tools and motherboards, his boxes of software and manuals, she was made queasy by the odor of the solvent he used to clean disc drives. And yet, when she thought of the smells of Russia, black bread and vegetable soup, the dusty and human smell of the subway in Moscow, the aroma of pielmeni, she wasn't reassured.

Her skin had broken out, too. It usually had a pale, almost luminescent appearance, which made her eyes seem bluer, but now she looked as though she were fifteen again. And so it wasn't only that she felt out of sorts because of the American odors, but she had broken out, too. It must have been from the airplane, where the air had been dirty and continually recycled. On the flight she had gone into the bathroom with the folding door and scrubbed her face with medicinal-smelling soap, but it hadn't done any good.

She longed, or so she told herself, to feel and smell that wind in the springtime in Russia when the earth was finally wet and green, but when her nipples began to tingle, and when her breasts hurt walking downstairs, she went into the kitchen and sat there, brooding as she stared at the black car parked in the yard. It didn't look like it was that hard to drive, and while she had never driven a stick shift before, she guessed she could do it. Her brother had been trained to drive a tank in the Soviet army, and he had talked about it all the time. It couldn't be that different.

Frank often went out for walks that lasted a couple of hours, patrolling along the brook for poachers and then taking a trail that went into the woods. There had to be a doctor in town, and perhaps there was a clinic she could go to if she could drive there. She sat in the kitchen and looked at that black car, which left her close to sobbing, and she was amazed that a black hunk of fiberglass could make her feel that way.

She began to think of those intense hours in Moscow when she had taken a chance with a young thug she had known there. But he had been sweet, even when they had done it in the park after getting drunk at a place called Yugoslavia, which was at the end of the Arbat, and he had told her that if she ever needed anything, she should get in touch. For reasons she couldn't quite understand, she believed him and wanted to call him, but then this grasping at remote possibilities, as though they were real, might have been just one more example of how disoriented she was, and how desperate. He had told her that he was going to travel to the States on "business," and that when he got there, he would look her up. Was this true, or just more talk? She looked at the car and tried to decide just what was certain, what was wishful thinking, and what she was going to do.

Katryna kept her tea from Russia in a jar with a red top. She brewed it in the afternoon, hoping that a familiar smell would help her, but sometimes she got up from the kitchen table and went into the bedroom to lie down after having just a sip.

Each day Kohler noticed how much less tea there was, and he was afraid that when it got down to nothing there would be a crisis, as though the black tea was the one thing that was keeping her attached to her sense of who and what she was, and when the tea was gone she would leave him. The glass jar had a way of commanding the room, as though it kept a running tally on what their chances were. He looked at the amount of tea. Then she did.

"There's a place in town that sells tea from all over," he said.

"Maybe they'll have some from Russia," she said, thinking that she should watch carefully when Kohler drove the car. "Who knows?"

Katryna and Kohler drove along the two-lane road that led from his house. She noticed that the pattern was like an H, sort of, and Kohler started the gearshift at the top left and then went straight back. He put in one pedal when he worked the lever and then let out the pedal again. She thought she could do that. Once, in Moscow, she had driven a Mercedes truck, a diesel that left a long trail of exhaust, like a cat's tail.

They went into the store that was filled with the dusty aroma of tea, and through the window she saw the flat, metallic surface of the river. The tea sat in a row of jars on a shelf, and a lot of it was black and shiny, just like the stuff at home, although there were other teas, too, brown and sere, or a green that was the color of an iguana.

"Can I help you?" asked the woman behind the counter.

While Katryna picked out tea from Russia, Kohler looked at some books on the other side of the room, histories of tea, and methods of brewing it, along with a cookbook that had a series of recipes in which tea was used to make sauces and marinades. As he turned the pages, Katryna said in a low voice, "Is there a doctor in town?"

"Sure," said the woman. "The one I use is up by the hospital."

"Where's that?" said Katryna.

"About a mile up this road," said the woman, who was busy scooping out the tea. "There's a sign. First Care of Vermont."

"I mean a doctor for women," said Katryna.

"Sure," said the woman. "Ask at the desk there."

Katryna looked out the window at the river. The geese were flying and she heard their call, at once plaintive, insistent, and trustworthy. She paid for the tea out of money that Kohler had given her, and then they got back in the car with Katryna holding the tea in her lap like a girl with a sack lunch. She saw the vees of geese against the sky, but their sound was lost in the growl of the engine. She watched how he changed the gears, first, then second, third, then fourth. A little gas. He started the engine by turning the key forward, toward the dashboard.

THE NEXT AFTERNOON Kohler said, "Would you like to have some of the new tea?"

She filled the kettle and put it on to boil, and she got out the cups and spoons and then they waited, hearing the subdued hiss of the gas in the stove and the ticking of the kettle as it heated up. The geese were honking again, so high up and so insistent.

She put the teapot on the table and they waited while it steeped. Then she poured it and picked her cup up and put it right next to her lips, sniffing it a little and then looking at Kohler through the mist that came off the surface. She couldn't stand the smell, and her breasts had gotten sore again.

"Isn't that something?" Kohler said. "And to think, you've only been here two weeks and you've found a way to get your tea from Russia."

Katryna swallowed with her eyes closed. She put a hand to her head and stood up with a woozy stagger that looked as though she was afraid of fainting, and with a rush that was like running through the rain, bent at the waist, she went through the living room and into the bathroom, where she closed and locked the door. Kohler followed and leaned his head against the frame of the door.

"Please," he said.

"Please what?" she said.

"I don't know," he said. "Are you all right?"

"Go away," she said.

"Isn't the tea any good?" he said.

"It was fine," she said.

"Then what's the problem?" he said. "Did it make you sick?"

She didn't say anything, and he imagined her making a gesture toward the door, an open-palmed movement that suggested the impossibility of trying to speak. Hands open, empty. He waited, hearing her muffled sobs, leaning against the door frame, listening. When she stopped crying, he wished she would start again, since it was better than the silence.

"It'll be all right," he said. "I'll make it be all right."

She was quiet in the bathroom for a while, and then he heard the sound of the water running. It sounded as though she was splashing water on her face, and when she was done, she said through the door, "Yes. It will be fine. I'm just not myself."

She came out of the bathroom.

"Maybe I'm homesick," she said.

"Well, that would make sense," he said.

"Mmmmmm," she said. "I've been thinking about my friends there, you know? Sometimes I miss them."

"Well," he said. "Sure. That's only natural."

"Maybe I could have one of them visit. Would you mind?"

"What's her name?" said Kohler.

"Dimitry," she said. She looked at his face. "He's a cousin. Would that be all right?"

"A cousin?" he said.

"Yes. He's about my age. A little older. He said he was going to come here on business."

"Sure," he said. "That's fine."

"I could speak Russian to him," said Katryna.

"All right," said Frank. "Write to him."

"Maybe I'll call," said Katryna.

At night Kohler sat at the table and read Caesar's *The War in Gaul*. As far as Kohler could tell, Caesar was a reasonable man and meant no harm, and the only thing he was interested in was fairness, justice, and doing the right thing. Katryna sat down opposite him and read a copy of *Vogue,* stopping to look at those women with long legs and perfect skin and shiny hair. When the moon rose, Kohler waited for the coyotes to begin.

Katryna went into the bedroom, leaving the door open, and when Kohler glanced up he saw her taking off her skirt and her blouse and standing there in that innocent Russian underwear, which she slipped off and dropped into the hamper in the corner. Then she got into bed and turned off the lamp, which left her in shadows and light, her hair disappearing into those coal-colored shapes, her skin looking almost tattooed with the geometric patterns that the moonlight made when it came through the lace curtains.

He stretched out next to her in the black and white of the geometric shapes.

"You mean so much to me," he said. "I never realized how much it would mean. . . ."

"Frank," she said. "I want to talk to you about something . . ."

"I know," he said. "You're homesick . . . You don't have to explain."

"But—"

"Don't worry," he said. "I love you. I really do. Everyone gets cranky now and then."

"In Moscow . . ." she said.

"Look," he said. "You don't have to say a word."

RUSSELL BOYD

EACH TIME A CAR WENT BY ON THE HIGHWAY, IT left something behind, not enough for Russell to feel at the moment, but the sheer number of cars added up, each producing this small effect, and when it got to be a million, ten million, a hundred million, it was another matter. Then, when Russell watched the road, he detected an agitated quality in the air, like static electricity. This effect was even more pronounced at night when the wind throbbed against the window of the cruiser.

He decided to move from one turnout to another, and as he drove to the next one, he saw a car parked at the side of the road. Lights on, one man inside. The dispatcher told Russell that there were no outstanding warrants to go with the plates, no priors on the owner, nothing. Just a car stopped at the side of the road.

Russell stepped from the cruiser into that keening sound of the tires on the road and a pulse of air that was left by each passing car. A cool night, not bad really, but filled with the promise of January. Then he walked toward the car that was parked at the side of the road, a Buick, a couple of years old. Russell stopped behind the driver, right by the post between the front seat and the back. The window was rolled down.

The driver opened the door and vomited. There were no cars passing at this moment, and the sound was loud in the momentary hush of the road.

"Are you all right?" said Russell.

The man shook his head.

"I'm taking chemo," the man said.

Russell went back to the cruiser and radioed the dispatcher, who said she'd get Rescue, and while Russell waited, seeing the Buick move a little in the pulse of a passing truck, he wondered if peopled died like this, at the side of the road, or was this man just having a reaction to the drugs? The dispatcher told him he'd have to wait. Rescue was busy on another call.

"It won't be long," Russell said to the man in the car.

"I should have stayed home," said the man.

"Someone will be here soon," he said.

"Do me a favor, will you?" the man said.

"What?" said Russell.

"Can you sit with me?"

"You'll have to wait," said Russell. "It won't be long."

"O.K.," said the man, then he swallowed. "I'm sorry about the smell," he said.

"It's all right," Russell said. "Don't worry."

"I guess you're trained not to get in someone's car?"

The stars shimmered at the end of the open place where the road had been cut through the hills, and when Russell looked back the other way, where the Rescue truck would be, it was dark, too. The Buick seemed all right, sitting on its springs the way it should, not scratched, no recently replaced panels, nothing to suggest that he was carrying anything.

"I'm pretty sick," said the man.

"I'm sorry," said Russell.

"It sneaks up on you," said the man. "You think you can go on taking this stuff, but . . ." The man made a gesture of resignation.

"You want a drink of water?" said Russell. "I've got some water."

The man shook his head.

"No, I don't want water. What gets to me is that I'm too tired to be scared."

The air pulsed as another car went by, and Russell felt it as a shove out of the dark.

"But I'm still scared anyway," he said. "Doesn't make a lot of sense. You know how I feel the fear? As a kind of loneliness."

"It won't be too much longer," said Russell.

"Yeah," said the man. "That's why I asked you to sit in the car."

Russell looked around. No lights from the south, where the ambulance would come from. Then he went around to the passenger's side. But as he did, he unsnapped the leather strap that went over the pistol in his holster. Russell didn't think the man could hear it, and then the holster was on his right, in the dark, so the man probably didn't see it. Russell thought that it wouldn't do anyone any good if he was scared, too. How can you help anybody that way? If you are scared, don't you just bring fear into the car, and what good is that? He wished he had the energy to bring something with him that wasn't tainted with fear. That is, if this man wasn't full of shit, and if he didn't have to kill him.

Russell opened the door and got in.

"Thanks," the man said.

"It won't be long," Russell said.

The car smelled, too, and Russell guessed the man must have been sick on the floor. There was the possibility, Russell supposed, that he could be sick here, too.

"No one tells you that there are things like this," the man said. "But I guess you see some of it out here."

"If you work out here, you see a few things," Russell said.

The cars went by at seventy miles an hour.

"There's some stuff I am going to miss," the driver said.

"Like what?"

"Oh," he said. He swallowed. He had a film of sweat on his brow, which turned golden as the lights from the cars on the other side of the highway went by. "Wind. The sound of wind. You know, at night, in the winter when the wind whistles around the house."

"Un-huh," Russell said. "I like that."

The night seemed to seep into the car, as though they were underwater and the black wet was leaking in, pushing the air out.

"Like what have you seen?" he said. "You know, out here, or on the job?"

"I don't know," Russell said.

"It might make me take my mind off of it," the driver said. "Tell me."

Russell thought about going up to a house a month ago where a boy, nineteen years old, had shot himself in the head. When Russell got there, the boy was still alive. He was on his bed and his mother was with him. The boy's breath made a heavy, grating sound as he died, and his mother held his hand and said, "It'll be all right, darling, it will be all right."

"I think we've got enough problems," Russell said.

"Have you ever shot anyone?" the driver said.

"No," Russell said.

"Have you wanted to?" he said.

"Not really," Russell said.

"That's something. But things change . . ." the driver said.

"Maybe not," said Russell.

"You believe that?" said the man.

"Maybe believing isn't what I'm talking about. Maybe it's more like hope," said Russell.

"Hope," said the man. He seemed to hang there, between being sick and just giving up. For a moment Russell thought that the man could die right there. He was sweating and breathing hard, not quite rattling in his throat, but it didn't sound good. The man looked at Russell. "Maybe," he said. He swallowed. "I don't know."

They sat there until the ambulance came, and when Russell began to get out, the man just turned and looked at him. Of course, Russell wanted to think that there was something in this glance, an essential feeling that made this easier, and then he realized the driver wanted to thank him. When Russell looked around, he thought that this small bit of gratitude was useful against the scale of the night, the stars, those pulses of dark air.

"Take it easy," the driver said.

"Yeah," said Russell. "Good night."

ZOFIA WIRA

ZOFIA LOOKED SICK WHEN SHE GLANCED AT THE horses and the roil of hounds through the crosshatching of bramble. Russell stopped running, but she shook her head, and said, "Don't worry. I'm all right. Maybe I had too much to drink last night."

"We didn't drink anything last night," said Russell.

"Well," she said, "That's what it feels like." Her eyes were glassy with fear.

They passed the leaves of sumac, which were the color of the reddest lipstick. Every now and then a leaf fell, twirling and then hitting the ground with an impossibly delicate tick. In the distance there was the occasional yellow smear of a stand of poplar. Each time Russell tried to stop her, she shook her head and went on running, even though she was pale and her forehead was damp.

The hounds were excited. Mixed in with their baying and yapping, their scent-hitting yelps, came the otherworldly clink of the tack, and then the sleek shapes of the horses emerged from the wall of brush. Zofia's skin was so white it looked powdered, and yet despite her blue lips she still sweated. She stopped and was mesmerized by the red jackets as they floated above the white horses, as though at sea, the motion so much like a boat riding on a swell. It seemed to make her sick, and she put her hands on her knees and retched with slow, deep contractions.

"I don't want to make a scene," she said. "So just ignore this. Can you do that for me?"

The clinking and yowling, the thudding of the horses on the bottomland sounded close, and from the cross-hatching of brambles Russell looked back, through the thorns and cane, and saw the hounds boiling into the edge of a field that was lined with cut corn. Zofia stood up and put the back of her hand to her mouth, her queasiness interrupted only by her nauseated panting.

"Stay here," he said. "I can finish."

She shook her head, her eyes looking backward.

"No," she said. "Let's keep going."

A fox came out of the raspberry canes. It looked over its shoulder, its head turned toward the hounds and the hunters, which were in the next field. It was so still that it appeared to be a color photograph of a fox. Not even its fur moved in the breeze. After seeing which way the hunt was going, the fox slowly turned its head to Russell and Zofia. Its eyes were the color of black licorice.

The sound of the hunt faded into that frozen landscape, and then there were just the three of them, Zofia, that animal, and Russell. It obviously knew precisely what should be done when you didn't have much time.

Zofia put her hand to the moisture on her forehead, as though surprised by it, but she still looked at the fox, which lingered there, moving its head once back to the hunt and then settling its eyes on her. It didn't move when Zofia was sick again, in one liquid upheaval after another. The animal looked at both of them with the most piercing certainty, and then it ran along the cane and brush, the shape of it defined in long, red arcs as it jumped impossible distances and covered a couple of hundred yards in a few seconds.

They started again, Zofia's face still white and her lips that alarming blue. Russell wanted to take her home and fill the tub with hot water, and then he would help her undress, pulling her T-shirt over her shoulders and arms, and then help her into the tub, where she could sit back in that steam and get warm. Then he would sit there, adjusting the water, seeing her legs waver under the silver water, as though she were dissolving into warmth and comfort.

On the way home she said, "Let's stop at the Rite Aid."

It was on the strip, not far from the indoor swimming pool where Zofia and Russell had gone whenever they could. Russell recalled the rubbery odor of her swimming suit, the taste of the chlorine on her skin, the rill of silver moisture on her neck when she got out of the water. The pool was covered with a transparent roof, like a greenhouse. The last time they had gone, Zofia had stood on the small platform, like one for races, and dove up and out, and for a moment she was suspended in the yellow light and the scent of chlorine, her arms out, toes together, the ankles just touching. When she had reached the height of the dive she appeared to hang there for one instant longer than seemed possible. Then she allowed herself to sweep down to that glassine water, where she entered without a splash. She came up from the depths, pushing a wave ahead of her as she swam, one arm sleek with water as it reached out and cut into the surface, followed by the other arm. She made the water boil where she kicked.

In the Rite Aid parking lot, she said, "Wait here." Then she went in and walked along the aisle until she came to the Coke syrup and Dramamine, Pepto-Bismol and Mylanta, all of it next to the section for pregnancy kits. At night, when Russell was asleep, she went into the bathroom and took the kit from under the sink where she had left it next to the Zud and Windex, and used it. Then she sat there, thinking about what she was going to do now that she was pregnant.

KATRYNA KOLYMOV

KATRYNA THOUGHT ABOUT THE FLAT WHERE SHE had grown up in Moscow, the stairwells of the building which were like those in a parking garage, the mishmash of sheds that people had put in the courtyard to store things because the apartments didn't have enough closets, and the old women who climbed the stairs with plastic bags from the market. From the window of the flat's living room she had been able to see a statue of the New Man and the New Woman, each a hundred feet high, muscled, sleek, and bold. One night the men in leather coats had pounded on the door for her father, at three in the morning, their appearance as bland and bureaucratic as that of deliverymen. Her father was disoriented at being woken up, humiliated and dizzy, his hair brushed up, his unshaven cheeks looking as though they had been sprinkled with salt and pepper. He had turned to look at Katryna, his expression one of love mixed with regret: What could he say to her now that would be useful? What fatherly advice could be compressed into one disoriented moment? She had been so afraid that she hadn't even clung to him as he went out the door between the two men in leather coats.

In Kohler's house, Katryna crossed her arms and felt the soreness of her breasts. Kohler sat at the kitchen table and signed the posters he had bought, which said, POSTED. NO HUNTING. NO FISHING. NO TRESPASSING. Each one had a place for the landowner to write his name, and he bore down on the dotted line, as though signing a lease. Then he picked up his nail apron and a hammer, and said, "You know the way to put up a posted sign? You do it like this." He dog-eared a corner, and held a nail against it. "That way they can't rip them down so easy."

"That's good," she said.

"Yeah," he said. "Deer season is coming up. I'll be back in a couple of hours."

The door closed behind him and she looked at the keys to the car on a little hook by the door. Out the window she saw Kohler as he walked through the field to the woods, as though he were whistling, his gait like a seafaring man. Then she looked at the car, parked behind the house. It seemed sharklike and powerful, more like a piece of military equipment than a car, but she realized it had come down to this moment: Either she was going to be able to drive it or she wasn't. She took the keys from the hook and went into the bedroom, where she had in her drawer a hundred and ninety dollars that she had brought from Moscow. She took forty and went out to the car.

The seats of the car were warm from the sunlight, and when she started the engine, the growl of it made her hesitate; it was nice to sit there, hearing the power of it before having to do anything. She was glad, at least, that she wasn't going to have to back up. The seat made a little whir as she moved it up and forward. She didn't know how to change the mirror at the side, but she reached up and adjusted the rearview. Then she put the clutch in, as she had seen Kohler do and as she had done in Moscow the few times she had driven. Then she let the clutch out and the car lurched forward and she felt as though she had been shoved. Her head jerked back. She began to shake, and her face felt hot as the engine died. She leaned forward, putting her head on the wheel.

She remembered her father's mustache and the stiff brush of it against her cheek when she was a child, the smell of his beer and smoked herring, the cigar smoke on the wool of his suit, and his pet names for her that made no sense, but still meant something to her. And when she saw anything made of gold, a piece of jewelry, a wedding ring, she instantly thought of that brushy embrace and then the sudden realization that he had died in a labor camp, in a gold mine. Now she remembered his look as she had last seen him. Well, he had probably meant that she should not be afraid, that she should try to get what she needed. She put the clutch in, started the engine, and let it out. The car jerked a little, but it went down the drive.

At the end of the drive she stopped and looked both ways before she put on the turn signal, which clicked like a metronome. She wished she had a more definite idea about where she was supposed to go in town, but this was the way she had to live, and she had contempt for people who could afford the luxury of taking a setback in stride. What did such people know about the small tolerances by which she lived? A breakdown, getting lost in a strange town, taking an hour too long—it wouldn't take much. The car stalled at the end of the drive, but she got it going again.

On the way to the highway, Katryna came up behind a tour bus that was rattling as it left a black cloud of exhaust that showed the path the bus had taken. It made her queasy, like everything else, the smell of bacon, the cologne Frank wore, and as she started to pass, she saw, in the rearview mirror, that a state police car was following her. It had green and yellow paint and a rack of lights on the top.

The speed limit was fifty, but she was pretty sure she had gone a little faster than that after turning out of the driveway, thrilled by the power of the car and the thrust of it toward where she wanted to go. She had probably gone sixty or more, since the car accelerated like magic. But had she done it in front of the police?

The cruiser turned on its lights.

Maybe she could pretend that she didn't speak English, but what good would that do? Sooner or later they would discover that she didn't have a license, and, surely the instant they found out who owned the car, they would call Frank. In Moscow you usually bribed a cop, and in fact, most of them preferred it that way when they stood on their little kiosk at an intersection and stopped you by pointing a baton in your direction. She wondered if twenty dollars would be enough? She would roll down the window and offer the money she had.

As she began to pull over, the trooper went by. Then the cruiser trailed the bus, lights flashing in that stream of black smoke, and as she followed, sick with the stink and the fear of being caught, she saw the bus turn on its blinker and make a slow, lumbering movement to the side of the road. The cruiser stopped behind the bus, its front wheels turned toward the road, and then the trooper put on his hat and got out, glancing at Katryna as she slowly went by, making a bad shift and riding the clutch.

In town she came up to a barrier where the street was closed for a fair. Kids were running around in animal costumes, rabbits and bears and foxes, and parents shepherded them with a weary good cheer. A small Ferris wheel went up and around, and the children waited in line, watching it go around and around. Katryna stopped the car just back from the barrier. The children, the bright colors of the Ferris wheel, the pink fluffs of cotton candy, seemed garish. A child came up to the window and waved a piece of cotton candy, like a small pink cloud, and beyond the airy confection more children shrieked. Then a policeman came up to her and motioned toward the lane that was open.

She shifted into first. The policeman beckoned, using just his fingers. To her right, people threw balls at aluminum bottles, where teddy bears sat at the back of a shelf, and where she heard the steady, repeated, and oddly reassuring sound of the shooting gallery. People laughed a little too much, and a few of them were carrying stuffed animals that they had won. She let the clutch out slowly and lurched forward. The policeman gave her a quizzical look, but continued beckoning. She heard the crack, crack of the shooting gallery, and for a moment she could almost smell the gunpowder.

But she managed to park the car, not perfectly, just a foot away from the pickup truck on her left. She got out, although there wasn't much room, and then she buttoned her short black leather coat, and looked around. She took a deep breath.

The front of the medical building looked like a greenhouse, and when she opened the door, she found herself in a room with two women behind a counter, each of them wearing a telephone headset and each looking at a computer monitor. The waiting room was to one side, the banks of chairs in it, all on one long piece of metal, looking just like the ones in an airport. The first thing she noticed was that her coat was wrong. It had been all right in Moscow, but here she could tell the collar was too wide and pointed. She stood up all the straighter.

One of the women behind the counter was on the phone, and after glancing at Katryna, she held up a finger, as though to say, Just one minute.

"Can I help you?" asked the receptionist.

"Yes, I'd like to see a doctor," said Katryna.

"Which one?" said the receptionist.

"One for women."

"Do you have an appointment?" said the receptionist.

"No," said Katryna.

The receptionist looked to the other woman behind the counter, who shrugged.

"I can wait," said Katryna.

"Do you have insurance?" asked the receptionist.

"What?"

"You know," said the receptionist. "Health insurance."

Katryna opened her handbag to look for the forty dollars she had there.

"You aren't from around here, are you?" said the receptionist.

A woman came through the front door and up to the desk, just behind Katryna. The receptionist looked at her and said, "Hi, Zofia."

"Hi, Darlene," said Zofia.

"I'll let Dr. Basinger know you're here," said the receptionist.

Zofia hesitated as she stood next to Katryna who was still holding the money out.

"Do you have a card?" said the receptionist.

"What kind of card?" said Katryna.

"Insurance," said the receptionist.

"No," said Katryna. "I have money."

"It would be better if you had insurance," said the receptionist.

Katryna held out the two bills. She did so as a way of stating the facts that weren't going to change.

"Here," she said. She held out the bills.

"That might not be enough," said the receptionist.

"I need to see the doctor."

The receptionist looked at the monitor.

"I can give you an appointment next week. How about—"

"No," said Katryna.

"Well," said the receptionist, "it might be more than forty dollars."

Katryna still held the bills out, and she knew that the instant she put her hand down, she would be defeated. She stood there, her posture perfect in that unfashionable jacket, her head up.

"I'll make up the difference," said Zofia.

Katryna turned to face Zofia.

"I didn't know about the insurance," she said.

"It's no big deal." Zofia turned to the receptionist. "Why don't you put her in for my time for Dr. Basinger. I just need a referral."

The receptionist shrugged. Then she typed and looked up and said to Katryna, "O.K. What's your name?"

"Katryna Kolymov."

"What?" said the receptionist.

Katryna spelled it and gave her address, too. Then she went into the waiting room and sat down, her eyes on the door that led to the examination rooms. She picked up a magazine that had been handled so often by sweaty hands as to look like it came from a lending library in Istanbul in the cholera season. Zofia, who had gone to the bathroom, came back and sat down next to her. Katryna felt a kind of panic, in that she didn't know if she could speak honestly if she had the chance. She had gotten used to lying, or at least protecting herself, and the possibility of doing otherwise left her a little disoriented. Maybe it was best to keep it for the doctor, but that would only be just the facts. She was used to denying herself ordinary pleasures, like speaking to people, and yet she was amazed that she sat there next to Zofia and thought, Please. Say something.

Katryna remembered driving by the fair, the cotton candy, pink as a dancer's tutu, the sound of the shooting gallery, the general hilarity of the place. It made her all the more ashamed that she didn't have the card, but how was she to know she needed one? The noise of the fair, the movement, the ominous creaking of the Ferris wheel, lingered in her mind like an indictment. People glanced at her. She sat up straight.

Then the nurse came out and called Zofia, who stood up and smiled at Katryna and then disappeared into the door. Then Katryna started to wait. There was a clock on the wall, and she watched as the second hand moved along, and wondered where Frank was now. Had he come into the empty house after seeing the car was gone?

Then she picked up the dog-eared magazine again, which she looked at without seeing any of it, and as she turned the pages, she thought of the woman, Zofia, who had helped her. The woman was perfectly American: the way the blue jeans she wore fit her rear end, the perfect and yet subdued sexiness of the man's shirt she wore, the beauty of her hands, which were strong and yet still graceful, the easy carriage and full-lipped smile, all of it vital and easy. Still, Katryna thought Americans had no sense of tragedy, no belief in the finality of fate, and if someone didn't have that, how could you make contact with them? How could you make yourself understood? Americans didn't have to look at war widows begging in the subway. Katryna looked around and saw that all the woman were wearing large gold wedding rings. Was it possible that the gold had come from Siberia? Maybe her father had dug some of the ore that went into these rings. Then she thought, Stop it.

Still, Katryna thought again of Zofia. But instantly she knew that the desire to speak would get her into trouble, and so she sat there, resisting it, concentrating on what she would say to the doctor. Should she mention the cancer rate among young women in Russia? Was that what was wrong with her?

Zofia came out of the door that led to the doctor's examination room.

"You're next," she said.

The nurse appeared and Katryna stood up. Everyone in the room glanced at her, and then she disappeared into the door that led to the offices.

"You'll have to wait," said the receptionist to Zofia. "You know, to see how much it's going to be for her."

Zofia looked at the card she held in her hand, which had the address and telephone number of a place where she could get an abortion. All she had to do was make an appointment to have the procedure done, and as she sat there with the card, she went through the obvious reasons. But before she even got to the end of them, she wasn't certain she was going to tell Russell about it. It was her decision, not his. But as she sat there, hearing the pages of those old, dead magazines being turned with weary exasperation by the other people in the room, she thought maybe that wasn't right. Could she dismiss his interest so casually when she decided *not* to have a child and include him so completely when she *did*? And as she considered not telling him about it, just taking an afternoon off work and being remote about what happened, just pleading a bad period and cramps, she knew that part of what made her enjoy being with him would disappear. This, she knew, was the nature of a secret. Not only did it have its own effect on the person who kept it, but it also did something to the way the person who kept it saw the people who didn't know. It was a cheap superiority she didn't want.

But all of that was on the surface. Underneath, there was another matter, which she tried to confront as she sat there in the relatively bland office with the people who were doing their best to seem indifferent. Wasn't that what she was doing? Then she opened her handbag and put the card into her wallet, and as she did so, she thought of the night where Russell worked, the malice and danger of his hour-to-hour existence, which she supposed could be seen in what he had described to her once: how the colors at night were so bright and those during the day so bland. She was frightened by whatever made those colors bright, whatever seemed to exist in the speed and the chase, and in the uncertainty of those people he pursued, and all of this had another quality, a fearful imperative that took courage to face, although this came at a price, and that was a steady, increasing fatigue. Was this how one had a child? Then she thought of how she waited for him to come home, and what it meant to her when she heard the car in the drive: a sweetness so deep and complete, so utterly essential, that it was like the sun rising.

Katryna came out of the door of the medical offices and walked through the waiting room with that same stately gait, at once mildly elegant and yet foreign. Zofia stood up and they both went to the receptionist's desk, where Katryna handed over a slip she had from the doctor, and Zofia got out her checkbook.

"Sixty dollars," said the receptionist.

Zofia wrote the check and ripped it from the book and handed it over. The receptionist reached up and took it while talking on the phone. Then Zofia and Katryna walked out to the front of the building.

"I'll get the other twenty back to you," said Katryna as she passed over her forty dollars.

"That's all right," said Zofia.

Katryna stiffened. It was as though she was willing to take a gesture of generosity, but not the notion that she couldn't ever pay it back.

"O.K.," said Zofia. "Here's my phone number. Have you got some place to write it?"

Katryna gave Zofia a small card, the same one that Zofia had for the referral, and on the back of it Zofia wrote her number. Katryna took it back. They stood there in the pale sunlight and then started to walk together into the parking lot, stopping in front of the low, black car, which was parked badly. Zofia looked at it.

"Where are you from?" said Zofia.

"Russia," she said. "Moscow."

"Oh," said Zofia. "Do you like it here?"

Katryna shrugged.

"Something is missing," she said. "Everything looks good. You can get everything you want. Like a hair dryer. You can get a great hair dryer here."

"I know," said Zofia.

"Have you ever wanted a good hair dryer and not been able to get one?" said Katryna.

"When I was a kid," said Zofia.

"Me too," said Katryna. "I used to cut my hair short so I wouldn't need one." She shrugged. She knew she should keep quiet. This felt too much like trying to explain a dream: all the objects were right, but the meaning, the import eluded her.

"There are twenty or thirty hair dryers to choose from here," said Katryna. "You can get the ones that look like a gun, or you can get one with a bag and a tube. Which do you think is best?"

"The gun kind," said Zofia.

"But not if you put your hair up in curlers," said Katryna.

"We don't do that so much anymore," said Zofia.

"Maybe not. But still a hair dryer is important if you want to go out and have a little fun. You know, maybe you go out where there are other people. Dance. Listen to music."

"Sure," said Zofia. "Do you get to do that?"

Katryna shook her head.

"Maybe later."

"So, what's missing," said Zofia, "aside from there being too many hair dryers?"

Katryna shrugged. "It's stupid of me to think about it. It doesn't make sense," she said. "How can you miss something that was horrible and hard?"

"I don't know," said Zofia.

"See?" said Katryna. "You don't know and I don't know." She swallowed.

"Do you know how to back it up?" Katryna said, gesturing to the car.

"Sure," said Zofia. "I think so."

Katryna held out the keys.

"Would you?" she said. "I don't think I can."

Zofia got into the car, started it, and backed it up. Then she got out, setting the brake, and being careful to put the car into neutral.

"Thanks," Katryna said. She hesitated. Then she said, "It's difficult being new here."

"Call me sometime," said Zofia. "We can go shopping."

Katryna touched the collar of her coat.

"I'd like that," she said. "I'll call when I have the money."

She got into the open door of the black car, pulled it shut, and drove down the rows of cars. When she stopped at the street, she turned toward Zofia and waved. Then she concentrated on the clutch. Let it out slowly. Give it a little gas. The car jerked into the street and left Katryna with the sensation of hanging on to the car rather than driving it, more like riding a wild horse than being in charge of a machine. Every now and then she glanced at the digital clock on the dashboard, which flicked by one second at a time.

FRANK KOHLER

KOHLER DROVE BY THE POUND, WHICH WAS ON THE strip between the Sandri and the Monro muffler shop, and then he made a turn and drove by it again. He had avoided the place in the past, but now he had a reason to go in, and yet he found it difficult just to go up to the door. He didn't like to think about that trunk at the side of the river, and coming here forced him to remember the dogs that had nosed around it. Now, as he drove back and forth, wanting to turn in and yet being repelled by the place, he thought, Katryna wants a dog. Are you going to get her one or not?

The pound had a flat roof with desert-colored stucco on the walls, which was already cracked, and a window with a broken venetian blind behind it. Two trees had been planted in front of it, but people had let their new dogs use them, and the trees were leafless even in summer. The local policeman instinctively found himself checking the place more than once on his rounds.

Kohler parked his car and went into a small room, which had a counter at the back, beyond which was a swinging door with dogs yapping on the other side of it. Kohler licked his lips. A man in a white coat, which made him look a little like a doctor, came out of the swinging door. The dogs barked with a new intensity.

"I came to get a dog," said Kohler.

The man looked Kohler over, and as he did so, Kohler smiled. Maybe that would help. Kohler wondered if there was a process you had to go through, like adopting a child, although on a much smaller scale.

"Well, you've come to the right place," the man said. "In here."

The room behind the door was filled with galvanized wire cages arranged in two rows, one on each side of the room, and as Kohler walked along them, he saw eyes, two by two, as dark as stove blacking, all of them carefully following his movement along the concrete floor. The man in the coat stopped at a cage.

The dog inside was part Lab and part shepherd, but its coloring was all black. It had a large head, black eyes, and a pink tongue with a ridge down the middle. The dog yawned and made its tongue curl before snapping its jaw shut with an audible click. Then it suddenly turned to its hip and bit it, as though it had been waiting to pounce on itself. It chewed there with a fierce intensity.

"This one is a good watchdog," said the man.

"Looks like it," said Kohler.

"No one is going to get by this guy," said the man.

The fluorescent light made everything seem to flicker, and in Kohler's mood he mistook the quavering light for the thing that was making him uneasy, which was a sense that there was more to this place than just a pound. Then he thought, This is just a place where the dogs are waiting. Nothing more. A dog is a dog is a dog. And yet, as he stood there, he was frightened. How did that happen? He swallowed and looked around, desperately looking for help. He wished the dogs would stop barking.

"Are you all right?" asked the man in the white coat.

"Yeah," said Kohler. "I was just wondering if my wife would like this one."

The black dog watched Kohler. It opened its mouth and panted. Kohler shook as the animal licked his fingers, the tongue warm and wet.

"Some asshole comes up to your house and this dog is there, well . . ." said the man in the coat. "You can imagine what he would be like in action."

"Yeah," said Kohler. "I can imagine. Is he housebroken?"

"Yes," said the man. "Had his shots, too. Good to go."

The dog's tongue had the texture of a wet emery board.

"Hey, boy," said Kohler.

The dog wagged its tail.

"So, you're a good dog, huh? Not going to cause any trouble?" said Kohler. "Hmmmm?"

The dog made a friendly, yearning sound in its throat.

"No stunts now, O.K.?" said Kohler.

The dog licked his fingers. Maybe, thought Kohler. Maybe we can come to an understanding.

The man in the white coat looked at Kohler with a quizzical air, but then he had seen all kinds in here.

"We understand each other," Kohler said to the man in the coat.

"Mmmmmm," he said.

"What do you say?" Kohler said to the dog. "Are you going to behave yourself?"

It barked and threw its head back.

"All right," Kohler said. "I'll take this one."

Outside, in the clutter of the Monro muffler shop, the Mobil and Sandri stations, the drive-in bank with the ATM screen, Kohler opened the door of the car, and the creature jumped in and sat on the passenger's seat, its tongue hanging out, its doggy breath filling the car. Kohler started the engine. The dog barked with a new, yowling, full-bodied intensity, and then the animal and the engine combined in one eerie duet, the elements of which, the voice of the dog and the growl of the machine, were so perfectly combined as to seem as if they had just been waiting for each other. Like lovers kissing for the first time. Kohler went up the road for a block and made another turn into the McDonald's entrance. There were large arrows painted on the asphalt, as though fate had found it necessary to leave signs on the ground.

At the microphone, next to a menu on a sign, there was a speaker, too, and from inside Kohler heard shouting voices, laughter, and then an expectant hum. The odor of cooking hamburgers hung around the building in a cloud, and smoke, which was a brownish color, rose from the ventilator at the back. The dog moved its nose back and forth, trying to locate the precise origin of that brown, mouth-watering odor.

The speaker said, "What can I get you?"

A boy with hair green on one side and purple on the other walked along the drive-through, but when he came close to the car, the dog exploded against the glass, barking, slobbering, head swinging from side to side, the strength of its barking seen in its back and ribs and in the raised fur on its back. The kid jumped back, and then put his head down and his face up against the window of the car before he barked, too, throwing his head from side to side, mocking the dog.

The animal instantly stopped. The kid mugged at the window, making a quiet yapping, which was a good imitation of the dog. But not a very loud one. Without even thinking about it, Kohler touched the button that let down the window, and when it had sunk a couple of inches into the door the dog exploded again—even Kohler jumped back, as though it was a good idea to allow the animal every possible square inch of space. The dog's mouth was so big that it had to turn sideways to be able to get through the only partially lowered window, and even then it couldn't open its mouth as wide as it wanted to. The kid was paralyzed with terror, at least for that instant when it looked as though the dog were actually going to compress itself into a black, cobra-like creature to get through the few open inches of the window. Just as the kid jumped back, the dog's teeth closed on his ear, not biting it, but leaving it wet with saliva. The kid backed away from the car, keeping an eye on the dog.

"What can I get you?" asked the voice again.

"Two double hamburgers," Kohler said.

"What?" she said.

"Two double hamburgers!"

"I can't hear with that dog barking," the voice said.

Kohler put his hand on the dog's head. It stopped barking.

Then he pulled up to the window, where he waited. Kohler looked out at the clouds in the sky, big dragging rags. The paper bag came out as though it was on a mechanical hand.

"Have a nice day," the young woman said.

Kohler pulled around and parked next to the building, but left the engine running. The double hamburgers were wrapped in wax paper, and as he opened the first one, the dog looked at him.

"Here," Kohler said, as he held out the first patty that he had taken from the sandwich.

The animal took it in one chomp. No chewing, just a voracious chomp, then swallowing and quick panting. Kohler held out the other patty so the dog could take it in another wet chomp-and-drool. The dog swallowed again and licked its chops and glanced over at Kohler with a kind of query. Was Kohler going to play ball or not? The dog had barked at the kid. Kohler had given it some hamburgers. Was that how they were going to continue—the dog providing the muscle and Kohler providing the burgers? There was another element in this arrangement, as far as Kohler was concerned. The dog had to protect him. Whatever happened, like what that kid had just missed, wasn't going to be coming Kohler's way.

"Hmm?" said Kohler.

Kohler unwrapped the second burger and the dog took the patties with the air of a deal signed and delivered.

It put its paw on Kohler's leg and then scratched at his arm and hand, and when Kohler put out his hand to take what was offered, the foot was heavy and rough, too, on the pads that dragged across his skin. So, the dog seemed to be saying, they had a deal. Kohler started the engine and went back into traffic. On the highway he let the car go up to ninety, ninety-five, and the dog slobbered as the landscape passed by. Kohler flipped on the radar detector, but then he realized that he wasn't worried about a ticket. The dog made him uneasy. Kohler's legs were a little shaky, since he knew that at any moment that creature could turn on him, just like all the times a dog had rushed out of a yard, barking and threatening, snapping at his legs. He thought about those black dogs, too, that had sniffed around that trunk in the mud by the river. Kohler glanced over at the animal from time to time with wary caution.

Frank turned off the main road into his drive and then drove up to the house, the dog not being interested in the fields or the side of the road, or anything at all aside from the amateurishly built house that looked like a jungle outpost. The car came to a stop in front of the door, and the dog looked through the window at the gravel around the front step, the snow shovel that was leaning at the side of the porch, and the bag of salt that was left there from the previous winter. Kohler needed the salt because the roof dripped by the door and the ice piled up.

Kohler got out and opened the door of the car and took the dog by the collar. Then he walked up to the front door. It was a warm afternoon, and the inside wooden door was open, but the screen door was latched.

"Katryna," said Frank. "Hey, Katryna. Come here."

Katryna came to the door. She looked a little pale and tired, and Kohler guessed she had been taking a nap. As she approached the screen, the dog lunged forward, barking, jumping up on two feet, trying to get through the screen, snarling and yapping and then making a steady, repeated barking sound.

"Open the door," said Kohler.

"What?" said Katryna. "What did you say?"

"The door," said Frank.

"What's *that?*" said Katryna, through the screen. She was wearing a bathrobe, and she held the neck of it closed with one hand.

"It's a present," said Frank. He turned to the dog, and said, "Quiet. Shhhh. It's O.K. It's fine. See?"

The dog stopped barking, but it looked through the screen door and growled, the hair rising on the back of its neck.

"It's for you," said Frank.

Katryna looked through the screen door, and then slowly reached over and undid the hook that held it shut. The dog curled around the door and pulled Frank into the house, putting its nose between Katryna's legs. She pushed it away. Frank pulled it back, and the animal started barking again. Katryna put one hand to her face.

"It just needs a period of adjustment," said Frank.

"Yes," said Katryna. "Sure."

"Let's give it some water," said Frank. "Maybe it's thirsty."

They went into the kitchen, where Katryna took a large bowl from the shelf and filled it, the running of the faucet drowned out in the animal's insistent barking. Katryna reached down to put it on the floor, and when she did so, her robe opened and the dog sniffed at her again. Then it lapped at the water.

"Look at him," said Frank. "Now that's a dog."

"Yes," said Katryna.

She glanced at the dog and then at Frank. Her skin was so pale as to seem almost blue, like shadows in the snow. Now she sat at the kitchen table, holding the robe shut with one hand at her neck, and looked at the dog.

"You've always wanted a dog," said Frank.

"Yes," she said.

The only sound in the kitchen was the dog's lapping of the water.

"Big and strong," said Kohler. "Unafraid. You know, the kind of dog you can trust . . ."

Katryna looked at the dog. It drank with a voraciousness that seemed to block out everything else in the room. Then it looked up and glanced around.

"You always wanted a dog, didn't you?" said Frank.

Katryna nodded. Yes. That was right. Then she looked at Frank. Maybe she could ask now, if he was in the mood to be generous.

"Yes," said Katryna. "Thanks."

"O.K.," said Frank. He reached down to pat the dog.

"I appreciate it," said Katryna. "But there's something else . . ."

"He's going to be a good watchdog," said Frank.

"Yes," said Katryna. "That's good. But there's something else . . ."

"What's that?" said Frank.

She pulled the bathrobe closer to her neck.

"I need some money," said Katryna.

"What for?" said Frank.

The dog stopped lapping the water and looked over its shoulder at the change in the voices.

"Can't I just have some money without explaining everything?" said Katryna.

"What's wrong?" said Frank. "Ever since the other day, you've been edgy."

Katryna shrugged. Every day for a week she had gone into the bedroom and looked under her underwear at the bills she had there, one hundred and fifty dollars, which she counted again and again. She'd need twenty dollars to pay back the woman in the doctor's office, and so she would need another hundred and seventy. It was as though she thought that by counting the money it would increase.

"I need a hundred and seventy dollars," she said.

The dog began a low, steady growling, the hair on its back rising like long grass in a wind.

"What for?" said Frank.

The dog barked now, putting its head back and giving full voice to its excitement. Its tongue was red and slobbery, and Katryna could smell its breath, which made her as ill as the smoke of the bus she had been following the day she went to the doctor.

"Can I have the money?" said Katryna.

The dog turned toward the intensity in her voice, barking with its head back.

"What?" said Frank.

"I asked you something . . ." said Katryna.

"What did you ask?" said Frank.

Katryna stood in the middle of the kitchen for a moment, and then she looked out the window. When she turned back, she seemed a little more certain. The dog was still barking.

"I've called my cousin," she said. "He can come now if I want him to. Can he come now?"

"What?" said Frank.

"My cousin," said Katryna.

The dog growled.

"Quiet," said Frank. "Quiet."

The dog still made that low, steady growling.

"Dimitry," said Katryna. "My cousin. Remember?"

"What's gotten into you?" said Frank. "What's the trouble?"

"Nothing," said Katryna. "Nothing at all."

"Shut up," said Frank. He jerked the dog, which turned on him and barked and growled.

"It'll be all right," said Frank.

"Did you hear me about my cousin?" said Katryna.

"Yes," said Frank. "That's O.K."

RUSSELL BOYD

ZOFIA SAT AT THE PHONE IN THE KITCHEN WITH the card she had gotten from her doctor and made an appointment. Then she felt the atmosphere in the house, which made her think of the mountains where the snow has piled up in winter and all it takes is a loud noise to make it crack and rush downhill in a white assault on everything below. The air in the house was like that: filled with the static of dangerous possibility.

Russell found her sitting in the kitchen when he came in. He turned on the light and said, "You know what tonight is? The Lowarys'. Do you still want to go?"

He sat down opposite her. She avoided looking at him.

"Yes," she said. "It would be bad if we didn't go. What would the party at the end of the season be without the foxes?"

"I don't know," said Russell.

"Let's go," she said. "I want to get out."

Zofia put on a black dress, and as she stood in front of the mirror, she saw that her skin had a soft luminescence. She realized with a start that makeup would only diminish the beauty of her skin.

———

THE DOOR of the Lowarys' house was black, with a brass lion-head knocker. The lion had a ring in its mouth, and you banged it against a brass plate on the door. The house was two stories with white siding and black shutters, and through the window Russell and Zofia saw the yellow light of the party, which was at once inviting and off-putting. The driveway and the road in front of the house were filled with Mercedes and Volvos and Saabs, and there had barely been room for Zofia's Subaru.

Virginia Lowary opened the door, dressed in a silk blouse and a skirt, her hair brushed and shining, her freckles making her look younger than she was. Jack Lowary came up to the door, too, his face flushed, wearing a sportcoat and a pair of brown pants, a shirt that looked as though it had been custom-made.

"Is the fox here?" said a woman in beige pants and a silk blouse who had come up behind Virginia.

"And the foxette," said a man who was behind her. All Russell knew about him was that he rode a bay horse. He was wearing a blazer now and was holding a snifter of brandy.

"Oh, Christ, don't be a bore," said Virginia. Then she turned to Zofia and said, "He's too stupid to mean anything."

The man blinked and had another sip. Then he shrugged and walked away.

"Let's get something festive for you two to drink to celebrate the end of the season," Virginia said to Russell. "Come on."

Russell followed her into the kitchen, where she took a beer out of the refrigerator, a German one. As she poured it, she said, "Zofia seems upset."

"I guess," said Russell. "I don't know."

She gave Russell the glass and said, "Well, here's to a wonderful season. Thanks for doing such a good job. Of course, I was trying to catch *you* all along. But I never did. Maybe next year."

"Maybe," Russell said.

"But I was close there a couple of times," she said.

"That's how it looked to me," Russell said.

"It wouldn't have taken too much more," she said. "If you had slowed down just a little. I wanted to catch you."

She said this with a smile, as though it was still just good fun.

"Which hunt did you like the best?" Russell asked. He looked around and saw that Zofia was in the living room, waiting. He waved.

"In the riverbottom," said Virginia. "I love that. The heat in the early season, and the colors later on. By the way, do you know how to ride?"

"No," Russell said.

"Would you like to learn?" she said. "I could teach you. Please. It would be fun."

"I think I need something for Zofia," said Russell.

"Of course," said Virginia. "I don't know what I could have been thinking."

Russell worked his way through the fragrance of liquor and perfume, wool and cologne, and found Zofia, who was looking down into the fire, which gave off a harsh plane of heat that scorched rather than warmed. She took the glass and said, not looking at him, "So, what did she try this time?"

"Come on," Russell said. "So what if she likes to flirt."

"It's not flirting," she said. She looked at Russell with a hot, teary glance.

"Oh, no," he said. "I'm sorry. I really am."

They stood by the fire. She swallowed.

"I don't want anyone to see me upset," she said. "I don't know what's gotten into me."

"Well, then, I'll tell you a joke," he said.

"What's the joke?" she said, her voice pleading a little, asking him to change her mood so that she wouldn't have to stand there and make a scene, which was all the more possible as she sensed how embarrassed she'd be if she did. Russell told her a joke about a genie and three wishes. When he finished she started to laugh, but that was worse, because it was that close to changing into something else. She finished her wine and said, "I don't know how much longer I can stay here."

"Look, she was just flirting. It didn't mean anything. Not to me, anyway," said Russell.

"I'm not a 'foxette,'" she said. "I don't drive a Mercedes. I don't have dresses that come from Calvin Klein. I work for a living."

"Me too," he said. "My dresses come from Wal-Mart."

"Don't," she said. "Don't make jokes."

They looked at some maps that were on a table between two sofas in front of the fireplace. The maps showed land where the people in the room had hunted, and Russell imagined running through the brush and along the edges of the cut fields. They knew which sections were too dangerous for the riders—the wet, slippery places where the fences were too high to jump, although in the excitement of the moment someone might try. Virginia came back now and took out a new map and showed them a section that they had just gotten permission to hunt. She sharpened a pencil and Russell smelled the bitter scent of the cedar out of which it was made. Virginia marked off the boundaries, and showed them sections that she thought would be good, more bottomland with rolling hills around it.

She looked at Russell and said, "Is the fox going to like that?"

"Yes," Russell said. "Very much."

"Excuse me," said Zofia. "Could you tell me where the bathroom is?"

"Right over there," said Virginia.

"I thought I'd freshen up," said Zofia.

"Of course," said Virginia.

Zofia walked away.

"You know, I meant that about the riding," said Virginia.

"Let me think about it."

"You won't regret it," said Virginia.

He looked over at the door of the bathroom.

"Excuse me," he said.

Then he went to the door and tapped.

She said, "Just a minute."

"It's me," Russell said.

"Oh," she said. "Well."

One of the hunters came up to Russell and said that he'd had a great season, one of the best. He was thinking of getting a new horse, but he wasn't sure. But he had a theory about horses, which was that if you were going to hunt them, the way they got better was to use them as much as you could. Still, he had noticed that when he got a horse just right, it died. So he guessed maybe the thing was to keep one coming along.

The door opened.

"After you," he said.

"No," Russell said. "Go on."

The man went in.

"Did she flirt some more with you?" Zofia said, as they walked away from the door.

"No," Russell said.

"Liar," she said. Then she looked around the room. "I'm pregnant."

Virginia came up and said to Zofia, "I was just saying to Russell that maybe he'd like to learn how to ride this winter."

"Oh," said Zofia. "He'd love that."

"If I have time," Russell said.

"You'll make time," Zofia said to him. "Surely you can do that?"

"That would be wonderful," said Virginia. "You'll encourage him, won't you?"

"Sure," said Zofia. "He knows what I think."

Virginia smiled. Then she excused herself and went toward the kitchen. Another member of the hunt came up and said, "The fox. Well, well. I've been waiting to meet you. You know, I've noticed that the way you lay the scent is like the real ones."

"Thank you," Russell said.

"Although maybe you are a little easier on us than a real one. I notice that you don't go over any six-foot walls."

Beyond him Russell saw the other members of the hunt, who were suspended in that yellow light which was perfectly filled with perfume and the odor of bourbon, and here and there he saw a woman's hair, blond or red, all perfectly combed and shiny. Sportcoats, bald heads, green ties, wool pants: there was something impossibly stilted about the room, a combination of L.L. Bean and Brooks Brothers. Zofia glanced at him and then at the man who said they had put down the scent like a fox. Even here, in this room, Russell had the almost tactile sense of something changing, and he wanted to touch Zofia, to put his hand on her arm, but she just stood there looking at him.

"Well," the man said as he left. "Keep up the good work."

"So," Zofia said. "Riding lessons, hmm? Is that what you are going to call it?"

"Let's get out of here," he said.

"Why?" she said. "Aren't you having a good time?"

"No," he said. "I just want to be someplace where we can talk."

"What's wrong with here?" she said.

"We don't have to do this."

"Do what?" she said.

"Here's to the fox," said a woman he had met once before. "Finally caught up with you. Well, I wanted to thank you for a lovely season. Exciting. Wonderful." She looked at Zofia. "And this is the other half of the team?"

"Yes," said Zofia.

"I wonder," said the woman. "You know, when you are running around out there, have you ever seen a fox?"

"Yes," said Zofia. "We saw one. Just once."

"No kidding," said the woman.

"It looked right at us," said Zofia.

"Maybe it was rabid," said the woman.

Zofia just looked at Russell.

"I don't know. Maybe it was trying to warn us."

"Well," said the woman. "What was it trying to warn you about? If that's what it was doing."

"Getting caught," said Zofia. "Being unprepared. Being surprised."

"Maybe it didn't mean that at all," Russell said.

"Oh?" said Zofia. "What else could it have meant?"

"That you don't throw chances away."

"It takes two to do that," said Zofia. "I didn't see any other foxes around."

"That's because foxes are solitary," he said.

"That's right," said Zofia. "Maybe one gets caught and the other is left alone. What then?"

The woman who was a member of the hunt looked from Zofia to Russell and then back again. She looked into her empty wineglass and said, "Well, it was nice talking to you. See you in the fall." Then she walked away.

"Come on," he said.

"Come on, what?" she said.

"You didn't have to tell me here," he said. "I didn't do anything to deserve that."

She bit her lip. A young woman who had been hired for the occasion came along with a plate of pieces of toast with caviar on them and salmon on small triangles of rye bread with a tiny slice of pickle. She put the tray out for Zofia, who just shook her head.

"I'm sorry," she said. "Oh, shit. What am I doing?"

"Come on," he said. "Let's get out of here. Let's go."

"Let me pull myself together," she said. "Just wait."

He tasted the hops in the beer. The liquid looked like sunlight on a fall afternoon, more like the color of wheat than anything else. He wanted to think about this as a way to slow things down, to get a moment to know what to say, or do.

They said good night. Then they were outside, in the cold air, and Zofia said, "I'm so sorry. I should never have done that."

"Let's get in the car," he said.

The engine turned over with only three or four gasps. On the back roads the lights picked out the shapes of the trees, large and bent. The whirring of the heater was like the sound of a desert wind: nothing but the hint of dryness and desolation. They came down to the edge of a field and saw a deer at the side of the road, eyes like green and blue membranes. Then it trotted off, into the scrub.

At home they pulled up in front of the house and then the lights from the car faded away. She got out and went into the house and Russell came behind her. Zofia turned on the back porch light and then reached into the trash and took out two bottles, a beer bottle and one for apple juice, and then went out behind the house where the chimney rose up from the foundation. She stood there and threw one bottle and then another, throwing the second into the glass *plosh* of the first, and as she did she said, "Goddamn it. Goddamn it."

Then she reached down and tried to pick up the pieces of glass and cut herself. She looked at the small rill of blood with a bright head that ran from her finger and then she held it out to Russell and said, "Suck it. That stops it," and then he tasted the blood in the cold under the stars.

In the kitchen, Zofia got a drink of water and then went into the bedroom, where she took off her black dress and got into bed in her underwear. Something in her attitude, in how she pulled the covers up to her neck and threw her head into the pillow, made Russell hesitate. He was certain that words weren't going to fix anything, and that the worst thing in the world would be to say, "What's wrong?" or "You know, I love you."

So he was left trying to show that he was alert. Maybe all it took, he guessed, was a lack of tension. Maybe he could reach her just by relaxing so completely as to be able to absorb all the tension in the room. He tried to fill the room with certainty. He was there. He knew something was wrong. He would keep his mouth shut.

He took off his clothes, as though being naked would help, as though she would realize there was nothing for him to hide behind, or any way for him to be devious. Then he went around and got into bed on the other side, slipping in behind her, trying to keep the rustle of the sheets down to a minimum. He tried to breathe in the same cadence, as though even the differing sounds of their breathing would be a distraction.

"We have just been playing, and this is not a matter of playing. It is serious. Do you know what serious is?"

"Yes," he said. "I do."

"But that's just about strangers," she said. "Just people who are breaking the law. I mean about us."

"I think I understand," he said.

"No, you don't," she said. "You don't understand vulnerability."

Don't understand *vulnerability?* He swallowed and found that he was trembling a little.

"I think I do," he said.

"No," she said. "You know why? You will never have to sit here at night with a child you love more than you can bear, hearing it breathe at night, maybe with asthma, with a cold, and while you hear that wet breath, you won't ever have to wonder if you are going to be left alone. You won't ever have to worry about being a cop's widow."

He knew it was a mistake, under the circumstances, but it was all he had. He said, "I love you."

"Great," she said. "Now, that's fucking great. And what is *that* going to do under those circumstances?"

Outside a car went by, and the tearing sound of the tires on the wet pavement came into the room.

"What do you want me to do?" he said.

"I want you to listen to me," she said.

He curled up behind her and put his head next to hers.

"What are you doing?" she said.

"Listening," he said.

She was quiet for a while, and then she said, "Well, I guess the problem is I haven't got much to say." Then she pushed back against him and started crying, saying, "I'm sorry, I'm sorry. I didn't mean to say such horrible things." She appeared almost too exhausted to speak. "I wish I had the energy to have this baby, but I don't. That's why I wanted to keep it a secret—I didn't want you to know that about me. But I don't think having a baby is the right thing to do now."

FRANK KOHLER

THE BUS STATION WAS ON THE NORTH SIDE OF town in a house trailer next to a Mobil station. It sat in the midst of a strip—a True Value hardware store, a McDonald's, a Price Chopper, a US Cellular store, National Auto Parts, all of which made for a collision between the familiar and the anonymous. Kohler parked next to the house trailer with the wooden steps in front, which looked like they went up to a deck, but it was just the aluminum door.

"Did you and Dimitry grow up together?" Kohler said.

"What?" she said. She moved in the seat, making it creak. "Yes. You could say that."

"Why does he want to come here?" he said.

"Moscow is a hard place now," she said. "They're pulling generals and bureaucrats out of the river every night, and desperate people are trying to make money, but they don't know how. Just outside of Moscow we have a four-lane highway, just like 91, the one you have here, and one day I saw a man there, in the rain, trying to sell mattresses. He was just pulled over like he had a flat tire, but instead he had his mattresses out there."

She shrugged.

"It's better here," she said.

Just now the sun came out behind the gray trees. The pattern of the trunks was a schematic of struggle, all of them reaching upward and competing for the light. The clouds were a soft brown underneath, like wood smoke coming from a fire damped way down. In the distance they heard the swish, swish of the cars as they went by on the highway.

"What's your cousin's name?" Kohler said. "I mean his whole name."

"It's a long Russian name," she said. "It would be hard for you. Dimitry is enough. Just plain Dimitry. He's probably not going to stay long." She smiled. "That's Dimitry for you. He likes to keep moving."

"Oh," he said. "What's he do for a living?"

"Dimitry knows how to take care of himself. He is clever that way," she said.

"Like what?" he said.

"He used to sing in a Georgian restaurant on the Arbat. It wasn't a lot of money, but he could get by, and then he had a shop in the subway, selling CDs and cigarette lighters. Pirated CDs, of course, from the gangs. And diplomas, too. If you wanted a diploma from Harvard or Yale, Dimitry could get you one."

Kohler thought about this for a moment. Maybe Dimitry could get him one from MIT. But then what good was the diploma without a transcript? Then Kohler tried to imagine just what she was thinking. Excitement at seeing her cousin, he guessed. That would be helpful, if only as a reminder of home. Or what used to be home. As he sat behind the wheel of the car, he understood her sense of isolation and banishment from Russia, since this was the way he felt about where he had grown up. It wasn't that he couldn't go there, or that he even wanted to, so much as that what he had known there had vanished, and living with the disappearance of what one loved, even if other people had thought it was tawdry, left him with a sense of having been banished. This, he thought, was one of the things that bound him to Katryna: it was an intimacy too delicate for words.

The bus pulled into the parking lot, lumbering over the apron that went into the street, and then it came up to the house trailer and stopped with a rush of air and a constant swaying from side to side as it rocked back and forth on its springs. Not a mainline bus like Greyhound, but an outfit Kohler had never heard of. Wayward North. The door swung open and the driver, a fat woman, got out and hitched up her pants and then opened the door to the compartment that held suitcases.

"There he is," said Katryna.

Kohler tried to imagine Katryna and Dimitry growing up in Moscow. Maybe they took the subway together. Kohler knew, from pictures in the *National Geographic,* what the Moscow subway looked like. Statues of the New Man and the New Woman. Escalators going down into the depths. The rumble of the trains as they came into the station. He glanced at Katryna as she put her hand on the door of the car and leaned forward, looking out the window. Everything about her was touched by that mysterious, unknown Moscow. He felt that if he took her fingers in his hand and strained, he would be able to feel the rumbling of the subway.

She opened the door and stepped out, running a hand through her hair. Dimitry was a man of about twenty-five or twenty-six, with high cheekbones. His brown hair was pulled back in a ponytail. He was tall, slender, wearing a long blue coat such as a sailor in the Russian navy might wear. He leaned over to get his bag out of the luggage compartment, but as he did so, he saw Katryna coming. He stood up and looked at her. His arms were outstretched and she moved into them with a smooth, filmic choreography, and then Kohler sat there, watching as Dimitry held her in the small of her back. He lifted her, so that she was off the ground, and he spun her around, laughing in her hair. He put her down and held her at arms length so that he could look at her. Then he kissed her. She smiled and pointed to the car.

The suitcase was small and blue, and had a mold stain on it. Dimitry picked it up and took a step or two in the direction of the black car, and as Kohler got out, the sensation of being sized up was so strong that he felt it like a blush. Then Dimitry smiled a toothy, Russian grin. He put out his hand and said, "Frank. Well. It is very nice to meet you."

"Yes," Kohler said.

They shook hands.

"Let me get your bag," Kohler said.

He took it around to the hatch and opened it and stuck the thing in.

"Get in," Kohler said. "Katryna will have to sit on your lap."

"This is a nice car," Dimitry said. "How many horsepower?"

"Three-ninety," Kohler said.

"That's a lot," Dimitry said. "Like a Russian tank."

He slid across the black leather seat. When Katryna got into the car, she had to pull up her skirt to be able to open her legs enough to sit on his lap. She was bent forward, awkward and yet turning to one side and smiling. Her legs looked white, even in their stockings, against the black interior.

"It's been a long time," she said.

"Too long," he said.

Kohler turned the key.

"Oh," Dimitry said. "Listen to that."

"I know how to drive," said Katryna. "He's been teaching me."

She turned a little more, trying to look at Dimitry, squirming on him to do so and then squirming back to look at the road ahead.

"That's great," he said. "You'll have to show me."

Then Dimitry looked out the window as they went along the strip to the entrance of the highway.

"Just like on TV," he said.

"Better," she said. "You can actually go into the stores."

"Oh, yeah," he said.

"How was your flight?" Kohler said.

"Long," he said. "You know, you have been flying for three hours and you realize you are only over Germany."

"Did you come right here?" Kohler said.

"No," he said. He looked out the window. "I had to go to New York. To Queens. To meet a business associate. Astoria. Have you ever been to Astoria?"

"No," Kohler said. "Is it nice?"

"Not to look at," said Dimitry.

"And what kind of business are you in?" said Kohler.

Dimitry glanced over and said, "Frank, let us wait. I will tell you everything. Right now, I am tired. O.K.?"

"Sure," he said.

"Import-export," he said.

"O.K.," Kohler said.

"How is Moscow?" Katryna said.

"Still filled with beautiful women," said Dimitry.

Katryna said something in Russian, and Dimitry shrugged.

"Not so much," he said in English.

On the highway, Kohler sped up to ninety. Katryna was hunched over, her back bent, looking around from time to time and smiling. The road ahead, after a rise, looked like one long ribbon draped over the hills. The river was on the right, shiny as polished ebony, and the hills looked fuzzy, like the fur of a dirty animal. Dimitry rested his hand on her thigh. Then they just drove, going up the highway.

"I hope you're hungry," Kohler said.

"Well," he said. "Yes. I haven't had any real food. Airplanes. Burger King. Taco Bell."

"I will make pielmeni for you," said Katryna.

"Oh, God," he said. "Not that. We're in America now. How about a steak? Yeah? And a baked potato and sour cream. That is American."

At the bottom of the exit, Kohler looked over at her as she sat on Dimitry, her hands on the dashboard, her small breasts in her black silk blouse. She stared out the windshield as though she had a delicious chocolate in her mouth. Watching her, Kohler rolled through a stop sign at the end of the exit ramp and hit a passing car with a *whomp* and the sound of tinkling glass. Katryna hit her head on the windshield.

"Oh," she said. She put a hand to her head.

Dimitry said, "What happened?"

The other car was a small red two-door, driven by a woman with a nose ring and a butch haircut. She got out of the car and held her neck, and looked at the crease in the door. Her car sat there like a bird with a broken wing. Water leaked from under the hood, and it made a kind of pissing sound on the asphalt that mixed with the hissing of the radiator.

Katryna had a welt on her forehead, and she put her hand on it. Dimitry opened the door and she swung her feet out, and stood in the cold air, still holding her head.

"Are you all right?" Kohler said.

"Yes," she said.

"And you, Dimitry?" he said.

"Yes," he said. "It takes more than that to hurt a couple of Russians."

The other driver came over and said, "Oh, my neck."

"Do you want an ambulance?" Kohler asked.

"I don't know," said the woman.

"Well," said Katryna to Dimitry, "welcome to the States."

"Let's pull over," Kohler said to the driver of the other car. "Let's get out of the middle of the street."

"Are they Dutch?" said the woman with the nose ring.

"No," Kohler said. "Russian."

"*Tovarich*," she said. "Comrade."

Katryna looked at her and then said something to Dimitry. He looked at the driver of the other car with weary disbelief. Then Katryna leaned against him, holding her head. Kohler moved the car out of the way, and the other driver did, too. Then they both got out and looked at the cars in the same way that people do when they are trying to decide to buy an automobile from a car lot.

"You should have looked where you were going," said the driver.

"There were two people in the front seat," he said.

"Well, that's not my problem," said the driver.

"Accidents happen," he said.

"Yeah," she said. "To people who don't look where they're going."

She went on holding her neck.

"Have you got an insurance card?" she asked.

"We're going up to the gas station," said Katryna. "Up there. The Mobil. Maybe they have coffee. And ice for my head."

"Here's my insurance card," said the woman with the nose ring.

She held it out as Kohler turned to watch the two of them walk away, Katryna's hips swaying in her short skirt at the side of the road, her hand just brushing Dimitry's, his broad shoulders in his jacket, and the look on his face as he glanced back at Kohler. Then, in response to something Katryna said, Dimitry shrugged.

When he turned back, a state police cruiser pulled over and stopped. The trooper had a microphone to his lips, and then he hung it up, turned on the blue flashing lights, and got out, putting on his hat. He had a little name tag that said R. BOYD. Trooper R. Boyd.

"Looks like you've had a little trouble," he said.

"My neck hurts," said the other driver. "He hit me."

Kohler kept looking into the distance.

"It was a mistake," he said. "I'm sorry."

Then the sheriff pulled up. He got out of his red and white car and said, "Hey, Russell, how are things?"

"All right," he said. "I thought I'd stop."

"Well, I'll take it from here," said the sheriff.

Trooper Boyd looked at Kohler and then up the road, where Katryna and Dimitry had turned onto the apron of the Mobil station.

"Well, O.K.," he said. "Looks like no one is hurt."

Kohler turned back to him.

"No," Kohler said. "I don't think so."

"What about my neck?" said the other driver.

"Do you need a doctor?" said Trooper Boyd.

"I don't know," she said. "No. I guess not. Let's just finish this up."

Kohler's shaking knees only added to his sense of shame and disorientation. Trooper Boyd looked at him. "You don't remember me, do you?" said Boyd.

"No," Kohler said. "Why should I?"

"I went fishing on your land," said Boyd.

"Oh," said Kohler. "You." He glanced at the Mobil station where Katryna and Dimitry had gone, simply vanishing into the blackness of the doorway. Why were they taking so long? "Yeah. I remember. How are your kids?"

"They're not mine," said Boyd. "But they're O.K."

Kohler nodded.

"Did they like it?" said Kohler. "Catching those fish?"

"Yeah, I think they did," said Boyd.

"Then come back sometime. It's O.K.," said Kohler. He swung his eyes toward Boyd, their glance like a beacon. "It's all right." He spoke with a little quaver in his voice, trying to say something more, but then he just stood there, blinking, and finally he glanced up at the Mobil station.

"Sure," said Boyd. "Maybe I will. Thanks."

The sheriff went on writing down license numbers. The woman with the nose ring glared at Kohler. Katryna and Dimitry came out of the apron of the Mobil, each with a foam cup of coffee, and as they walked along they took small sips. Every now and then one of them spoke, but not much, just a word or a phrase, which even from a distance seemed to imply an irritated confrontation with a difficult fact. Dimitry shrugged and avoided looking at her, and then she spoke again and then again. He was quiet, sipping from his coffee.

"People catch a lot of fish there," said Kohler.

"It's a good place," said Boyd. He glanced at Dimitry and Katryna. "Who's the couple?"

"They're not a couple," he said. "That's my wife and her cousin."

"Oh," he said. Then he turned to the sheriff. "Well, O.K. See you later." He turned back to Kohler.

"Take it easy," said Boyd.

"Sure," said Kohler. "Yeah." Kohler looked around at the dented car. "As soon as I get out of this mess."

"It's not so bad," said Boyd.

Kohler didn't say anything. Instead, he watched the slow, intimate loco-motion of Katryna and her cousin.

Boyd got into his car and turned around, and after he did so he turned the lights out and went up to the entrance to the highway, getting on and accelerating. Then Kohler took his license back from the sheriff, felt the other driver glare at him again, and got into the car. Katryna got in, on top of Dimitry, hiking up her skirt again.

"I'm sorry," Kohler said.

"What do you have to be sorry for?" said Katryna.

She shrugged.

"It's so nice to see you, Dimitry," she said. Then they spoke Russian, a slow, sibilant conversation that went back and forth, with Dimitry looking out the window, nodding, asking a question now and then, and finally say-ing nothing at all as the landscape went by.

"So," said Dimitry. "This is the States. Where do all the movie stars live?"

"Over in New Hampshire," said Kohler.

RUSSELL BOYD

SHEFFIELD, VERMONT, WAS BUILT AT THE JUNC-
tion of the Connecticut and Charles rivers. It was a railroad town, but not
many passenger trains came through these days, just one that went from
New York to Montreal, although there were still a fair number of freight
trains. The bridges in town were often scouted by movie companies looking
for antiquated locations, but the bridges were too run-down to suggest any
period other than this one. Still, even in this state of slow dissolution, the
sense of the past in Sheffield was so palpable that you could imagine the coal
smoke of the trains that had come through here seventy years ago, and the
piles of railroad ties, which were stacked in the train yard, gave off a tar-like
odor of creosote that permeated the town. Sheffield had a diner, and two
places that sold secondhand furniture but were trying to pass themselves off
as antique stores. It also had a hotel.

Russell stood in front of it, looking up at the mansard roof and feeling
the failed promise of the abandoned railroad yards behind him. Everything
about the hotel—the dirty curtains behind the windows, the door with a
piece of yellowed tape over a crack in the glass of one pane, and the air of
just hanging on—was the kind of thing he saw all the time, neither better
nor worse than a lot of it.

Russell had awakened this morning thinking about coming up here. As
he heard Zofia's soft breathing and felt the warmth of her against his side,
he thought of the woman at the side of the road and how she appeared in
the flickering blue light from the cruisers, just as he recalled the slowly rising exhaust, which was the haunting blue color of a shadow in snow. Even
then, in the warmth of bed, the memory of a torn nipple and of the frost on
the dead woman's eyelashes left him straining, trying to come up with something useful, but he found that he ran up against the same few details and
an all-pervasive sense of the tawdry way that this woman had been left in
the cold. The tawdry senselessness of it, which seemed to exist in the memory of the colors and the half-frozen landscape, left him at once restless and

fatigued, and so he hung between the two, mystified and yet thinking of the hotel in Sheffield. After the woman had been found, a description of her had run in the paper, and the manager of the hotel had called to say that a woman who looked like that had checked in, stayed for a couple of days, and then gone away. She hadn't taken her things, which she had left in her room, and she had paid for a month in advance, in cash. New twenties.

Russell had gotten out of bed, put on a pair of jeans and a shirt and sweater, made a cup of coffee, and left a note for Zofia. Then he had driven to Sheffield, but the instant he saw the hotel, he wished he hadn't come. What was he going to find out that the men who had been assigned to this job hadn't already discovered? And if he was going to find out nothing, then why come up here on a Saturday morning? Two men came out of the diner down the street, both of them laughing over a joke, the punch line of which one repeated. Then they both laughed again. The odor of coffee hung in the air, and Russell could see the frosted-up window of the restaurant, which looked warm and fragrant inside. He could almost smell the cinnamon rolls, the baking apple pie.

He opened the door to the hotel and found himself in the lobby. It had high ceilings, now stained by smoke and leaking water. A reception desk with a large marble counter stood at the back of the room beneath a clock with roman numerals on its face. The hands were stuck at three-thirty. There was a desk set on the counter for guests to register, which was a large piece of green plotting paper held in a leather frame, but instead of a fountain pen, there was now a ballpoint that said along its side, in type like palm trees, YAN'S CHINESE TAKE OUT.

The manager was a bald man with scabs on his head that he picked as he sat beneath the stopped clock. And now, when he looked up, he found Russell, who looked around the lobby and then said, holding out his identification, "I'd like to talk to you for a minute or two. That is, if you've got the time."

"Sure," said the man. "Time is something I've got plenty of." He pointed at the clock. "We've got so much of it that we don't even bother to count it anymore. Like millionaires."

"Uh-huh," said Russell.

"There were some other men here," said the manager. "They already looked at the room. You know, the rent is still paid on it."

"That's what I heard," said Russell.

"Well, I guess you want to see her room. The other two did. Let me get the key," said the manager.

When he stood up, he was very short—in fact he wasn't much taller standing up than sitting on his stool. He turned and reached for the key from the rack beneath the empty slots for mail. Russell looked through the glass of the front door at the tracks, which curved away in a silver pair of rails. He had no illusions about what he was going to find, since he knew that he was like a blind man trying to get someplace and who kept going around a room with no door. The movement in the dark, the touching of the few familiar features on the wall, the molding, the picture in a frame all suggested advancement and might even be momentarily reassuring, but in the end, sooner or later, he'd have to admit to how things really were. And yet even that eluded him, since that frigid air, that blue smoke of exhaust, the woman's face, which had been reduced to something no longer human, were so impenetrable in their emptiness as to suggest a profound and appalling vacuum. It was this emptiness that had sucked Russell into this place, and while he knew that more knowledge of it would only make him feel worse, he still tried to grasp that appalling vacancy. He saw hints of it in the dusty stillness of the lobby, in the wet breathing of the manager, and Russell supposed he would see other details in the woman's room, although they would be far worse.

"You coming?" said the manager. He was wearing a brown button-up cardigan, and there was a stale odor around him, like in an old people's home.

"Yes," said Russell. "I guess."

Both of them climbed the musty padded stairs, which muted their footsteps. Russell tried to imagine the sound of the woman's shoes on these stairs. And yet there was nothing to connect the woman at the side of the road with the woman who had walked out of her room. The detectives who had been here said that the clothes in the room had been bought from the thrift shop in town, and that there was no way to find out anything beyond that.

Russell and the manager went down the hall and along the carpet, which was new and bright pink, although the carpet on the stairs was brown. The manager unlocked the door of a room and pushed it open and then stood back. "There you go," he said.

Russell stood at the threshold. The room itself was distinguished by the dim light that came in from the side of the shade. A green carpet, a double bed with a white spread textured with lines of fuzz, a dressing table with a chrome-framed kitchen chair in front of it. The manager made a sound of wet breathing, winded from climbing one flight of stairs. Then Russell tried to understand the sense of desperation that seemed to exist here like a hidden force, unseen but still powerful. He stepped into the room as though someone were sleeping here.

In the closet he found a couple of dresses—one blue, one black, and one with a red and yellow pattern of flowers. Underwear in a drawer, which looked like it had come from Kmart. No books, no paper, nothing that showed anything about where she had come from or what her plans were. There was a toothbrush in the bathroom and a stick of deodorant, but that was it. Russell guessed that she must have taken her cosmetics bag with her when she had left.

"She was polite," said the manager. "Always said good morning and good afternoon. Had a little accent, you know. Maybe South America. Spain. Very refined, in a way. Didn't say much beyond good day."

Russell looked at the mirror, which was covered with dust, and then at the bedstand. A newspaper from a month before still lay there, turned back to the want ads. Surely she had been looking for something, but what? An apartment? A car? Another kind of life? Then he just stood in that sad atmosphere of the room, and as he waited, he could sense the evanescent nature of the woman's presence, as though she was slowly disappearing, even now, and that the last of her things would soon be gone and then there would be nothing. He tried to resist this, as though by concentrating on the few things that were still here and on the presence that was left, he could slow the process down. His inability to do anything more than that only increased his sense of the enormity of what had happened to this woman; he knew that one of his struggles was to keep this murder from being absorbed into the mundane details of his job. Soon, if nothing turned up, she would be forgotten, and being absorbed into that, into the simple ability to forget, left Russell with a greater sense of a vacuum that existed just beyond the appearance of things.

Russell went over to the window and put up the shade. Maybe a little light would do some good, but the room was one of those places that was better in the shadows. As he looked around, wanting to pull the shade down again, he felt a rumbling, a trembling that shook the entire hotel, and then he turned to the window, where he saw the engine of a freight train, not the black and glistening and huffing train of the past, but a new diesel, vibrant and seemingly unstoppable. It came along those silver curves of track, the engineer visible inside the engine, behind the window, reaching up to work the horn, which sounded in long, piercing blasts, and then the engine disappeared and Russell was left with the sound of the passing freight cars—click-ah-clack, click-ah-clack—and as he stood there in that room, remembering the woman, he recalled what a man had told him years before. It was what the sound of a freight car's wheels really said, which was "Cut your head off, cut your head off, cut your head off." Russell looked around the room again. He sat down on the bed hearing the low squeak of the springs, and as the sound of the train slipped away, he imagined that sound when the woman got into bed alone in this room. He remembered the taste of blood from the night before, when he had sucked Zofia's finger, the saltiness of it like fury itself. For an instant he wished Zofia were here so he could say, I understand. I really do. What isn't uncertain?

"Do you think she was the one they found?" said the manager. "You know, by the road?"

"I don't know," said Russell.

"Well," said the manager, "I hope they get the bastard."

"Yeah," said Russell. He pulled down the shade. "Thanks for letting me look around."

"Any time," said the manager. "I'm always here."

FRANK KOHLER

KOHLER LIKED THE ISOLATED LOCATION OF HIS house. When he was alone, the landscape seemed to spread out from him as though he lived at the center of everything. It was where he could be clear-minded. He had been thinking of taking advantage of this privacy in late June, when the fireflies came out in the evening: that would be the time when he and Katryna could take a blanket down by the brook so they could lie there in the sparkling darkness, under those greenish and flickering streaks.

Kohler came up to the house after taking the dog for a walk along the property lines. The dog had seemed to understand that the purpose of the walk was to surprise a trespasser. They had looked for an hour, but had been disappointed, and now, with the habitual stealth of patrolling the property lines, they came up to the kitchen window. The window caught the afternoon sun, and it was easy to see into it when the light was at the back of someone who looked at it from the outside. Kohler and the dog came up to the window and stood next to a tree there, a maple that was eighty feet high.

Inside, Katryna stepped from one side of the room to another. Dimitry was sitting down, at the table, reading Kohler's copy of *The War in Gaul*. Katryna wore a short black skirt and a white blouse, appearing almost for-mal as she walked back and forth, pacing with a brooding and sultry urgency. She had perfect posture, which came from the years when she had studied ballet. She stopped at the sink and got a glass of water, looking down toward the brook. Kohler saw her full lips pushed against the glass, slightly open to take a drink. Finally, with a shrug, she put the glass down and turned back to Dimitry.

She spoke to him. He looked up with an expression of surprise, as though she was making an offer he had always wanted, although not quite the way he had anticipated it. Then he nodded, yes, yes, of course, if that's what you want. He reached into his pocket and took out his wallet, from which he counted out a hundred and seventy dollars. She picked it up and counted it, too, quickly and yet making sure that the amount was right. She put it on the table. Eight twenties and one ten, as nearly as he could tell. A hundred and seventy.

Then she reached under her skirt, hiking it up to her waist. She was wearing thin, black underwear, so fine that the shape of each hip was visible under the mesh. With both hands she slipped the underwear down to her ankles and then stepped out and put them on the book, lying open on the table. Kohler looked from the small ball the underwear made in the middle of his book to the money.

The desire to flee and yet the horrifying impulse to watch were the same as when one of Jerri's men, a Bob Jack, had given him twenty dollars to hide in the closet and watch what Jerri did. Kohler had held that twenty-dollar bill there in his confinement, there in the tickle of the stockings that hung on the back of the door. The closet had been redolent with sweat and perfume. The clothes had a musty quality, which seemed hot around him as he had wanted to get away, but didn't know how. He had folded the bill up, trying to make it smaller and smaller, and when he did so, he still glanced out the crack of the closet door, where Jerri's head went up and down as Bob Jack winked at him.

Outside the window, Kohler looked down at the black dog, who stood there without making a sound, or moving. The landscape was quiet and indifferent, as though nothing were happening at all. The sky was gray, illuminated by the muted circle of the sun, which was the milky color of a lightbulb. Then Kohler turned back to the window.

Katryna stood just back from Dimitry's face. She stepped a little closer and then put one hand at the hem of the skirt, lifting it a little. He said something, but Kohler couldn't hear it, and even if he could have, he guessed it was Russian. She bent down, her lips not quite touching Dimitry's. They both waited here, at this moment, as though the distance between them and the attraction that was pulling them closer together were not only overwhelming but pleasurable, too. They seemed suspended between two worlds: the proper one in which they behaved, and the one in which all things were pleasurable and inevitable. It was the confinement of watching that Kohler recognized, the same as being trapped in that dark closet. He trembled with the realization that it was the same as before, as though this experience had a knack of repeating itself, and that he had to stand there and watch, no matter how much he wanted to get away. Then, with an effort that left him exhausted and sick, he turned away.

It was easy going down to the brook. At the bottom there was a flood-plain where the brook overflowed in April, although now it was dry and filled with driftwood, entire trunks of trees that had washed down here in the spring flood. Kohler sat on one, with the dog in front of him. Then he wondered if Katryna got down on her knees and looked Dimitry right in the eye with it in her mouth, the way she had with him. Then he thought that this was probably right. That's probably what was happening. He guessed Dimitry was going to get his hundred and seventy dollars' worth.

"Is that what she's doing?" he said to the dog.

It put its paw into Kohler's lap, and Kohler felt the rough pads. Then he held the dog's foot, thinking about how Katryna had appeared with her skirt hiked up as she stepped into the bedroom, looking back at Dimitry over her shoulder and speaking a language Kohler didn't understand and never would.

Kohler knelt by a pool in the brook and splashed water on his face, the cold shock of it diminishing as he did it again and again. He thought of the fluid movement of her hips as she walked, the quiver in her bottom as she went out of the kitchen. The dog yawned and made a little chomping noise when its jaws snapped back together—in the midst of the yawn its tongue curled out like the shape of the neck of a violin. All he could think about was the woodsy sensation of the water in his mouth, and that it reminded him of what it was like to kiss her between her legs. The differ-ence was the coldness. She was much warmer.

He listened to the sound of the running water in the brook, and he heard, too, the chirping of birds that hadn't cleared out for the south yet, chickadees, he supposed, little black birds with a white mask. Like small Lone Rangers, or did the Lone Ranger have a black mask? At the moment, he wasn't sure. He hadn't ever really seen the Lone Ranger on TV, since it was before his time. He had only heard about it.

The paleness of the sky had a new quality, which he thought was more like the white of bleached bones. He faced the prospect of a bland landscape while he sat there in the stink of the dog's breath. The fatigue of it washed over him, and left him thinking that it would be hard to lift a hand or move, or even swallow.

He looked at the dog.

"Sit down," he said.

It sat down.

"Roll over," he said, and it rolled over. Then he picked up a stick, as though it weighed ten pounds, and threw it into the stream. The dog went after it, grabbing it in two strides, and came back, dripping, and put the wet thing into his hand. Perfect obedience. Then it put its paws out on the ground, as though stretching, but really crouching, eyes on Kohler, wanting to play.

Then Kohler stood up and started walking back toward the house, the black dog at his heels. The metal roof glinted in the mild sunlight. He guessed that the sunset would be beautiful this afternoon, when the light would be soft and indistinct and looking like the smoky residue of desire.

RUSSELL BOYD

ZOFIA AND RUSSELL WENT TO THE FOOD CO-OP IN town. They took a shopping cart, like the chariot of the domestic, and when they walked by a mirror, Russell saw the two of them together, Zofia in her blue jeans and man's pink shirt, her shiny hair and thin hands looking at once ordinary and yet romantic, too. In the mirror he saw a man with a flat-top haircut. He had a narrow waist, and big hands, and wore blue jeans. Her doubts about having a child had infected him now, since he trusted her, and if she was clear-headed about this—why, then maybe he was the one who was making a mistake, and yet, if he was, if that was really the case, was what he did just vanity and a swaggering impulse? So, as he stood there, seeing their reflections, he was left with a sense of a collision between common sense and his beliefs about what he should do.

They bought dinner, which they were going to fix together: lettuce and tomatoes, cucumber, salad greens, mesclun, radicchio. She said, "Radicchio." Something wet and vibrant in her lips, like a salacious promise. He knew, when he heard the word, that when he was alone on the road late at night and thinking of her he would say "Radicchio." They bought chicken, which they were going to make with Marsala and sautéed garlic.

A man stood with a plastic basket at the end of an aisle, his face scarred with acne, his hair pulled into a ponytail. He had a tattoo on one arm, not the decorative kind that young people got these days, but a crude prison tattoo. Russell looked at the man's pale face, his stooped shoulders, his feral alertness. Russell turned back to the basket, and realized that he had arrested this man when he had been stationed up north, and yet he wasn't certain what it had been for. Drugs, he guessed. Now, he supposed, the man had moved his operations farther south.

Russell and Zofia bought other things, aside from what they needed for dinner. He thought, Yes, maybe this is a way that we can begin. Isn't there magic in these things, some indication of the person who uses them? By

magic, he meant that a thing had some meaning when it was used by someone he cared about.

They went along the ends of the aisles, although Russell could still feel
the glance of the man he had arrested, like the pressure of sunlight. Zofia
stopped in front of bins of coffee, and then filled up a small bag and said,
"Do you like the Colombian?"

"Yes," he said. "That sounds good."

She poured the beans into the machine that ground them, just like one
in a general store years ago. He looked up and saw the man with the tattoo
and the bad skin. Russell thought of saying hello, but maybe it was better
like this.

In the next aisle she picked up a box of pads to use when she had her
period. She was going to need them soon, rather than the tampons she usually used. He looked around the store, struck by the beauty of the ordinary,
people just living in the moment, not posing, not showing ambition, not
being devious. It was like an exercise in which two things were blended, the
unbelievably mundane and the profound and mysterious.

He wanted to buy something that showed a small aspect of himself. She
looked at a list she had pulled out of her pocket, standing there in her tight
jeans, moving her weight from one hip to another. She glanced up and Russell reached over and took a box of Q-tips off the shelf and dropped it into
the cart. She took a strand of her hair that had gotten loose and tucked it
behind her ear. This was a gesture she made when she was thinking things
over. If she asked him what the Q-tips were for, would he say, "To clean my
pistol. It's hard to get the oil off the safety catch"? Or, "I use them to keep
my ears clean"?

Then he saw the man from up north talking to a kid, about twenty, who
also had a homemade tattoo on his forearm, a messed-up cross that made
him look discounted, like a young man who has already made the mistake
that he is surely going to make not only once, but again and again, although
each time it will get worse. Zofia opened the glass door of the freezer, all
misted on one side, the frigid air flowing out. It was so cold Russell imagined it was water spilling from the case onto the floor, and the touch of it on
his shoes, around his ankles, left him considering that tattooed kid and his
friend. Zofia folded up her list and stuck it into the pocket of her jeans. She

had to lift up her shoulder and make her arm straight to get it in. He stood there in that pool of cold air.

"That's it," she said.

At the checkout counter they heard the beeping of the machine as the clerk scanned everything. Then they paid, sharing out money in a comfortable, easy way, Zofia's coming out of her pocket in a series of crumpled bills, Russell's neat and crisp from his wallet, both of them giggling at the difference. He picked up the brown paper bag and went out through the door, which opened automatically, and as they went, she said, picking up the Q-tips, "What are these for?"

"My . . ." he said. "My ears."

"Oh," she said, careful now as she dropped the box back into the bag.

They went to the dry cleaners, then to the hardware store. They got into the car that was parked at the curb, and as he closed the door the sound scared some pigeons, which rose in one flickering mass and wheeled around, their wings seeming to have a green tint in the sunlight. As he saw the filaments of light in her hair, as he looked around at the chrome of the cars parking nearby, he was almost disoriented with the sense of being here, in this moment, as though he stood at the bottom of an enormous funnel that brought down to him so much life he felt the keen buzz of it.

FRANK KOHLER

KOHLER STEPPED INTO THE HALL BEHIND THE
front door. The house had a particular peacefulness that only comes after
one thing. The dog was quiet, too. They walked into the kitchen, where
Katryna's underwear still sat in the middle of *The War in Gaul.* The dog
went to its water bowl and started lapping, and the clicking of its nails and
the noise of its tongue in the bowl changed the silence from one of peaceful
exhaustion to expectation. And in the middle of the transformation, Kohler
opened the cabinet at the side of the kitchen door and reached inside for his
Mannlicher rifle. It had set triggers, a forearm that extended to the muzzle,
and a stock with a cheekpiece. As Kohler felt the weight of it, and when he
opened the bolt and pushed a brass hull into the magazine, feeling the
engagement of the cartridge, he had the sense of the object offering something necessary and right: it was going to give him a little control and defi-
nition in the face of everything being up in the air. He felt a little less ethereal
and drifting, like a phantom, when he touched the weight of the rifle.

Katryna's cheeks were a little reddish and her hair needed to be combed
as she came into the kitchen, where she picked up the underpants and put
them into the pocket of her house dress, which she then held together at the
throat.

She started when she saw Frank.

"I thought you'd be gone longer," she said.

"I guess," said Kohler.

"Did you find any trespassers?"

"No," said Kohler.

The dog put its nose between her legs, but she pushed it away, although
the dog did it again. Kohler pulled it back. When he did, she stared right at
him. How much did he know? How much had he seen?

"Well," said Katryna. "Let's have a drink."

She got out a bottle and poured some brandy into three mismatched
glasses. Dimitry came out of the bedroom, wearing just a pair of black jeans.

He looked from Katryna to Frank and back again, and then at the dog. He sat down, as though that would make this more casual. Katryna sat down, too. The dog panted. Kohler took a seat between Dimitry and Katryna and put out his fingers for the glass. His hand was just opposite Katryna's, and she slid her fingers closer, not quite touching him. He had the rifle across his lap.

"Why did you have to charge money?" said Frank.

"Money?" she said.

"The hundred and seventy dollars," said Frank.

"Oh," she said. "That."

"What a mutt," said Dimitry. He reached out to pat the dog. "I bet that thing will chew your ass off if you let it."

"Yes," said Kohler.

"We don't have to let this get out of hand," said Dimitry.

Katryna took a large drink. The dog started barking, its body and head still, just the mouth opening and closing and the ribs heaving. It wasn't barking at anything in particular so much as giving voice, as though everything in the air was distilled into this insistent yapping. The sound was wet and hoarse, like a barking seal. Katryna looked at the dog and then at Kohler and at Dimitry.

"Everyone makes mistakes," said Dimitry.

"That's right," said Frank.

Katryna put a hand to her head and looked down at the floor, and then the dog came up to her and tried to nuzzle under her hand, but she pushed him away once and then again, harder the second time, and when he came back again, she kicked him, and the dog made a low growl.

"Don't be stupid," said Dimitry.

"You do this with my wife and then you call me stupid?" said Frank.

"I didn't mean it like that," said Dimitry.

"How did you mean it?" said Frank.

"We can work this out," said Dimitry.

"It's not what you think," said Katryna.

"No?" said Frank.

The dog started barking again and it roiled around now, jumping up on Katryna and going over to Dimitry and licking at him and coming back. Then Kohler saw that she had reached into the drawer of the kitchen table and taken out the punch that Kohler had stolen and now she started click-ing it, the sound, that click, click, click, like finality itself.

Dimitry said, "This is no big deal. Really. We can talk it over. We can work it out. Everything can be worked out."

"Yes," said Kohler, bringing up the rifle. "You're right."

The dog went wild, going from one side of the room to the other, and then it stood right in front of Kohler, barking, drooling, jumping up. The sound of the rifle, in the confined space, was louder than the loudest explo-sion of thunder he had ever heard. It was like a physical presence that washed over all of them, and existed like a scrim that covered up how things had changed forever. Dimitry's chair was tipped over now, and Kohler instinctively avoided looking at the disorder on that side of the table. Only the dog jumped around that shape on the floor, howling and barking, and then coming over to Kohler.

"Get away from me," said Kohler. "Get away. Get away."

Then Katryna stood up, still holding the punch, but not using it any-more. She looked down at the thing as though suddenly realizing its use-lessness, and then she put it down on the table.

"What do you have to say?" said Frank.

She shook her head. How could she explain the tolerances by which she lived, the small difference between getting something to work and ending up like this? What was the difference? A hundred and seventy dollars. The money was on the table and she picked up the first bill and ripped it in half and then again before letting the square, rough-edged bits flutter away from her fingers into the dirt and the crimson stain on the floor.

"You aren't sorry, are you?" said Frank.

"What does that have to do with anything?" said Katryna. "That's too big for me. Everything is smaller than that. A few dollars here. An hour there. That's all."

"For a few dollars you threw this away?" he said. "For a few lousy bucks?"

She shrugged again.

"I loved him," she said. She motioned to the floor, which she wouldn't look at either.

"Well, that's great," said Frank. "Then why did you charge him money?"

"Why?" she said. "I needed it."

"Oh?" said Frank.

"So you and I could go on living together. See, that was the difference. A hundred and seventy dollars."

"A hundred and seventy dollars," said Frank.

"Yeah," she said. She starting ripping up another bill, the green and white shreds drifting away from her fingers like confetti that is dropped after the party is over. "What do you know about being trapped? Confined in a place that you can't get away from?"

She looked up at him.

"Well," she said. "Can you understand?"

He thought of that closet, and the wink of the man who had paid him to watch.

The dog threw its head back as it barked, showing its white teeth and red tongue and a hole at the back of its mouth. The sound was so perfectly repeated as to seem like the same thing over and over, like a stuck record.

She started ripping another bill, and as she did so with impatient, frustrated movements, she said, "It was so close . . . just that close . . ." She held the bits in her hand.

"You mean you almost got away?" he said.

"You can't understand," she said.

"Oh," he said, "I think I can."

That sound went through the kitchen again, as loud as the loudest thunder, and with his ears ringing, he turned away, although he saw those shreds of bills, green and white, in disorder on the wet and darkening floor. The dog went from one dead shape to the other, sniffing, barking, jumping around, whining. Then it turned to the door and scratched at it with an insistent, hysterical desire to get outside. Kohler opened the door, just to stop the thing from making that noise, and watched as it went around the half-open door with a magical flash of speed. Kohler came outside, and the dog ran down the drive in a sprinting rush. It looked like a streak of black. Kohler drew a bead on it, but then he just watched it go.

He went over to the stove and turned it on. The flames jumped up, blue and yellow. There was a lot of newspaper around, and he started rolling it up into balls and throwing it around the room, over the shapes on the floor, going outside to get more from the place where he kept newspaper to recycle. Then he piled up the balls all over the kitchen, around the stove, and finally began to throw them onto the burners, where the blue and yellow flames spread into the newspaper, changing color, becoming yellow and red and trailing smoke.

Outside, he put the rifle and some ammunition in the back of the car. The crackling of the fire was lost in the sound of the engine, and then Frank put the car into gear and went down to the road, where he turned toward town. He concentrated on the yellow lines in the middle of the pavement, following them while seeing that everything, the hills, the trees, the beaver pond at the bottom of the hill, all looked precisely as before. This calmed him down, at least for a few moments, and when he got to town, he was able to get out and fill the tank with gas, premium, $26.61 worth, which he put on his credit card so he wouldn't have to go inside. The cool metal of the nozzle, under his hand, was as good as splashing water on his face.

HE PARKED at the side of the town square and then got out and slammed the door with a hard *whomp*. Then he did it again, before standing there, looking over the black top of the car at the square itself. He walked around along the asphalt paths that went through the grass and between the wood-slatted benches. The fountain, where tourists came to throw pennies in the summer, was empty now. In October, when the fountain was drained, the custodian of the town hall swept them into a pile and picked them up with a dustpan, which he emptied into a garbage bag.

Kohler sat down on a bench in front of the fountain and thought of the good intentions of every one of the pennies that had been thrown in here, just as he imagined the copper-colored arcs, like smears of hope, that had accompanied each wish. There was always the possibility, he guessed, that there was a residue in the air from all of that wishing and that he might get some benefit from it, but then he realized that thinking this way was just making things harder.

The fire whistle on the square was like a klaxon in a war movie. It started its whining drone, but Kohler didn't flinch, or look around. He guessed someone had seen the smoke from his house and turned in an alarm, but he knew that if anyone said that it was Kohler's house, the firemen would take their time. That was how things had been in town for a while. And yet he had tried. Every year the town had the Christmas Club, which raised money to put up decorations on the common, and Kohler had worked with the committee that ran it, although recently they had written him a letter telling him that while they appreciated his interest, he wasn't going to be needed this year. He guessed it had to do with his desire to have more tinsel than they'd had before. The other members of the committee had wanted lights. He was a traditionalist. Was that what had been at the heart of it? Then he sat there, hearing the fire whistle, which kept him anchored to the spot.

The church was directly in front of him. It looked even better than the pictures of it that were for sale as a postcard in the general store. White siding, green shutters, a steeple, a flagstone walk in front, large windows on both sides that let the light in. It was the kind of place that Martha Stewart would suggest for a country wedding, and people came from as far away as Boston and New York to get married here. That was in the spring, summer, and early fall, and now the church looked deserted. One spring he had seen a bride and groom come out of the church and go up to the fountain with a handful of pennies. Thinking about those coins in the air, like copper scales, Kohler put his hands together, trying to find a way to know what to do, to have an instant's clarity. It was all he really wanted.

He walked across the empty green. The door of the church should have been locked, but when he pulled on it, the heavy slab of wood swung open and he saw the gleam of light on the pews and the flagstone floor, which gave the interior a sandy odor. Kohler drifted up the aisle and sat down just behind the first bench, one row back from the alter. The hush there was different from the sound in his house, or what had been his house.

He put his head down and thought, Please, oh please, I tried so hard to be human and turned into a monster. If I could just have a clear sense of what I need. If I had a sign. If I could just see God. Just a glimpse. Then he concentrated, trembling, sick with the effort of trying to demand an audience of some kind. After a minute or two he heard the creak of a door on an old hinge, and then a whoosh, whoosh, whoosh, at once soft and reassuring, like a warm breeze. When he looked up, he saw a young woman who had emerged from a door at the side of the altar.

She had hair the color of cherry Kool-Aid, and was about twenty. One eyebrow was pierced and she had a silver ring in it. She wore a T-shirt and black jeans, and she had a broom. At the altar she began to work toward the door, sweeping the dust on the flagstones into a small pile, which she then moved down the aisle toward the door. Light shot up and down the polished handle of the broom as she worked, swaying her hips, going up the aisle. As she got farther away from Kohler, he felt her presence diminish in a way that he didn't like. Then, at the rear of the church, near the door, she stopped and turned back, her voice resonant in the gloom of the entrance as she said, "The door is unlocked 'cuz I was gonna sweep. We're supposed to be closed."

"I'm sorry," Kohler said.

"No skin off my nose," she said. "Go on. Sit there if you want."

She pushed open the door to sweep the dust out, and when she did, she said, "Is that your car out there? The black one?"

"Yeah," Kohler said.

She turned now and started back toward Kohler, still sweeping, doing so with a variety of sulky indifference. She got closer, pushing a smaller pile of her sweepings, and Kohler looked down and thought, Ashes to ashes, dust to dust.

"I have to lock up when I'm done," she said.

"I just came in to . . ."

"I know," she said. She looked around. "I know. It's all right."

He put his head down on the wood of the pew in front of him.

"A lot of people come in. Like they just sit," she said. "You know, like Isaiah. We look for light, but there is darkness. For brightness, but we walk in blackness . . ."

He wanted to speak, but then when he opened his mouth, nothing came out, and so he shut it and made a gesture, as though there weren't words. She shrugged. Then she stood there, leaning on her broom.

"How fast does it go?" she said.

"What?" he said.

"Your car. Does it go fast?" she said.

She sat down in the pew on the other side of the aisle, and leaned on her broom, looking at him. "How fast?"

"Pretty fast," he said.

"Like, give me a number."

"A hundred, a hundred and ten. A hundred and thirty."

"That fast," she said. "Huh."

"Maybe more," he said.

She leaned on her broom handle and stared at him.

"Are you from around here?" she said.

"Yeah," he said.

They both sat there, the girl resting on her broom, Kohler smelling the flagstones, which were like wet cement, although there was something else to it, a sort of certainty, as though people could come and go, but that presence, that damp atmosphere would last forever. Then he thought about his house, how the flames had started inside, but when he'd looked at it from the outside, they'd appeared as though an enormous red and yellow bird with a tail of smoke had sunk its beak into the kitchen.

"This job is part of my probation," she said. "But it's kind of homey. My father was a preacher, in Island Pond, and we had to learn scripture. Like, if we had barbecued ribs, we had to give a line of scripture before we got one. I liked those ribs, when I was young. Now I'm a vegetarian."

She reached into her pocket and took out a joint, wrapped in white paper, which she put in her mouth, looking like Humphrey Bogart with an unfiltered cigarette hanging from his lip. She lit the joint and inhaled deeply, then offered it to Kohler, who shook his head. The smoke rose in a lazy, blue shape, like a big S, and then she exhaled, too, as though she had been diving and had come to the surface. The light from the window slanted onto her face, which made her skin seem radiant. With her eyes closed, she said, "Who coverest thyself with light as with a garment, who stretchest out the heavens like a curtain, who layeth the beams of his chambers in the waters: who maketh the clouds his chariot, walketh upon the wings of the wind . . ."

She held out the small cigarette.

"Sure you don't want some?" she said.

He shook his head. Then he remembered the barking dog.

"I've learned something else, too," she said. "One of the secrets is moderation. See?"

She licked her thumb and forefinger and put out the tip of the joint with the two of them, giving it a quick squeeze. It made a *pfft*. Then she put the thing in her pocket. The smoke rose and hung above them like a small, horizontal island, which slowly dissipated. The words she sang came out in a low, throaty voice, which Kohler wouldn't have thought she had, but it was hard to hear what she was really singing. Kohler put his hands to his head, and when he looked up he saw her smiling at him. She ran her hand through her red hair and giggled.

"Don't worry," she said. "Hey. I forgive you. Hey. See? It's O.K. Whatever it is, it's O.K."

He tried to speak again, but couldn't. She was wearing a musky perfume, and it hung there with the smoke. He felt a little better, hearing her voice and her giggle. She smiled again and went back to sweeping.

A cloud of dust hung in the aisle, the mass of it delineated by those same brilliant motes, which surrounded her as she worked all the way up to the end of the aisle and swept the pile into a dustpan, which she took over to the side of the room and dumped into a plastic trashcan she had brought in.

"That's really a nice car," she said.

"I used to think so," he said.

"Yeah," she said. "You're always looking for a new one. Like you see the advertisements on TV, and the next thing you know, you want the latest model. There's always something."

"I can't stand the color," he said.

"Well, you can always have it painted," she said. "Or if you got a new one, you could get it in red or yellow. And then maybe you could get mag rims."

Now she stopped and looked at the windows on the side of the church where the sun shone. She took Kohler by the hand and pulled him up. Then the two of them went to the side of the church and stood where the light came in, the slight warmth of it and the luminescence hitting Kohler on the face. "Close your eyes," she said.

The sunlight lay on his face like a bright film, and he stood in it, trying to concentrate on the warmth.

"Let's go for a ride," she said. "What do you say?"

Kohler opened his eyes. All he could see was the bright cherry-red hair of the young woman. She smiled in that crooked, half-high, totally reassuring way. She still had her broom. She took it over to the corner by the trashcan and leaned it there.

"All right," he said. "What's your name?"

"We don't have to get into names, do we?" she said.

"I guess not," he said.

"Let me get my coat," she said.

She went into the door from which she had emerged, and Kohler was left alone. He looked around and then reached into his pocket for his keys. She came back wearing a down coat that was leaking a few white feathers, and as she walked up to him, she reached out her hand and took the keys.

"O.K.?" she said. "Let me drive."

They came to the car and she opened the driver's side door. She saw the rifle in the back.

"What's that for?" she said.

"I don't know," he said. Then he threw a jacket over it.

"Well, all right," she said. "Let's go."

She got in, adjusted the seat, and put the key in the ignition.

RUSSELL BOYD

ONE AFTERNOON, WHEN RUSSELL HAD BEEN A state trooper for a couple of years, he was called to investigate a burglary that had taken place at what had been his grandfather's hunting camp. After Russell's grandfather had died and then Russell's father, too, the camp had been sold, and he hadn't been back since the sale. He pulled up in front of the place and found the door open. Although the new owner hadn't been there to show Russell the broken window, Russell had a pretty good idea what had happened, and now that he was here, he was more certain than ever.

When the camp had still been in the family it had existed as a physical place, but it had an emotional gravity, too, since it had been the center of family life. This was so palpable as to leave Russell a little disoriented when the place was sold. Even now he didn't know what he missed the most, the geography or the tug the place had exerted on him all year.

Often, before the camp was sold, he went there in the summertime, attracted by the moody atmosphere and something, else, too, which he didn't quite understand. He usually stopped when the stone building first came into view in the same the way one naturally hesitates at the first silence of a churchyard, among the gray stones and the damp and shady atmosphere of such places.

When the house wasn't used at the hunt, it was usually empty, punctuated only by an occasional break-in by young people who knew the place was deserted. For Russell, when he arrived in late August or early September, the first moment after crossing the threshold was always mesmerizing. Maybe it was the lingering presence of the young people who broke in to use a bed. Their delicious privacy, made all the more pleasurable by the breaking glass and the quick undressing, seemed to hang there in the silence as a footnote to the other things that had happened in this house. Maybe the young people who broke in had never been completely naked together before the privacy they found here. Anyway, when Russell came about the burglary, he guessed young people had broken in. Just like always.

When he stood there, as a policeman, Russell remembered the summer when he was eighteen. Then he had gone back just like the other times. He'd stepped inside, into the musty silence of the place, which seemed connected to the ashes in the fireplace. This silence was reassuring, and yet it left him with an ache that he couldn't quite feel completely, a hint of mortality or loss, which was compensated by the almost-comfort of being here. The door made a squeaking sound behind him as he shut it and then walked in and stood in front of the fireplace. Outside he could see that the sunlight was fading, and that shadows were sweeping into the clearing in front of the building. The tall grass outside was mowed once a year, in the late fall. Now the highlights in it from the sunlight disappeared as the clouds covered the sky, not in the usual collection of lumps of mist and uneven clots, but all at once in the purple wall with which a thunderstorm arrived in the mountains. Russell sat down to wait.

He thought of his grandfather's story of a snake that was supposed to live in the house. Of course, Russell thought that his grandfather had been telling tall tales, and let it go at that. Russell had never seen the snake. The light in the room dimmed, and then turned gray tinted with purple. Russell felt dampness and the electric charge of the air that seemed to seep in through the cracks in the door and down the chimney. The purple light darkened.

He sat on the fender that was next to the fireplace, and as he did so, he saw an array of sparks of static electricity, little bits that seemed to bloom suddenly, in the way snowflakes appear at the beginning of a snowstorm. A sound accompanied the appearance of these hot yellow specks, a crackling that Russell heard in the midst of a needling rush over his arms and shoulders, a chill that seemed to be composed of points that were as sharp and as sudden as the sparks. He supposed that this was ball lightning, and that it was flowing down the chimney and spreading around the room. It came in pulses. First the particles of light, then more static as the room was charged again, the invisible presence growing until the electric arcs, just as bright and as visible as those of a Fourth of July sparkler, returned with a ripping sound, like Velcro being pulled apart. And with this progression there was the increasing odor of ozone. Everything about this was at once soothing and frightening, in that as the tension went up and then was released, Russell thought that he had survived another bad moment, but instantly it started all over again. Finally the room was filled with a keen purple light, as though a fluorescent fixture had been turned on, and outside the air exploded with lightning so close that Russell felt the charge on his skin.

The static charge built again. At the back of Russell's mind, he felt mild curiosity about what it was like to be in a building that was struck by lighting. It was this curiosity, he knew, that was keeping him from real fear. As the sparkles appeared, producing a sense of the ominous that made it hard for Russell to breathe, he looked up at the top of the stone walls on which the rafters were set. The walls were a couple of feet thick, and that meant there was a flat place about two feet wide at the top. There, in that sparkling rip, in the chill on his skin, Russell saw the black snake.

It was moving with a glistening slink, the coils of it sliding through the same places, as though they were going around pegs. Its skin had a silver cast that was set off by the golden sparks that crackled in the room. The snake kept going along the wall, not seeming to be headed anywhere so much as trying to get away from the place where it was. Outside, the air exploded, but the movement of the snake was constant: it didn't flinch or stop or do anything at all but move along with that constant slinking flow, as though it wasn't the sound that was bothering it, but another unnamed, unknown thing.

Russell stood about ten feet away, and the first thing that came to mind was that the snake wasn't nine or ten feet long. "It's got to be twelve or fourteen feet," he thought, as though putting a name or a number on this thing could help him with the other unknown presence, which he was too frightened to make sense of, or name, or even fully comprehend. He watched as the thing slipped down the wall, its tongue flicking out, tasting the ozone that filled the room as though the place were a power plant, rank with the sparks from the brushes of a generator. The snake went down the wall like a swaying, mesmerizing rope, and then slid across the floor, still not flinching when the explosions of lightning came outside or when the purple light pulsed through the room. It went across the concrete floor and stuck its head into the wooden frame that had been built around a sofa bed in front of the fireplace. Then, with a kind of legerdemain, it found a place to enter it, and Russell watched that slinking flow, the skin black and glistening, surrounded by sparks as it disappeared, all of its amazing length, into that wooden frame.

Then the purple light and the clouds vanished. The light of the sun came down with a soothing, fluid presence, and when Russell looked out the window, he saw balls of moisture on each blade, each one silver and perfectly shaped, as to suggest an essence of grass and light, like a handful of diamonds spread on a green cloth. For one horrible instant he was afraid that he had imagined the entire thing, and that he was experiencing the first symptom of a disorienting mental disease. Then he knew that this was utter nonsense, and that what he really was afraid of was not the precision of the way his grandfather spoke, such as when he had described this snake (which Russell had dismissed as the story an old man told to a young one to scare him), but rather that the old man had probably been right about the mesmerizing arrival of those events when one's beliefs no longer applied, no matter how fiercely one clung to them.

FRANK KOHLER

"HEY," THE GIRL SAID, "THIS SUCKER REALLY GOES."
The interstate stretched away in front of them, and Kohler glanced at the speedometer, which swept up to a hundred. She drove with her arms fully extended, like a racing-car driver, and Kohler reached down and flipped on the radar detector. The first thing he noticed was that his sense of time had changed, and that it didn't seem to rush forward in a smooth arc, but now was made up of ragged bits that didn't fit together. The future didn't seem to have the depth it had possessed just a few hours ago, and this absence, which felt like a vacuum, left him straining for something that just wasn't there. That was part of the difficulty. He wanted something that was gone, which was the notion of one thing naturally leading to the next in a long chain of the ordinary.

She glanced over. "Am I scaring you? Something wrong?"

He swallowed. "I feel sick," he said.

"You want to throw up? I can pull over."

"I don't know."

"You have a fever?"

"No."

"Anything else?"

"I'm just shaky."

"You mean like scared?"

"It's hard to describe."

"I know," she said. "Like you've done something you shouldn't have. Is that it? I get that all the time."

He nodded.

"Yeah," he said. "That's pretty close."

"There's nothing you can do about it," she said. "Not a thing. It's goes with the territory."

"What territory?" he said.

She shrugged.

"Look," she said. "There's nothing you did that hasn't been done before. That's a promise." She reached over and put her hand on his. "Does that feel better?"

"Yes," he said.

"Well, sure," she said. "There's no mystery there." She put her hand back on the wheel. "This is really cool. One-ten and gaining."

"It's just a sick feeling," he said.

She glanced at the oil pressure, alternator, gas, tach.

"Well, at least everything looks all right here," she said.

"I think you should slow down," he said.

"Come on," she said. "I've just been sweeping all morning, thinking about my troubles. Are we going to have fun or not?"

"Fun," he said.

"Yeah," she said. "Like being in a fast car."

He looked directly at her.

"What are you on probation for?" he asked.

"This and that," she said. "I don't want to go into it."

"Well, it couldn't have been that bad," he said.

"Yeah?" she said. "How about possession of stolen property? Is that bad? Or possession of a controlled substance with intent to distribute?"

He shrugged. No. Not from his perspective.

"No," he said.

She smiled.

"And other stuff," she said. "But they didn't catch me for everything."

"Do you have a license?" he said.

"Me?" she said. She giggled.

The wolf-colored landscape slipped by, streaked with yellow from the last of the poplar and the occasional willow, which drooped over itself near the side of a road. He put his head back and thought that maybe, if he took a minute, he could come up with . . . with what? As he sat there, he was uncertain what he was looking for. He confronted that oncoming landscape, which was different now, and it left him with the sensation of being lost. Where could he go? It was like being inside out: not that he didn't know where he was, but that he didn't have a clue where to go. Then he watched as she put out her cigarette.

"So," she said. "What's really eating you?"

He shook his head.

"No?" she said. "Well, I told you about the possession-of-stolen-property rap."

"I don't know," he said.

"'I don't know what's wrong,' or 'I don't know if I should tell you'?" she said. "Say, have you got any money?"

"A little," he said.

"Why don't we pull off here and get a little something to drink?" she said.

"I need to get away," he said.

"That's what I'm talking about," she said. "A little trip to the seashore, courtesy of the booze manufacturers."

She got off the highway and pulled into the empty, dusty parking lot of a state liquor store. She tapped on the steering wheel and then looked over. Next to the liquor store was a motel, not part of a chain, but one that had been built here in the late seventies. A couple of cars were parked in front of it, and the effect was like a man who had only a few of his teeth. The girl looked at the motel and then at the liquor store.

"I think I'll wait here," she said. "You know what I mean?"

He got out. When he stood on that dusty apron, under that sky, he wanted to take action, or to find a way to produce one small point of reference that would allow him to . . . then he came back against that disjointed sense of time, one thing being ripped from another, like the past and the future. He swallowed. Maybe the girl was right. A drink might help. Then he had the sensation of being exposed and obviously not belonging here.

The store had metal racks for liquor, a cash register, posters about drinking and being responsible, and when he came in from outside, it seemed to him that he was just a guy who came into a liquor store, and the fleeting sense of the ordinary, which lasted only a few seconds, left him dizzy with an understanding of his new circumstances. What, after all, had he lost but the sense of living from hour to hour in a connected way? He took a bottle off a shelf and walked back to the cash register and paid the clerk, who was watching a basketball game on TV. He didn't even look at Kohler.

In the car the girl said, "I was thinking about getting a room." She gestured at the motel. She took the bottle out of the sack, twisted the top off, and took a big sip. Then she wiped her lips with the back of her hand. "If we drive around drinking like this, we're going to have trouble. I'd like to take a shower. There's no doors on the bathroom in the halfway house I live in. No privacy."

He sat there, staring directly ahead. He could see those shreds of money falling like leaves from those shaking fingers.

He took the bottle and had a sip, and the only thing that he could feel, the only thing that seemed to exist in his life, was that hot, burning taste. Vodka. The transparency of it was mesmerizing, as though he could see, in the clear liquid, a hint of the unseen. Surely the liquor appeared one way, clear and harmless, but was really another. Then he took another drink, just to feel the burning presence, the heat in his face, and the long, warm descent into his stomach. He held out the bottle and she took it, her fingers touching his with a nice frankness.

"Everyone looks at you," she said. "Do you have a tattoo, do you shave under your arms? You know?"

"What?" he said.

"In the shower," she said. "Where I live."

He glanced around. It was probably a good idea to get off the street. Maybe then he could think for a moment.

"I'll get the room," he said.

"Good," she said. "I'll wait here."

He opened the door of the office, which was so small as to seem like a compartment on a spaceship. The counter was right in front of him, classic motel style: veneer paneling, a ballpoint pen in a holder, a form held by two little clips, ready to be filled out. A woman of about fifty was reading an *In Style* magazine and glancing up at a wrestling match on the TV on a shelf in the corner. Kohler had trouble remembering the number of the license plate of the car, his home phone, and his Zip code. He did the best he could and gave the woman three twenties. She took them and gave him a key and two bath towels and two washcloths. Then he came out and got into the car.

"Maybe you should pull around to the back," he said.

"Anything you say," she said.

The room had two double beds, a greenish mirror, a lamp on a nightstand that was made out of veneer and had plastic knobs that were treated to look like they were metal. A painting was attached to the wall with screws. The girl came in with the bottle of vodka and sat down on the bed, where Kohler had left the two clean but threadbare towels. They both had a sip and she put the bottle on the floor while she lit up the last of the joint she had in her blue jeans.

"Here," she said.

He took a long, deep drag and held it. Then he had a drink of the vodka and she said, "It won't take long."

She went into the bathroom and closed the door. He heard the squeak of her feet in the tub, the running of the shower, and after a while the generic perfume of the soap, not quite lavender but something like it, came into the room, too. The smoke in the air, the lights here, which were probably seventy-five-watt bulbs, the sound of the girl's voice as she sang a hymn in the shower, all left him trying to decide what he was going to do. The effort came at the cost of exhaustion, which made him relax a little. That, he guessed, was the upside of depression. Or maybe there was something else here, too. The girl made even this ugly room with the dim lights seem warm and lovely. She came to the end of the hymn and then the water stopped running.

He wished that he had a map in the car, since he could bring it in here and put it on the table that was screwed to the wall and plan which way to go. He had a credit card and five hundred dollars in cash. He guessed he could go to the bank and take out what he had, but was that a good idea? He didn't know.

She came out of the bathroom with the towel wrapped around herself, tucked in between her small breasts. Here and there she had a mole. She sat down opposite him and took a drink, tipping the bottle up and making a long bubble in the neck. Then she opened the drawer and picked up the Bible there, which she flipped back and forth.

"You know," she said. "Sometimes you can get so close. You read the scripture and it's all jumbled up, like poetry, and you can almost see it. But it just bleeds away."

"I know," he said.

"But, if you're feeling bad, if you just grasp it, just for a moment, it helps," she said.

While she sat there in that cheap towel, her hair wet, her lips at the mouth of the bottle, he thought about the disorder of the kitchen, Dimitry's chair going over backward, and then the explosion after that, all of it coming together in such a way as to leave him with a sudden, unexpected desire.

"You know," she said, "that was the first good shower I've had in months. I can tell you this. I don't want to go back to the place I'm staying, or to that sweeping."

He took the bottle and had another drink.

"Maybe we could go someplace," she said. "Maybe we could just get the fuck out of here."

"Where would you like to go?" he said.

"Out west," she said. "Washington State."

"It would be nice," he said.

"Yeah, Cheyenne," she said.

"That's in Wyoming," he said.

"That's good, too," she said. "You know what I'm saying."

He swallowed. When her red hair was wet it was dark, almost purple, and her skin seemed so white that it was close to the color of the towel.

"You look pretty scared," she said. "Are you afraid of taking a chance?"

"No," he said. "It's not that."

"When I'm scared, I just take the first step. That's all. Break things down into small pieces. Do them one at a time."

She took another drink.

"What could we do out there?" he said.

"Start over," she said. "Get a house trailer. You know. A job. What do you do?"

"I fix computers," he said.

"That's perfect," she said. "They've got broken computers out there. I guarantee it. You can take that to the bank."

"Uh-huh," he said.

"Give me your hand," she said.

He put it out, the fingers trembling a little. She took it and held it in hers and looked him right in the eyes.

"Can you feel that? It's like my fingers are buzzing."

He closed his eyes.

"Yes," he said. "I can."

They sat there, just holding hands. He smelled the soap, the bleached bedspreads, and then they looked up in the mirror and saw the two of them together.

She wants to go with me, he thought.

"Now?" he said, his voice breaking a little. He looked around the room where everything seemed hazy, as though seen through heat on a road. Quavering, he thought, or is it wavering? He just sat there, trembling like a wet dog.

"Yeah," she said. "Why not? What's the big deal?"

"You mean it, don't you?" he said.

"I don't want to go back to that group house. And you've got money and that car. Just the basics. That's enough."

"Is it?" he said.

"Yeah," she said. "Let me tell you, I've been in so many things that had less going for them than money and a car that . . ." She stopped and looked him over. "My best stories are about men, but it's probably a good idea to keep my mouth shut."

He closed his eyes again and concentrated on the coolness of her hands.

"Washington. Aren't there big mountains out there?" she said. She hesitated. Then she looked right at him, leaned close enough to him so that he could smell her hair and that soap. "You don't think I know you're in trouble. Of course I do. So what? I'm in trouble, too."

"So what?" he said.

"Yeah," she said. "Come on. I'm saying we can do it."

She took the last of the joint and lit it and took a long drag and let the smoke go. Then she watched the cloud of it float away and vanish into the air of the motel room.

"Right now," she said.

She dropped the towel and stood up, her skin white, her breasts small, and then she turned and went into the bathroom, where she got her clothes and put them on, wiggling into her tight pants. She buttoned up her blouse.

"That was the best shower I ever had," she said. "You sure you don't want one?"

"No," he said.

"Look," she said. "You've got the money and the car. That's cool. I can give you something, too."

"What's that?" he said.

"Come on," she said. "Let's go and I'll show you."

She stood up and looked at him with that half-mad smile and that funny red hair. When she spoke, it wasn't so much that she made everything simple, but that she made it clear and resonant, and while she reduced things to the smallest elements of a problem, she didn't appear to diminish them.

"I forgive you," she said. "Does that help?"

"You don't know what I've done," he said.

"Well," she said, "I'll worry about that some other time."

They left the key to the room on the bed and went outside, where the light seemed very bright. The car was behind the building, and they got back into it, the girl behind the wheel, Kohler in the front seat. She started the engine and said, "All right. Pacific Coast, here we come."

He had the bottle and she reached over for it. Then they went down the two-lane road, through the middle of town, and got onto the four-lane highway.

"Am I still going too fast for you?" she said.

He stared straight up the road.

She lifted herself up from the seat and reached into her pocket for another joint, which she lit with a cigarette lighter from her other pocket. In the small space the odor was very strong, and the smoke was like a scene in a World War II movie about a fighter pilot whose plane has been hit and the cockpit is on fire. She offered it, but he just shook his head.

She glanced over at him, took a deep pull, and said, in little puffs of smoke, "Trying to figure things out, huh?"

He nodded.

"Yes," he said.

"And you shall grope at noonday, as a blind man gropes in darkness; you shall not prosper in your ways; you shall be only oppressed and plundered continually, and no one shall save you."

Then she exhaled.

"I'll tell you this," she said. "Once you learn that stuff, you don't forget. What I like is the scale of it, you know? Big, booming, like from way out there . . . all jumbled, but almost there."

She took it up to a hundred and ten. The dials all steady, the landscape animated by the speed. It slid by.

"I don't know," he said, feeling that burning sensation on his tongue when he had a drink. "Did you ever have a dog?"

"No," she said, "but I know scripture about them. I used to play the game with my dad. He'd say, like 'dogs,' and I'd come up with something. You want to hear one?"

"Yes," he said.

"And I will appoint over them four kinds, saith the Lord: the sword to slay, and the dogs to tear, and the fowls of the heaven, and the beasts of the earth, to devour and destroy. You think I'm kidding? Jeremiah."

The speedometer held at a hundred and ten. The girl looked over and said, "Well, we're going pretty good now. We'll hit 84 and then we'll go west. Maybe we'll stop in Hartford for a map."

He nodded.

"You know," she said, "getting a fresh start makes you think. Like what the hell am I going to do with the rest of my life? Like should I go back to school? Education is such a cool thing."

"It depends on what you learn," he said.

"Well, how about computer science?" she said. "Web pages and all that stuff."

He nodded. Yeah.

"Uh-oh," she said. She glanced in the rearview mirror. "Oh, shit."

Kohler looked back, too, over his shoulder. A state police car had turned out from behind a screen of trees, and had its lights on. Kohler looked at the flashes of blue. Then he turned back, put the cap on the bottle, and put it under the seat, as though that was all he had to worry about.

"How fast does this thing go?" she said.

"I don't know," he said.

"Well, we're about to find out," she said.

The cruiser came along, not quite at the speed of the black car, but fast, and as Kohler looked forward, he felt the sense of pursuit, as though there was a long trail, invisible, that streamed back from the car. The numbers on the speedometer swept up to a height that Kohler had only seen in a dream. Was that really a hundred and twenty? The girl looked right ahead, her dyed hair against the window. The lights of the car behind them showed as a blue flickering in the sideview mirror. Kohler smelled the pot, and he could still taste the raw vodka he had bought. The car held the road in the next turn, although it seemed light, barely gripping the pavement. Kohler looked around, and there, in that moment, he had that teary sense of the unknowable, or only knowable by its fleeting, maddening presence: up ahead, to the south, the sun came through the clouds, just like a painting one would see in Italy, the masses golden at the edges, the rays piercing, and all of it left him sitting there, blinking, trying not to let it get away from him. He swallowed, and yet it still lingered, that operatic sense of everything, of a vast apprehension of . . . he didn't know, really, perhaps just the feeling itself, which he clung to in the face of disaster. And when he was thinking of that sensation, that state, he said, "Oh, please. Stop."

"Yeah," said the girl. "Yeah. Shit."

She slowed down and pulled over. Kohler sat there, still blinking. He remembered Katryna's expression when she looked him right in the eyes, not even noticing the dog anymore. "So, you saw," she said. "Too bad."

The cruiser sat behind them for a long time.

"What are we going to say?" said the girl.

Kohler shook his head. He didn't know what to say.

"Oh, they are going to fucking kill me," she said. "You know what my probation officer is going to do?"

He shook his head again. He still had that sense of the beautiful and the ominous that was just beyond his ability to comprehend. Its scale was large and he was obviously in the presence of it, but that was all he knew.

The trooper came up to the car. He had his gun drawn.

"Stay in the car," he said.

Kohler saw that his name tag said TROOPER DEUTSCHE.

"Do you have some identification?" he asked the girl.

She reached into her pocket and took out a social security card and an expired driver's license. The trooper took them both, and when he did, he looked inside at Kohler, too.

"Is this your car?" he said to the girl.

"No," she said. "It's his."

"Oh?" said the trooper. "Was there any reason to drive that way?"

"No," said the girl.

"And you?" said the trooper. "You let her do that?"

Kohler shook his head.

"I asked you a question," said the trooper.

"I couldn't . . ." he said.

"You couldn't what?" said the trooper. "Have you been drinking?"

"A little," said Kohler.

"Wait here," said the trooper. "Don't get out of the car."

He turned and walked back to the cruiser and got inside and picked up the microphone. Kohler swallowed. The girl started tapping the steering wheel with her open hand, glancing in the rearview mirror.

"That's not my real ID," she said.

The trooper came back.

"Get out of the car," he said to the girl.

She got out. As the trooper started to put handcuffs on her, she turned and started running. He grabbed her hand, but she got away, and then the trooper took a step toward her. He had his gun drawn. Kohler reached behind the seat for the rifle, and then the girl broke for the side of the road, where there was a field, beyond which rose a line of trees about a hundred yards away. The trooper looked at her and said, "Stop. Stop."

Then he turned and saw Kohler, who had gotten out of the car.

"You don't want to do that," said the trooper. "You really don't."

Below, at the edge of the field, the girl was still running, her hair bobbing in the otherwise dull landscape: it appeared like a bit of red yarn blowing across a piece of damp concrete. Above her a hawk wobbled in a thermal, its movement like anxiety itself. The girl had almost gotten to the trees at the edge of the field when she heard the rifle and felt the shock wave of it, too. The sound was deep, loud, and seemed to permeate everything, only to bleed away into a hum, which in turn vanished and left behind a new and ominous silence. When the girl heard the sound, the light became brighter and the colors more crystalline. Even the hawk seemed to flinch, wheeling over on one wing.

She looked over her shoulder, one hand to her lips. From her perspective, she saw the flashing lights, the two cars, and one figure standing there at the edge of the highway with that funny-looking rifle. She turned back to the woods, running into them without looking where she was going. The brambles and cane, the brush at the edge were like a wall, but she ran right into it, falling once and getting up, her legs always moving, as though she was still trying to run even when she was falling.

When she emerged on the other side of the woods, she saw a service road where an occasional car went by, and when she came to the edge of it, she waited, unable to make sense of what had happened. Something had changed. She knew that. Time had become short. She had the feeling of being in a tunnel. She sat down in the wet leaves at the side of the road, and as the moisture seeped into the seat of her pants, she kept blinking, looking around, unable to sit still. She could still taste the vodka in her mouth and the ashy tang of the pot. Then she looked around and thought that it would be best to keep moving.

RUSSELL BOYD

RUSSELL AND ZOFIA SAT AT THE KITCHEN TABLE, just opposite one another, the sound of their raised voices slowly vanishing, and when it was finally gone they just sat there, hearing the dripping faucet in the sink, the ticking as the house cooled and the furnace came on with a throb. They both looked up at the clock at the same time. Then Zofia went to the sink and leaned on the faucet, but she only slowed the drip.

"I guess you're going to have to go soon," she said.

"Yes," he said.

"I'm sorry," she said. "We just go around and around. It's not that I don't want a child. You know that."

The furnace throbbed again, and outside he saw that the sun had left a film of light on the brown grass, a kind of pink film. There were places, here and there, where the tint came up against a blue-black shadow that was so dark as to look like a hole that had been cut into the ground.

In the shower, Russell stood under the hot water and hoped that the noise of it would obliterate everything, and while he grasped at the soap, which kept slipping through his fingers, he found himself confronting the fact that he did not know what was going to happen, and each new event, each new detail, each time he stepped out into the wind of the highway required that he look at things as though he had never seen them before, even though they looked precisely like things he had. And when he walked out into the kitchen, what could he see that was new, that would help him, or her? The sound in the shower got louder and louder and then he turned it off and stood there, hearing the drip from the fixture and feeling the cool air.

"You had a call," said Zofia. "From Mason. You know, the sergeant. He wants you to call right back."

Russell picked up the phone, called, and listened for a moment.

"Oh, no," he said. "What kind of shape is he in? Shit. Sure. Right away. Sure."

He put the phone down and went into the bedroom, where he started to dress, pulling the body armor over his head and fastening the Velcro straps, which stuck to themselves with a tearing sound. Zofia stood in the doorway, her arms crossed.

"What was that about?" she asked.

"Tony got shot," he said.

"Oh, no," she said.

She looked past him and out the window.

"Is he all right?" she said.

"No," said Russell.

He pulled on his pants and took a shirt out of the box from the cleaners. The plastic sack came off with a whisper, and when he put the shirt on, it still had creases in the front. Often he thought that part of the discipline of being alert began with shaving closely, shining his shoes, making sure his hat was clean, too. Now, though, he just put on his clothes as fast as he could. Then he went out to the kitchen, where Zofia was now standing by the sink.

"Did they get the guy who did it?" she said.

"No," he said. "They're looking."

"Oh," she said.

She swallowed.

"I'm sorry," she said.

"Me too," he said. "But not half as sorry as that asshole is going to be when . . ."

He stopped and ran the water until it was cold. Then he had a drink.

"Look," she said. "I just have a funny feeling about this. Maybe it's being pregnant."

"I've really got to get going," he said.

He knew, though, that he had to make a lunch. If nothing else, he was going to have to eat.

"I don't want you to feel bad," he said. "I don't want anything like that."

"You're not listening," she said.

"I don't think this is the best time," he said.

"I don't want you to go," she said.

"I've got to," he said. "It's my job."

"I've just got a bad feeling," she said. "Don't you see? I'm asking you not to do this. How often do I ask you, straight out, to do something that is important to me? Stay here."

"Not now," he said. "We don't have to talk about this now."

"No?" she said. "This looks like the perfect time."

He turned to face her.

"I'm good at what I do," he said.

"So?" she said. "What the hell does that have to do with anything?"

He took bread out of a drawer and luncheon meat from the refrigerator, and began to make a sandwich, which he could eat in the cruiser. Sometimes he went out to lunch with other troopers from the barracks, but he knew there wasn't going to be any of that tonight.

"It doesn't have to be this way," he said.

"I'm asking you . . ." she said.

He stopped and opened up a package of ham, the marbled stuff slippery under his fingers. He dropped a piece and picked it up again and put it on a slice of bread. "I'm trying not to lose my temper, but there are times when you are—"

"A bitch? Is that what you want to say?"

She stood next to him, staring out the window. Then she turned to him and said, "Here. Let me do that." She took the lettuce and the mustard from him and said, "Do you want cheese?"

He put a hand to his head.

"You didn't answer me," she said.

"Yes. Yes, I want cheese," he said.

She slapped down a piece of cheese, and the sound hung there between them and bled away. He got out a brown bag and they put the sandwich in. He felt the pleasurable buzz on his fingers where she had touched them, and the sensation was like the lingering buzz from an emery board.

"I'm sorry," she said. "I don't mean to talk like that."

He nodded.

"I know," he said.

"Who did it?" she said.

"I don't know," he said. He shrugged. "Heroin dealers travel in pairs. When the first car gets stopped, the driver of it starts an argument. Then the second car pulls up and the driver of it gets out and says to the cop, 'Do you need assistance?' just before shooting him."

Russell shrugged.

"It could be something like that," he said.

He got to the screen door, which he had planned on replacing with the storm door insert this weekend, and then she was inside and he was just on the other side of the screen, with the mesh between them. He stood there, not moving a muscle, holding that bag. She looked through the wire.

"Don't go," she said. "This is the last time I'm going to ask."

"I'm already late," he said.

Then she put her lips next to the mesh and said, "Be careful."

He stood in front of the cruiser, momentarily disoriented. Then he put the sandwich in the car and got out the tuning fork he used to calibrate the radar, doing so because he wanted to slow everything down, to do one thing that he had done before and that gave him the feeling of doing the right thing in the right order. Then he got into the car and pushed the sandwich over on the seat and saw that she had turned away from the door and gone inside. He could see her through the window with her arms crossed under her breasts as she stared out into space.

FRANK KOHLER

THE DOOR OF THE CRUISER HAD OPENED WITH A click. Kohler had gotten behind the wheel, putting the rifle next to him, its butt on the floor, its forearm leaning on the edge of the passenger seat. It took a little fumbling to turn off the flashing lights, and as he put his hands under the dashboard, pushing one switch and then another, he heard a click as the lock on the rack that held the shotgun behind his head opened. He toggled the switch back and forth, hearing that sound, which came and went with a cold finality. He left the rack unlocked.

The radar was on the dashboard, and below it he saw a microphone and the radio. A wire mesh cage was behind him. The voice of the dispatcher gave a number and what sounded like an abbreviation for a town. He didn't know what that meant. If he responded, what would he say?

He went north at a steady seventy-five miles an hour. Occasionally he came up behind another car, and for a while he just followed it, and then there was a moment when the driver in the car ahead looked in the rearview mirror, saw the cruiser, and got out of the way. Kohler accelerated, letting the cars slip by, one after another. Then the woman's voice came on.

He was glad to be away from the black car, which was filled with the smell of the cheap vodka and the cigarette the girl had been smoking, but there had been something else, too, about the interior of the black car. It was confining, and just sitting in it was a punishment of some kind, which had, at its heart, his sense of being in the place around which everything had collapsed. It was the locus, or so Kohler thought, of pressure. It didn't take long, however, for that sense of being at the bottom of everything to come into the cruiser, too. He thought the voice of the dispatcher produced this atmosphere, as though she was a part of a chorus, and what she said was an ongoing, steady commentary that he couldn't understand. It reminded him of the language that Katryna and Dimitry had spoken, and so he reached down and turned the thing off. The quiet of the car was instantly soothing, and for a minute he just drove in it, but then the silence began its slow, steady change from relief to something that was confining and inauspicious.

What seemed odd was that he still existed at all. When he looked around, everything was at once mundane and still filled with meaning, and when he tried to take a deep breath, if only to calm down so he could think, the relief was momentary, since he went through it again, the girl running away, his hand as he reached for the rifle, the soles of the trooper's shoes, which were visible as he lay at the side of the road.

He knew that the smart thing would be to pull over and to get out of the car and find a way to turn himself in. To make an appointment to do so. An *appointment*. How could he use such a word? And he knew he wasn't going to do any such thing. As he drove, all he could think of was the scale of what had it in for him, something keen and malicious that he saw even in the vista ahead of him. The woods and sky seemed dangerous, and he knew that giving up was a matter of surrendering to what had so perfectly singled him out. This was a matter of faith. He swallowed and tried to look around, to calm down, and when he did so, he found himself trembling and feeling drained and barely able to keep his eyes open.

He got off the highway and turned toward the Green Mountains. They were attractive to him, and he drove west, thinking it over.

He remembered Katryna when she had made tea in the afternoon, sitting there at the table and sipping from the cup he had bought her, her eyes far away, as though she were seeing Moscow, the river with lights smeared across it, or those Soviet statues of the New Man and the New Woman.

The wood road was about five miles from the main highway. It wasn't much to look at, just two ruts that ran uphill into the trees. Kohler slowed down and looked at it, and then turned into it, slowly climbing along the hard earth, which was mostly frozen. He didn't know where he was going exactly, although what he thought was that he would park the car at the end of this road, or as far up as he could go. Sooner or later the cops would come up here, looking for the car.

RUSSELL BOYD

RUSSELL SAT IN THE CAR IN A PULLOUT AT THE entrance to the valley. He took off his hat and put it on the seat while he looked ahead. This country was full of these places to park, mostly next to a stream that, in September, was so low that all you saw was a collection of brown and blue rubble. Here the stream turned away from the road and ran along the edge of a floodplain, which was fertile land, although there wasn't much of it. You could see where it ended by the hills on each side of the valley. Russell put his hand to his head and looked at the house that was not too far from the road, about a quarter of a mile beyond where he sat.

The house was sided with clapboards, but they hadn't been painted in a long time, the effect of which was to make them seem scaled with peeling paint. The house was two stories, and it had a porch. The roof was made of slate. The overall impression of the place was that it had been a lot better off forty years ago, and now was slowly disappearing. A barn behind the house was missing shingles, and the cupola on the top, where pigeons still lived, looked as though it was going to go next winter.

Russell knew that Deutsche's parents were home. A lazy pennant of smoke rose from the chimney. A woodstove had been attached to it in the kitchen, and Russell recalled the afternoon when he had come for a turkey dinner, when both the kitchen range and the woodstove had been going and the house had been warm and fragrant with sage. The valley and particularly the house looked different now. Now it looked, in the harsh landscape, like an outpost that was about to be overrun.

He knew that he didn't have much time. But he sat there looking at the smoke and the pigeons that circled around it. Having to do this, to tell Tony's parents about what had happened, left him with the sensation of becoming something he had never wanted to be. He had hated events that left people with the sense of being overrun, whether it was someone beating someone else, or the slower but equally devastating work of heroin. He had always put himself on the other side and had been glad to do it, too. But having to go up to the door with this news made him feel as if he had become part of what caused the trouble.

He started the engine. He knew that slowing things down wasn't going to do much. Even so, he found himself trying to gain an extra minute before pulling up in front of the house and going in. The drive wasn't paved, just dirt with puddles that had frozen and that reflected the silver-gray sky. In one of the puddles, as he stopped the car and glanced down, the pigeons were reflected as they flew around the house in fluttering, anxious-looking movements. Russell sat in the car and looked at the kitchen door. One light was on. The others, in the living room and upstairs, were out.

He got out of the car and put on his hat. Then he walked from the cruiser to the small wooden porch where there was a screen door that hadn't been replaced yet with a glass storm panel. It made him think of Zofia as she had stood on the other side of the screen when he had left, that faraway look in her eyes. Then he opened the screen door and knocked a couple of times, before he looked through the glass and saw that Deutsche's mother and father were standing in the kitchen, both of them turned toward him. The woman wore the same brown sweater that buttoned up the front, a gray skirt, and her hair was in a serviceable bun. She had one hand to her lips. Her husband stood in overalls, which he didn't really need for work, since they had sold their herd of fifty cows ten years before. The husband came to the door.

"Hello, Russell," he said.

Russell nodded and came in, holding his hat. He felt the room change, as though he had brought in a presence that, while invisible, still made everything seem a little washed out and a little heavier. He swallowed and looked from one of them to the other, feeling that room as it seemed to become someplace he had never seen before, not in the arrangement of objects, but in the way they felt.

"Come in," said Mrs. Deutsche.

Russell closed the door, hearing the suck of it in the frame.

"We were just going to have tea," she said. "Wouldn't you like to have some?"

Mr. Deutsche leaned on a chair, his hands gripping the back of it so hard that Russell could see that the nails of his fingers were white under the pressure. Mrs. Deutsche didn't wait for an answer. Russell was certain that they knew—that his coming to the door at this time of day had been enough.

The kitchen still had the odor of breakfast, a mixture of oatmeal and toast and maple syrup, all of which seemed to bleed away now into the stone of the chimney, into the walls that needed painting. Mrs. Deutsche held the teapot up to the kettle, putting it over the steaming spout, and then she turned to Russell and said, "Did you know that the most important part of making tea is to warm the pot?"

"No," said Russell. "I didn't."

"Well," said Mrs. Deutsche. "You'll remember now, won't you?"

She tried to smile, but it was as though the skin of her face was heavy. Even so, she managed it and said, "And then you add a spoonful of tea for each person and one for the pot."

He watched as she did this, the water making a sloshing sound as it went into the pot. Russell tried to concentrate on the sound, as though it could protect him. Mrs. Deutsche put the pot and three cups on the table and then they all sat down.

"It takes about five minutes to steep," she said. She put one hand up to her hair and patted it, to make sure it was in place. Mr. Deutsche sat down and looked out the window. In the distance the pigeons flew around like shreds of dirty cloth. Russell put his hand on his cup and moved it around, but the grating sound made him stop. A log collapsed in the stove. The house made little noises, as though in the wind. Maybe, thought Russell, maybe I could tell them how much I liked their son. He looked at one of them and then the other. No, he thought, they just want to drink tea, to do anything they can to keep what I've brought into the kitchen away, to make it slow down.

Mr. Deutsche closed his eyes.

"Oh," he said. Then he shook his head.

Mrs. Deutsche poured out the tea and gave a cup to her husband, who took it and cradled it in his hands to feel the warmth, even though it was scalding. Russell took his cup. Mrs. Deutsche held hers, too, and blew softly across the surface. Russell looked at her pursed lips as she blew, and remembered when he had seen it before, in a house where a woman was having a baby without being able to get to a hospital. Her lips had been pursed like that when she panted to control the pain. Mr. Deutsche took a sip of the tea.

Russell bit his lip. The silence in the room was like a physical malicious thing: if anyone spoke, they would have to say things that no one wanted to say and hear things no one wanted to hear, and yet the silence sat right there, demanding, making it hard just to drink the tea. Russell swallowed and had the wild impulse to tell Mr. and Mrs. Deutsche that Zofia was pregnant, but then he stopped it, swallowed again, and had a sip of the tea. It was strong and good. He realized that what he wanted to do by telling them about the baby was to share some hope. It was a small thing against the way the house appeared there, perched on that landscape, like the scene of a crime.

"We just tried to make ends meet here," said Mr. Deutsche. "You know, we were almost able to make a go of it. When Tony was young."

"He didn't like to work on the farm," said Mrs. Deutsche.

"Yes," said Mr. Deutsche. "That's right. It's hard work."

"I'm sorry," said Russell.

"No," said Mrs. Deutsche. "Don't say that. Don't."

Russell took another sip. They finished the tea. The house creaked, and outside, on the road, a car went by, the sound of the tires hissing on the cold asphalt.

"Well," he said. "I don't want there to be any misunderstanding."

Mrs. Deutsche shook her head.

"No," she said. "There's no misunderstanding. The sergeant called before you got here. He said . . . he told us about Tony."

"I'm glad you were the one to come here," said Mr. Deutsche. "At least you had the sense just to drink your tea."

He put a hand to his face.

"How's your girlfriend?" Mrs. Deutsche asked.

"Fine," said Russell.

She nodded, putting a hand to her face.

"I think you better go," she said.

He stood up and she did, too, clinging to him. He could feel the thinness of her under the old sweater, the trembling against him, even through the body armor. Then she turned away.

Outside on the porch, Russell looked at the frozen puddles in the driveway and walked to the car, where he threw his hat onto the seat. Then he thought about the tea, which he wished he had never tasted. He started the car and turned around, and at the main road he went back toward the highway.

FRANK KOHLER

KOHLER SAT IN THE CRUISER. WHEN HE GOT OUT, as he did from time to time, he looked back the way he had come. There were ruts in the wood road, which were the color of clay, and between them rose a high center strip on which a fringe of grass grew. About a hundred yards back, the road curved around a hill and disappeared. He guessed that soon he should walk back that way and climb up on the hill so that when they came in here, looking for the car, he would be behind them, and uphill, too. The police would be going for the sound of the car, which they would hear because Kohler would leave the radio on, good and loud. He had decided on that, anyway. When they approached the car, he would be behind them. They wouldn't know he was there.

He got back behind the wheel and turned the radio on again. A lot of it was in code and numbers, but every now and then he heard his name, that people had reported seeing men who looked like him. Well, he thought, that was fine. By the time they got up here, they would be more tired, less alert. He had the shotgun and the rifle. He also had a uniform that had been left in the car, fresh from the dry cleaners, and a trooper's hat that was in the backseat. Kohler turned the radio up as loud as it would go, and put the trooper's hat on his head. If they saw him, up there on the hillside, they would think he was a policeman and hesitate before shooting one of their own. That hesitation would give him an advantage. I'll do everything, he thought, to make this more confused, more difficult, more uncertain.

As he put the shotgun on the roof of the cruiser and reached in to get the Mannlicher, he had the sense of making order out of this mess. He was going to climb uphill to find a place that had a clear view of the wood road and that was far enough away from the cruiser so that he could hear them coming, even with the radio on. There, up the hill, he'd feel the weight of the rifle and the shotgun. The light would be behind him when he put the forearm of the rifle against a tree to steady it, and, of course, a lot of other things would occur to him as he went along. He had had it up to here with vagueness and uncertainty and his inability to understand what was wrong. The weight of the rifle was ballast against all that. What he was interested in, he realized, was a moment of clarity, which he anticipated as golden heat and super brilliance, more platinum than gold, but whatever it was, it would be bright, clean, and filled with something knowable. He would emerge from the shadows he had lived in for years.

He picked up the rifle and walked back along the road he had driven in on, looking for a piece of high ground with good cover, below which there wouldn't be much brush. He stopped when he came to a clearing in the woods, above which, on the bank, a couple of old pine trees grew, each as big around as a barrel. He began to climb. At least he'd have good visibility.

The sun had come out in the afternoon, and it would be behind him. It felt good as he sat there, waiting. He knew that they would come, since the tracks of the cruiser at the beginning of the woods road would show that someone had driven up here, and when they began to check every road off the main one, they would surely see the marks. When they came along, they would approach from his left. He was about thirty feet above the road they would be on. A tree would give him cover and a rest to keep the forearm steady. He knew that the best way to hit someone who was moving wasn't to move the sights with him, but to keep them steady and just ahead of the man he wanted to shoot. Let him walk into it.

Kohler began to push the leaves away from his feet in a widening circle about five feet across. He wanted to have just the bare earth under his feet, since if he didn't have to worry about stepping on the leaves, he would be much quieter. No one would hear if he moved a little. He looked down at the brown dirt he stood on, soft and a little loamy. His feet moved in it without making a sound. Then he looked around, feeling the sunlight on his back. The caress of it made him think of the girl with the red hair.

She had a gift for reducing problems to their basic elements, and while she was superficial, with her Kool-Aid-dyed hair, her slang, and her teeny-bop clothes, she made him think that other, larger matters could be easily understood. It wasn't the simplicity of his circumstances that made him try to recall her red hair and her goofy smile, but how she would have made sense of this. The weight of the rifle and the certainty of what was coming was her kind of clarity, and even though he was glad she was gone, he still missed her. But the more he thought about her, with his feet on that circle of earth, the more he realized that this was about understanding. Or doing something that was to the point and definite.

The sunlight slanted through the woods, and in the long, cathedral-like lines of it, he saw the shadows of the trees delineated as though they were part of an art-deco design. The lines of light and shadow, the absolute stillness, hit him with a sense of longing and regret. No one wants to die. You always think of it as coming sometime, and everyone knows it is coming, but even so, in that final instant, you think, Not now. He swallowed. Well, this is another item to make definite, his fury about this last, horrifying regret. He stood there shaking, looking down at the wood road, ready to face everything that he couldn't shake.

He imagined the smell in the house where he had grown up, the aroma of rum and coke and the scent of perfume too expensive for someone like his mother to use. He remembered his uncle's house, too, and the bags from the fast-food places, McDonald's and Taco Bell, which was the best part: the paper had been clean. Then he thought of one of the Bob Jacks who had told him that he should never back down in a fight, that if he was going to have to fight, he should fight to win, and that there was nothing to do but to realize that that was the way things were. This brought him to a teary state again. *The way things were.* Well, he had some ideas about what to do about that.

He thought of Katryna's desire to be a train conductor and how she wanted to have a blue uniform with a hat with a gold badge on it and with brass buttons on the tunic. That was the word she'd used: *tunic.* He said it out loud. Then he thought of that click, click, click of the paper punch. He could remember the sound of it from the few times he and his mother had taken the train from Northampton to New Haven to go to the discount mall there, where he had been so happy to get a North Face coat that was a second. No one could see that the zipper didn't work. The reason Katryna had wanted to be a conductor was—or so she'd said—that on a train you were always getting away from somewhere. But now, as Kohler stood there desperately trying to remember the sound of that paper punch, he realized that yes, you can get away, but one day you are going to arrive, too.

He wondered how long it would be. The sun lay across his back and he closed his eyes from time to time as he trembled in the warmth.

Kohler noticed that the shadows of the trees all moved along together with the inexorable sweep of a sundial. As the sun moved, it settled in directly behind him, or that was the way it would seem to anyone walking on the road. Every now and then, no matter how hard he tried not to, he still moved his feet around in that brown circle.

He looked at the empty sky, just as he noticed, too, that these woods were unusually quiet. Even the smallest sounds and movement, which was a matter of small birds, like chickadees, had vanished, and as he sat there, trying not to move, he wondered if these creatures were able to sense something about to happen. He guessed it was possible. But he wished the birds would return, not because he cared about them, or wanted to see the small shapes of them, the chickadees flitting around like torn bits of black and white cloth, but because he didn't want the unnatural lack of sound to give him away. The dirt had thawed out in the circle at his feet and he smelled the acrid odor of it, like something at once familiar and yet unknown. The odor, perhaps, of a newly dug grave.

He had often seen vultures. They circled over the dump on the other side of the river, lifting together in a slow, wheeling circle, like bits of ash rising from a smoldering fire. He guessed that their feathers were black and as shiny as those long-playing vinyl records they used to have when he was a kid. That wheeling circle, those somber colors, or the spectral sunlight on them as they turned around and around, all meant something to him: that movement, around the attraction of a particular place, was precise in the face of everything that was vague and uncertain, and of course it was a sign of a final thing. He thought he should be able to take comfort in finality, which was all he had, but it was just another item that left him concentrating on the weight of the rifle.

He thought of those times in winter when he'd had to go out on a call and hadn't had the time to do a good job cleaning the snow off his car, and then, when he'd turned on the defroster, the snow had blown into the front seat. The golden and spectral particles revolved around him, like chaos visible, and yet like a hidden mystery that had just decided to let him have a glimpse of itself after all. And what was that mystery? Then, in a teary moment, he tried to say to himself, I don't have time for that anymore. I am going to solve it. I am going to know.

No birds. Nothing. Not a sound aside from the occasional rush of a jet overhead. The trails those planes left were white scratches in an otherwise pale blue sky, and they reminded Kohler of the time he had seen a piece of glass scored with a diamond. He was glad the girl had gotten away. She was so skinny and had those funny moles. Then he went back to waiting. He wished he had slept with her, but then, pretty soon, he was going to find a way to do something about regret.

From the main road, he heard a dog bark. In the cool air the sound seemed to float, to come and go, and then to disappear altogether. Kohler stared in the direction from which the barking came, and as he turned his head now, putting an ear toward the road rather than his eyes, he imagined the open mouth, the red tongue, the sharp teeth. Then he tried to feel the warmth of the sun, but there wasn't anything on his back except that slow, constant breeze, which came and went with an intermittent pressure. The dog went on barking.

RUSSELL BOYD

THE COMMAND POST HAD BEEN SET UP AT THE SIDE of the road in an old logging stage. At least it was a flat place, but now there were so many cruisers, from Vermont, New Hampshire, the Department of Fish and Game, and other outfits, like the U.S. Border Patrol, that it looked like a used-car lot for cruisers. In the center, two of them were parked side by side, nose to tail, one from Vermont and one from New Hampshire. That way the drivers could talk to each other just by speaking out the window. It was a method of trying to deal with the fact that Vermont and New Hampshire used different radio frequencies.

Russell looked at the two of them and glanced away. It was makeshift, and not very reassuring. Still, the men here began to work their way through the reports that came in, sightings of Kohler, or small robberies that could have been done out of desperation, but then there were always a fair number of these. The troopers tried to act as though everything was business as usual, but many of the men had known Tony and liked him.

Russell was assigned to look into a report that Tony's cruiser had been abandoned in the woods with the radio blaring. A boy had been out looking for his lost dog and heard the radio and seen tire tracks on the grown-over logging road. At least he'd had the sense not to go look for himself. The boy said that something about the un-naturalness of the noise made him walk down to the main road where he called the police. Still, it was hard to know what he had really seen and heard, since by the time Russell had been told to take a look, the report had gone through three dispatchers, a couple of troopers, and an administrator who had been called in to take charge. So, Russell drove to the beginning of the wood road where the tracks had been seen and waited for the other men who had been assigned to go along with him. At least, he thought, he wouldn't have to go up there alone.

While he waited for the others he ate his sandwich, taking a bite, chewing slowly, and thinking about Zofia. He wished that he could have said something before he left, but what? That he cared about her? Would that have been sufficient? He didn't know. The sandwich had been in a brown bag, and now he held the empty thing in his lap, not knowing what to do with it. He folded it up and left it on the seat.

The others began arriving. The first was a dog handler, a Vermont state police officer with graying hair. He was a tall man with a face that looked weathered, not by being outside in the winter, or in the heat of summer, but by looking into trouble. His name was Richard Bonowski. His German shepherd stood at the beginning of the wood road, tall at the shoulder, narrow in the hips, with very black eyes and pointed ears, and from time to time it looked in the direction they were going to go and barked. A man from the Department of Fish and Game arrived, too, Peter Michaels. He was in his forties and he was wearing the dark green uniform of a game warden.

"What's it like up there?" Russell said to Michaels, who, he guessed, as a Fish and Game officer, must have walked over every square foot of Vermont. He gestured up the wood road.

"I don't know," said Michaels, who had red hair and blue eyes. "I've never been up here. But that's where the cruiser is. I know the kid who heard it."

"Heard it?" said Santini, a blond trooper from a northern barracks, whose car had pulled up after Michaels's. "He didn't see it?"

"No," said Michaels. "He just heard a blaring police radio and came back out of there."

The four men stood at the beginning of the wood road, and there was an air of uncertainty about them, although each one looked in the direction they were going to go. It was as though they were wired together: one looked up the wood road, which disappeared in a V of the two hillsides, then the next looked, and then the others. After that they checked a firearm or tried to see if a portable radio was working, but there was so much traffic on the airwaves that they couldn't get through very often. The dog looked up the road, too, mesmerized, taking the air. They had started the dog on Kohler's jacket, which had been in the black car.

Russell wished that one of them had a topographical map so he could have an idea of what the land was like, and how high the banks on either side of the road were. He wanted to know if they were steep right along, or if they flattened out, or if there was a seasonal swamp up there, although he guessed that it might be frozen now. How frozen? Enough to walk on? Would they have to walk between these banks right along, or would the landscape give them room to move around? Now, though, he just stood there, looking up the road and imagining what it was like, but this was a matter of guessing. That wasn't the way to approach this, and he looked around again, trying to find the right attitude to walk up there, but what was that aside from trying to anticipate what he couldn't see? Then he wished he had said something to Zofia. I'm lost without you. I couldn't live without you. Was that true? Russell looked around at these hillsides and thought, Yes. It is. Well, maybe law school is the answer. Is that right?

The wood road looked like any other in this part of the state, two ruts that went between two hillsides covered with hemlock, pine, maple, and birch. The ground between the trees had a layer of cinnamon-colored leaves. Rhododendron and wild berry canes were at the side of the road and on the steep hillside. Everything about the place was unremarkable.

Everything here was so bland and unknown. What can you tell about a place that is undistinguished? Russell and the others had heard of sightings of a man who looked like Kohler in places a long way from here, and some of those reports had come from good observers. This only made for more vagueness, and none of the men here knew what they were really doing. Were they just checking out another false report, or was this something else? When Russell tried to think about it clearly, he couldn't tell what, if anything, was concealed by the lousy radio connections, the lack of a map, the different sightings and the terrain, which forced them into the bottom of a V.

The air wasn't very cold, and yet the shadows here hinted at those nights when it was ten below zero. Russell was hoping, he realized, that the guy was already dead, that is, if he was here at all. That was the likely thing. Then he thought that this was another useless desire. Nothing moved here, not a bird, not anything at all, and this left Russell considering how much he didn't know, rather than what he did. He looked down at the dog again.

At least Russell had had a chance to eat the sandwich.

"Well," said Bonowski. "We haven't got all day."

"No," said Michaels. "I guess not."

They started walking.

"What are you going to do for lunch?" said Santini.

"I don't know," said Michaels. "There's a diner in the next town up."

"Is it any good?" said Santini.

"Not really," said Michaels, putting the back of his hand to his lips as though it gave him indigestion just to think about it.

Bonowski went first, with the dog. Michaels followed next in his dark green uniform, which stood out incongruously against the landscape, and Santini walked along after him. Russell came last. He heard the sound of the dog panting as it went along the ditch at the bottom of the hill, head down, sniffing. Santini had a rifle. The others had handguns. They stayed on the side of the road that the dog worked, that is, the right-hand side, and they looked uphill from time to time, where they saw the whitish sky and the timber that was as gray as an elephant.

The half-frozen leaves made a soft crunch. As they went, Russell thought about escape, or the keen and yet panicky pleasure that people took in living in the moment, when they were trying to get away on the highway. What was it like for a man and a woman to get lucky, to slip by him and then pull into a motel? Russell imagined the sound of the clothes being removed, the sudden, impatient whisper of underwear slipping down a smooth leg, the creak of a cheap bed, the sound of the distant highway. Did they feel love then, or was it just excitement? Then he thought, Stop it, stop it. He watched the moving heads on the wood road, going in and out of those slanted rays of light.

The dog went back and forth along the ditch at the side of the road where water had collected and frozen. The ice in the ditch made a white and shiny curve about five inches wide, that ran up the road and out of sight. The air from the hillside flowed down and pooled by the ice and then probably seeped along the slight grade the men had climbed. Russell thought, Being on this road is a mistake. It is the way in. If someone is waiting, he knows we are on it. Then he looked around again at the blue sky, which seemed to form a wall just behind the trees. Russell couldn't tell if they should stop and think this over or if they should just keep going. It all looked so ordinary.

He was angry, too, and wished he wasn't, since all he wanted was to see the hillside through the perspective of an ordinary mood. Any other perspective was going to get in the way. The dog started barking and moving from side to side. The action of it, at the end of the leash, was like a kite in a wind, swinging this way and that.

"What's that?" said Michaels.

"He's got something," said Bonowski.

"Well, let's mark it," said Michaels. His green uniform stood out there as he looked down at ice at the side of the road. "Rub your foot in the dirt here. Then we can check it out on the way back. I think the first thing is to get to the car."

Russell waited, looking up the hill.

"All right," said Bonowski.

He put the heel of his boot into the soil in the middle of the road, and made a line with it, turning up the dirt in a small furrow, just like a line that a child would make at the beginning of a game. They went up a little farther, with the sun just setting at the top of the ridge. White on a cream-colored sky, like sun above a desert. The dog started barking again.

"He's got something," said Bonowski.

"Well, all right," said Michaels.

Everything about the wood road was stale. There was something in the air like fatigue from dirt and water that had frozen and thawed too many times. Russell looked around again at the white sun, which was the pale color of a snake belly.

"He's got something," said Bonowski.

"Mark it," said Michaels.

FRANK KOHLER

THE DOG APPEARED ON THE ROAD JUST BELOW
Kohler. A German shepherd with black fur on its back, although it was
tawny brown on its legs and part of its face. Kohler steadied the rifle against
the side of the tree. It was made of good German steel, and it had set triggers, or two triggers, one to make the other more delicate. The road was
tedious in its ordinary colors, in the banality of the dead grass and the clay
soil of the ruts. Then Kohler saw that the dog wasn't alone. It was being led
by a man.

The man and the dog fell back, and another man, in a green uniform,
came up the road and stood there, looking at something in the ditch that ran
parallel to the ruts. Kohler put one finger against the first trigger and used it
to make the second trigger more delicate. The rear sight was a flat piece of
metal with a V in the middle, and he put the bead at the rifle's muzzle so that
it perfectly filled that geometric opening. Down below the men moved under
this alignment, the dog going one way and another, the man in the green uniform less active, more pensive. Soon, Kohler guessed, the man would stop
puzzling over the ice in the ditch at the side of the road and realize that there
was someone just above him, or at least he would look uphill and see Kohler,
the rifle braced against the tree and wearing the trooper's hat.

Kohler saw, out of the corner of his eye, a little flash of movement, a
sudden appearance and then disappearance of red, and in a sudden awareness of that color, he thought that the girl was here, that they had caught her
and had dragged her in here to talk to him. But then he realized it was just
a bird, a cardinal. In this recognition that she had not arrived, his notion of
isolation was suddenly larger than it had been before, since if there was one
thing he would have liked, at this time, it would have been to see her. Or to
hear that throaty, out-of-character voice, that ability to sing in a deep register. He realized that it was a voice that would have left a low, vibrant resonance in the wood of an old church. More than anything else he craved her
ability to talk about the mysterious by using everyday details. Her charm

had been to combine the enormous and the ordinary, just like that. No big deal. Let's take a chance. If you're scared, break what you have to do down into small tasks. Want a hit of this dope? And what, he wondered, would she have made of this?

In the reassuring odor of the oil with which he had cleaned the rifle, in the sense of everything funneling around him, he thought, with angry horror, that the girl would have reduced this to the obvious. She would have said, Well, what's happening? What are you doing here? He looked around, thinking of her voice, of her way of making things clear, and he thought that this road, this moment, those men below, the fire in the house, the shooting at the side of the road were all obvious signs, and that each one came from one person, and that was him. These events showed how he had come into the world and what he had done here. His desperation, which he hadn't been able to control, had attracted everything that he hadn't been able to handle. And while he couldn't see what details he had muffed, what had been wrong in his perception, what impulses had been erroneous and sentimental, he nevertheless suspected with a trembling thrill that this was just one more flaw. Well, he would take responsibility, even for this last infuriating fact. His last hope and his last sense of beauty, which was the girl, had brought him to the certainty that this was all an expression of him. Where, he wondered, did knowledge stop and self-loathing begin? About right here, she would have said. Up against this tree.

Then he strained against all of the memories, the sounds, the silver bubbles in the water glass by his mother's bed, all of them blending together in one keen, bright instant, which arrived with a shock and a noise that sounded like the end of the world.

RUSSELL BOYD

MICHAELS FELL BACK WITH HIS HAND ON HIS LEG.
He didn't swear. He just fell on his back and then worked his way to the
side of the road, where that ditch was. The dog kept barking, and Bonowski
moved back, too, trying to get the dog and himself out of the way. The other
men looked up the hillside, where they saw a shadow by the tree against that
sun. Michaels was bleeding from the back of his leg, and he said, "Shit. He
shot my leg off. Can you believe it?"

Russell came up to him, his gun drawn, still looking up the hillside, and
as he knelt there, hearing another shot and seeing where it hit in the middle of the road, he heard Michaels say, "I can move my toes. Well, that's
something. How fast do you bleed out?"

"I don't know," said Russell. "You'll be O.K."

"Can you see him?" said Michaels.

"No," said Russell.

He stayed against the bank where they had a little cover. Michaels
looked up the hill and asked, "Is he coming down to finish me off?"

"No," said Russell.

"I think that's what he's going to do," said Michaels.

Russell looked around, back the way they had come, and wondered how
far it was. Then Santini sat down, too.

"I'm shot," said Santini. "That son of a bitch. That dumb fuck."

Michaels lay on his back, his feet toward the main road, his head toward
the hill where Kohler was. He couldn't turn over on his stomach, so he had
to point the pistol from where he was, on his back, so that from his perspective, the hill appeared upside down and disorienting. This combined
with the buzzing edge of blood loss and fear.

"I don't want him coming down here to get me. Is he going to do that?"

"I don't see him," said Russell.

"Does that mean he's coming?" said Michaels.

"No," said Russell. "It's going to be all right."

"Bullshit," said Michaels. He moved his boot again. "I can still feel them. But it's changing. It's getting a little numb." He looked up the hill, still on his back. "If he comes down here, you'll kill him, won't you?"

"Yes," said Russell.

Michaels lay there, his uniform green against the cinnamon-colored leaves on the bank and the grayness of the ditch. Russell knelt next to him, looking uphill, trying to see where Kohler was.

Santini sat farther up the road, and when Russell tried to get closer, another shot came from the hilltop. He pulled back and lay against the bank, hugging it, looking up but wanting to be careful about even that, since he wasn't sure if he was exposed. Santini said, "I'm lung-shot." He looked around, trying to see the hillside, and he said, "Is he going to come down here and kill me?"

"No," said Russell.

"I bet that's what he's thinking. He's got us down and now he's going to finish us off," said Santini.

The dog looked uphill and barked, and then Bonowski took out his radio and tried to speak and then listened, but all he heard was static.

"We can't receive here," said Bonowski. "But does that mean they can hear us?"

"I don't know," said Russell.

"Is he coming?" said Michaels.

The dog went on barking, moving from side to side on the leash, lunging uphill, its feet slipping on the ice at the side of the road.

"I'll be right back," said Bonowski.

He crouched over and started walking quickly, pulling the dog and still trying to stay low, against the bank, and when he was far enough away, he stood up and starting running. As Russell leaned up against the bank, he turned his head and saw the man and the dog as they disappeared in the V the hills made as they came down to the road. They just vanished, and when they did so the landscape seemed darker, the grays looking sootier and the browns appearing wetter and redder, too.

Russell tried to move closer, to get beyond Michaels, who still held the pistol on the hillside, and when Russell passed him, Michaels said, "What are you doing? He'll kill you. Don't you see?"

Russell could only see that pale sky and the shapes of the trees, and then when he tried to look at the spot where he thought Kohler was, his perspective had changed and all of the trees seemed to be in different places.

"I'm getting numb now," said Michaels.

"It'll be all right," said Russell.

"No," said Michaels. "What happens if I pass out and then he comes down here?"

Russell tried to get a little closer to Santini.

"I'm lung-shot," said Santini.

"You've got to promise me that you won't let him come down here," Michaels said to Russell.

Russell looked up the hill again. All he saw were those gray trunks and the light, the leaves, and all of it had the smell of dirt and rotting vegetation. And as he hugged the bank, Russell saw those long streams of light, filled with dust and looking as though they were drawn with a ruler. Then he tried to think of what to do. He found that he was waiting, looking to see if the man up above would show himself, and then he was hoping that he would, but he knew that this was going to get him nowhere.

Bonowski came back alone, running along the road and crawling along the bank, coming along until he stopped right at Michaels's feet.

"I got through on the radio out at the road," he said.

"Did you?" said Michaels. "What the hell did they say?"

"It won't be long," said Bonowski.

"Yeah," said Michaels. "Well, you know what, that depends on your point of view."

"Come on," said Bonowski. "I'm going to try to get you out of here."

They crawled along the road, keeping to the bank, starting and stopping, and then looking up. Russell thought maybe when they moved along like that, they'd have a chance. Michaels held his leg with one hand while he held his pistol in the other, and he and Bonowski kept moving and stopping, moving and stopping, and then they disappeared around the V of the hillside, leaving Russell and Santini alone. Russell wished that he could reach out for Santini and pull him in, and as he sat there he saw, about ten feet away, that the ice in the ditch had long threads of blood on it, seeping down toward him, and mixed in with the slow ooze there was water, too, which had melted because of the warmth. Then he looked up the hill again.

He guessed that help was coming, but he still felt the sluggish drag of time. It was so slow that he seemed aware of the space between his heartbeats, which he could hear as he kept his head down against the ground. More shots came from up above. Santini said, "I'm getting a little hazy. Kind of buzzy."

Russell had the sensation of being underwater too long, and that he needed to come up. He kept trying to make it to the surface, but he found that he was still down in the green depths and still desperate to breathe. He saw the light that came down in long rays from between the trees, and as he watched their milky illumination, he smelled the dirt. He wanted to move over to Santini, but when he did, there was another shot. And when he tried to wiggle back away from the place where he was exposed, down in the dirt and the damp, half-frozen ditch, there was another shot for that, too. So, he was stuck.

"It's so buzzy," said Santini. "Like everything is made out of bits."

"We'll get you out of here," said Russell.

"Just watch that guy so that he doesn't come down off of that hill," said Santini.

Russell looked around, when he dared, trying to stay still and yet looking for a moment when he could reach out there and grab Santini, but what then? Russell would have him in the same spot where he was, but the two of them together might stick out so much as to be exposed. Then Russell pushed up against the bank, trying to think. What settled over him, with a sensation of something like mist, was the certainty that he was here without knowing a thing. He didn't know if there was only one man up there, or how much ammunition he had. He wasn't even sure how exposed he was. Everything he had known, all the precision that he had learned, such as the ability to know what was going on without even really being aware of it, wasn't anywhere near enough. He was still down there in the green depths, desperate to inhale. Should he just step out there and get shot?

Then he looked up again and saw at the top of the hill, at the side of the tree, a man who was wearing a trooper's campaign hat.

"He's wearing a trooper's hat," Russell said to Santini.

"Well, maybe he's a cop," said Santini.

"Do you think a cop would do this?" said Russell.

"Not on purpose," said Santini.

"What is that supposed to mean?" said Russell.

"What it means is that I don't know if that's a cop or not. Or what is going on," said Santini, "aside from the fact that I'm getting shaky and everything is buzzing."

The silence oozed down the hill, like cool air. The radio from the cruiser was quiet, and he heard Santini's ragged, wet breathing. A slow, steady tick, tick, tick came from Santini's belt as repeated, rose-colored drops fell from it onto the ice and then flowed back toward Russell. He had the sense of claustrophobia that came from two things: the desire to sit tight, to do nothing, to stay right there, which came on him with a weight and that ugly sparkle which filtered down through the woods. The other impulse, which was as strong as the first, but intermittent and horrifying, was the desire to reach out to the rifle that Santini had dropped.

Russell's knees, arms, and face were cold from hugging the dirt, which smelled like the cellar of an old farmhouse. He looked at the rifle.

The coldness of the ground was irritating and unfriendly, too, since as Russell pressed against it, the cold dirt was unyielding and wouldn't let him get in where he wanted to be. As he struggled, thinking of how it would be good if he was down inside the ground, just a little, he suddenly wanted to push himself away with all the horrified revulsion one feels at a grave. And as he waited there, the odor of the earth changed, too, no longer just the ammonia-like stench of leaves rotting from the fall, but the smell of a newly dug hole in the ground where someone was going to be left forever. Then he glanced at the sky and the shapes of the trees with all the horror of obliteration. All of the vagueness disappeared in the realization that one specific man wanted specifically to kill him. And what was the next thing to discover here, in that now thoroughly illuminated fragrance of the earth?

Santini had dropped the rifle when he fell back, and the muzzle had leaves around it, which could have been just debris, but then it was possible that there was mud stuck into it, too. The ice and the oily metal of the rifle were lost in the glare of sunlight.

It couldn't be too much longer before other men showed up, and yet sitting here was wrong: the silence overwhelmed him and left him with a sense of being reduced, pressed down to nothing. He listened to the ragged breathing and turned on his back to see if anyone was coming up the road, and realized he couldn't see very far that way, either. What he needed, in that moment, with that flowing silence and the sense that it was impossible to breathe, to think, to do anything correctly, was a sense of certainty, which was the last thing in the world he had. So he looked at the glare of the ice, saw the blood drip onto it in that appalling cadence, and heard the sound of the breathing. Then the radio in the cruiser came on again.

He heard the radio and the voice on it, the steady, repeated, unempathic voice of the dispatcher. Then Santini started a slow, constant swearing, a cursing that missed no one and nothing. In the sound of that despairing voice, Russell thought of the white horses in the hunt, which had come along beyond the screen of brush. All he knew was that he was disoriented by his contradictory, constant impulses, which mixed so perfectly with the smell of the dirt.

He reached out and took hold of Santini's black boot. It was soft and had been shined that morning. Russell could smell the polish. He put his hand out there and realized that he had shoe polish on his fingers. Then he pulled himself closer. Santini grunted and said, "What the fuck are you doing?" Russell stumbled beyond him and picked up the rifle, and sat back down against the bank. He tried to think, Put on the safety, put it on before you dig the leaves and the mud out of the muzzle, because it makes no sense to shoot your fingers off. Then, as he picked the leaves and muck out, lying on his back and hearing Santini's breathing, he had the sensation of having been suspended in a moment in which nothing had happened at all, an emptiness, that left him trembling. He swallowed and looked around, and then rolled over and put the bead on the side of the tree, and when the man in the blue shirt leaned around the trunk, Russell shot. It was the recoil and the obvious impact that seemed to clarify everything. The noise was loud, and as his ears rang, the man slumped back behind the tree, but Russell kept shooting, keeping him there, and when the man looked around again, Russell shot and saw him snap back and drop.

A station wagon backed up the road. Bonowski and other men were using it as a shield, all of them coming along slowly, and when they were pretty close, Russell went on shooting and the others picked up Santini and loaded him, although they dropped him once. Then, when the station wagon drove away, two other men took places around Russell, one looking on one side of the tree and one on the other, and all of them waiting: what

Russell had was that sense of everything and nothing, that coming and going, that silence and noise like an A-bomb.

After a while they began to work their way up the hill, a group of men giving fire while one of them moved closer, and finally Russell saw that Kohler was lying there in a circle of dirt where the leaves had been pushed away. He wasn't moving. Then the other men came up and looked, too, and after a while they walked right up to him.

"Do you recognize him?" one of the men asked.

"Yes," said Russell. "I recognize him."

"What the fuck was wrong with him?"

"I don't know," said Russell. "Who knows?"

"Is he dead?" said one of them.

A man reached down and put his finger against Kohler's neck.

"Yes," he said.

"Well, that's something," said the one who had asked.

RUSSELL BOYD

RUSSELL OPENED THE SCREEN DOOR AND TOUCHED it with his fingers so that he could feel the coarse weave of it, which felt like the texture of a nylon stocking. He was determined to replace it with the glass insert. Then he went into the kitchen and felt the absence of Zofia: it wasn't just a lack of noise, but the presence of something else, a stillness that was filled with what it is like to reach out for someone who isn't there, and this was endless, since the impulse to find her came again and again and was answered with the same quiet oblivion. It permeated everything, and if he had gone to her closet and looked at her clothes, her absence would have been even more palpable. Then he sat down at the table.

He thought of the explosions on the wood road, the dripping of the blood on the ice, and the misty light as it slanted down between the trees. His ears were still ringing from the shots, and that only made the transition from one place to another all the harder. But, at the same time, he didn't want to move, or do anything at all. He waited. Once he put his hand to his face and smelled gunpowder.

The first thing that announced Zofia's arrival was the car coming into the drive, and when he looked out the window, he saw her pull up to the door behind the house and get out with a bag of groceries. Greens were sticking out the top, and the paper was brown, practical stuff, which Zofia saved. She had the bag in one hand and a gallon of milk in a glass bottle in the other. She always said she was reassured by the old-style glass container. She came up to the door, and he opened the inside one, and then they stood opposite each other with the screen between them. He pushed it open, and she came in, carrying the bag, which she dropped on the table along with the milk. Celery and lettuce spilled out, and she just left it there, putting one hand to her face. Then she tried to kiss him, but her lips were shaking and it wasn't a kiss so much as a fluttering, wet touch. Then she put her hands on his arms, on his neck and chest, his head, going over him to make sure everything was all right.

"You know, I thought . . ." she said. Then she stopped, her superstition and her delicacy bringing her to an abrupt silence. She didn't want to say, I thought you were dead.

"Shot," he said.

"Yes," she said. "Or worse. I heard there was trouble up there halfway to Canada, and when I called, the dispatcher said you were up there and that as far as they knew, you were trapped . . ."

He swallowed.

"It's over," he said.

"And then a cruiser came up to the door, and when I saw it wasn't you, I thought they had come to tell me," she said. "But they said you were all right . . ."

She kissed him on the cheek and then they both sat at the table with their chairs pulled up to each other. Their knees were about a foot apart.

Russell looked around the kitchen, and as he sat there he couldn't shake the way the woods had looked. If he closed his eyes, the bland and stark blacks and whites, the grays and light grays, all came back, like something on the inside of his eyelids.

"So, you're all right," she said.

"I wouldn't say that," he said. "No."

"But not hurt," she said. "I mean not injured . . ."

He shook his head. He wanted to be able to say something that made sense, or that could convey anything at all, but he didn't even know for sure what had happened there: it was as though everything had opened up and let him have a look, but here it was hard to say what it was. He recalled the intensity, and when he did, he found that he was looking at her, blinking.

"What happened?" she asked.

He looked at her again.

"I don't know. I don't know what was worse, that noise, that shooting, or the waiting, the knowing I had to do something, but it wasn't obvious . . . just, I don't know . . ."

"That's all you have to say?" she said.

Her hands were shaking as she touched her mouth.

"No," he said. "I just need to think about it."

She nodded.

"And there's something else. I'm going to fix that screen door right now."

"What?" she said. "You're going to do what?"

"I'm going to fix that screen door," he said.

He stood up and went down into the cellar where they kept the glass panel to put in place of the screen, although down there in the dark, he stopped at the smell of dirt. Then he brought the glass back into the kitchen.

"Do this some other time," she said.

"No," he said.

"Look," she said. "I want to know what happened."

"It wasn't like that," he said. "It wasn't like something that happened at one moment and it was done. It was something else."

"Like what?" she said.

"I don't know," he said.

He put the glass panel down and opened the door.

"Don't," she said. "Just wait."

She sat there, shaking. He began to unscrew the tabs that held the screen in. She stood up, still shaking.

"We've got to talk," she said.

"Of course," he said. "I just don't know what to say."

"Were you scared?" she said.

"That doesn't do it," he said. "That doesn't even come close."

"Then what comes close?"

He shrugged and tried to undo the tabs.

"Great," she said. "That's great."

"Please," he said.

"Please what?" she said.

He stood there, undoing the next tab with a small Philips screwdriver.

"Well?" she said.

He took off the next one: it was important to get rid of the screen, of the thing that had been between them, and even though he knew this was probably not the right thing to do, it was all he could think of to get a moment's relief. Zofia watched him and went over to the kitchen sink and picked up a glass from the sink and threw it on the floor, where it shattered with perfect symmetry, the rays of glass shooting out in all directions and skittering across the floor like ice. Then there was only silence in the kitchen. Russell stopped what he was doing and came over to the sink and said, "Is that what you want? You want to break things?"

"Yes," she said. "Yes."

He picked up a tumbler and threw it on the floor, the glass shattering just like the first time, although he threw it much harder and the glass spread across the floor in those same rayed patterns, only going farther this time, hitting the half-open door and going into the next room, leaving the two of them in the center of those icy rays, which, even as they lay there on the floor, still suggested movement, as though somehow or other this was an ongoing explosion more than one that had come and gone. He reached for another glass.

"Why stop?" she said. "Why not break everything?"

She stepped back and bumped the table, where the groceries were, and as the table lurched, the glass milk container rocked back and forth at the edge before falling and shattering on the floor, the milk coming out in a white, almost beautiful wave, before splashing on the floor and leaving both of them standing in a pool of it.

"Goddamn it," she said. "Look what you made me do."

"Me?" he said. "You're accusing me?"

"I don't know," she said.

She stepped forward in the milk and broken glass.

"Please," she said.

"Please what?" he said.

She tried to kiss him, but it was the same shaking half-attempt, trembling and not really a kiss at all. He put down the glass, but when he held her it was awkward with the body armor and the fact that they were standing in the broken glass and the milk. As they clung to each other, he said, "What do you want, what the hell do you want?"

"I don't know," she said. "Or I know. Or I don't know."

She swallowed and put her hand to her face.

"Well, which is it?" he said.

"I don't know," she said.

"Well, I do," he said. "You don't have someone try to kill you without being sure of—"

"Stop," she said. "Please."

She leaned against him in the body armor.

"O.K.," he said. "All right."

But then it started again: he looked at the glass in the window and thought about throwing a bottle through it. He stepped through the mess and slammed the door, the house trembling with it.

"Don't," she said.

She put a hand to her face.

"Well, are you going to tell me or not? What do you want?" he said.

"I want . . ." she said.

"What? For Christ's sake."

"I want to have this baby," she said.

He heard the ringing in his ears.

They got down on the floor with towels that Russell brought in from the bathroom and started sopping up the milk, and when they had gotten most of it, they picked up the glass pieces, putting them into the brown bag that had held the groceries, the large ones going in first, although there weren't too many of those, since the glass had shattered more than broken. Zofia cut her finger and then watched as the blood ran from it onto the glass, the red throbs of it making splashes there, just like bleeding onto ice. Russell got a dish towel and gave it to her and then started sweeping up the glass as quickly as he could, getting it into the dustpan and then into the bag, before going back and sweeping the kitchen, looking for the small bits of it and trying to get them all. Then he threw the bag in the trash, put the broom away while she sat at the table with a napkin wrapped around her hand. He pulled up a chair.

He put his hand in hers and both of them sat there, not trembling exactly, just sitting there and listening to the house. It was cold and the furnace throbbed.

After about a minute, Zofia looked up at the answering machine, which was by the telephone. The red light on it was blinking.

"Maybe you better see who called," he said.

"Later," she said. "I don't want to deal with anything now. That's something from this morning."

He got up and pushed the button.

There was a beep and then a woman with an accent said, "Hi, Zofia, this is Katryna." She was silent, just holding the phone. "I . . ." Then she stopped again. "A friend is visiting from Russia and he's going to give me the money today, I think." She stopped. "So, I'll have it for you." Then she went back to waiting. "There's something else. I was wondering if you could help me look for a job." She was quiet again, obviously weighing whether Zofia could be trusted. "The railroad seems like a good idea. I have been thinking about it. At night, when the wind blows the right way you can hear the whistle of the engines. Anyway, do you know how to apply? Do you start at the union, and is there one for conductors?" She paused again. "It doesn't have to be that, though. Anything would be O.K." In the background someone spoke Russian. Then Katryna used a couple of phrases of Russian, too. "I've got to go," she said. More Russian could be heard in the background. Katryna said into the phone, "O.K. *Poka.*" She laughed. "I can't tell if I'm speaking Russian or English. *Poka* is Russian for, um . . ." A man's accented voice in the background said, "So long, see you, *ciao.*"

"So long," said Katryna, as though she were trying to memorize it. "So long."

ZOFIA WIRA

ZOFIA WAS SURROUNDED BY SHADES OF WHITE,
from cream to shell, from china to a hue that was like the arctic, tinted with
an almost impossible-to-see blue. And along with the colors there were tex-
tures, too, where the dresses were hung, one against another, chiffon, cotton,
chenille, silk, satin, and other fabrics she had never seen before. It was like
looking at a selection of clouds. Her fingers touched the bone-colored material. She hesitated at the rustle of each dress, and as she stood in the cloud-
like masses of white and the miasma of sizing, she felt the attraction of the
color. Surely she was grown up and modern enough to be able to dismiss the
dresses in this store as being antiquated and silly, and yet she found it exciting to be here, so much so that she blushed.

The first thing she wanted was to look attractive, not sexy, not innocent,
but womanly and beautiful in a way that could be felt as well as seen. And
how was she going to suggest this secondary quality? She wanted to have a
kind of luminescence, which she guessed would come from her, separate
from the dress, although there were some shades that might be better than
others. She was drawn to the purity of the color, but purity, as far as she was
concerned, had nothing to do with innocence, since she perceived purity as
being one and the same with certainty. Her lack of innocence allowed her
to be intense in her desire to be married, and it was all the more pure for not
being ignorant. She thought of this difference as being the critical one
between girls and women.

Then she went back to looking at the fabrics, wanting a dress made of
cotton in case it got wet, rejecting satin as gaudy and not much better than
chiffon. In the shades and hues of white, she detected something else, which
was the scale of what she was doing, just as she was struck by a hint of mortality in all of this: the dress she picked out would be recorded in a photograph of her that would be shown to a member of a future generation, yet
unborn, a granddaughter or great-granddaughter. What subtle message,

what delight and pleasure, what restraint and beauty did Zofia want to send across time?

She had considered wearing her mother's wedding dress, which had been put away, but she had looked at it with a certain unnameable queasiness. The yellowed fabric was evidence of the passage of time and a staleness, too, in how people began to take each other for granted. She didn't want a reminder of that.

Then she continued from one dress to another, and as she touched the white material, as she held it up to the light and carried it to the front of the store where she could see it in the sun, she felt charged by possibility. The sunlight on a white cotton dress in the front of the store seemed to waver with a variety of brilliance, and as she turned away, she was more certain than ever of how broad the spectrum of possibility really was, from the whitest desert to the most shocking white of the arctic, from material that showed blood on a martyr's robe to the glare that produces snow blindness.

White, as far as she was concerned, was the blankness of the beginning, as cool as starlight and untroubled by ugly necessity. It had other associations, like the color of the belly of a snake, or the pallor of the albino, and yet these things detracted not at all from the gravity of the color. In fact, the ugliness of these hues, so imbued with deformity and danger, only made white more substantial and compelling.

Then she picked up a dress, more simple than not, not low-cut, but trim around the waist and ribs, a little lacy. It wasn't for a sedate bride, but for a woman who knew something about herself and was glad to have the chance to see if she was right about what she knew. In the color, as white as sand at midday in the Sahara, she realized that this hue was the opposite of everything she had previously been afraid of. This, of course, had been the speckled darkness of the night, the sparkling gloom that was Russell's companion on the road, not to mention another quality, hard to describe but still noticeable. This emotional essence, which she thought of as a shadow, at once inky and ill-meaning, was at the heart of events gone wrong. The whiteness of the dress showed her defiance and her delight.

She went up to the saleswoman, who had obviously spent one too many days with women who couldn't make a decision.

"I'll take this one," she said.

Outside, in the street, she found Russell waiting, and when she came up to him with the oversized white bag, filled with the dress and the pale fluff of tissue paper, he said, "Uh-oh, what's wrong?"

"Nothing," she said, putting a hand to the side of her face, next to her eyes. "It just wells up like that from time to time."

"Oh," he said. "But is there something wrong?"

"Oh, no," she said. "There's nothing wrong."

"Then why do you get teary?" said Russell.

"It's just hard to describe. That's all." She reached into her handbag for a Kleenex. "Cut a girl a little slack, will you? Can't you see when someone's happy?"

Both of them turned to the window of the store they stood in front of, where she blew her nose into a Kleenex and stood for a moment, taking a deep breath.

"Well," she said. "I hope you like the dress."

RUSSELL BOYD

RUSSELL HAD A MONTH OFF AFTER THE SHOOTING
on the wood road. He got up early, with Zofia, who was in a hurry to take
her shower and dress, doing so with an air or perfectly controlled impa-
tience. They had coffee together. That was it. She got up and put on her coat,
the rustle of it a little sad, or so it seemed to Russell, but then he thought this
was just a mood and that it would pass. She went out the door, and he sat at
the table, looking out the window at the snow. It was winter, and snow had
piled up around the house, and the fields of white were like a desert.

Then the sound of her car disappeared and he waited while the silence
came back. It arrived like a toothache. At first he noticed it only a little, but
then more and more, and finally he got up and slammed the ice box door
and sat down again, looking around as though the sucking of the rubber seal
and the slap of the metal door would change the way things appeared. All
he wanted was certainty. This was the first thing, but as he looked out the
window, he realized that this was an impossible desire, and yet, as he admit-
ted this to himself, he was only more uncomfortable.

He didn't like the idea of luck, either. What was certain about that?
Luck offended him through its connection to the chaotic. Everything he had
taught himself had been designed to avoid the surprise of the chaotic, and
now he realized his error had not been what he had taught himself, but that
he hadn't really known what chaos was. Now he did.

He tried to read such books as Livy's *War with Hannibal* and *The March
Upcountry,* which he tried to understand as men making effort in the face of
impossible odds, and yet it wasn't the effort he needed or wanted. He was
ready to make effort. It was a notion of certainty that he craved, and the
desire to know what kept these human beings from panic.

The weeks passed. He thought that his task was to distinguish between
anxiety and fear, and how do you do that? In the midst of a snowstorm,
when the stuff came down in long, white ropes, like twine, he realized that
he would have to go back to work. What else did he have?

The first afternoon he dressed and went out to the cruiser, where he took the tuning fork from the glove box of the car to check the radar. Then he got in, behind the wheel, with the sandwich in a bag on the seat next to him. At least his desire to be alert was informed by an understanding of loneliness, which was something new. A knowledge of loneliness goes hand in hand, he thought, with a knowledge of the chaotic. He swallowed when he sat in the car and put the tuning fork away. He was slowly working his way around a central, essential matter, and he didn't know what made him more uneasy: the circuitous way he was working, or the thing that he was going around. He had to do and not do at the same time, to be afraid and not afraid, and how did that happen in the moment, in the instant that was about to shatter?

He had a dream that was so obvious as to leave him ashamed of its lack of symbolism. He dreamed he was with a good friend. A long, white, fingerlike tentacle, about twenty feet long, came into the room and reached out for Russell. He knew that he had to take hold of it, no matter what it would do to him, and when he was about to do so, he woke up with chills on his neck and back, which recurred in constant, repeating thrills as he recalled that white tentacle. Then he got up and walked around, knowing what the dream meant, that something had come into his life and he had had to take action; the impact of the dream hadn't been just the fact, though, but the atmosphere, which was that of being in the midst of pure malevolence. The chills came on him even during the day when he thought of being at the thing's mercy.

He parked in a turnout on the interstate and faced the car toward the south. It was just dusk, and he found that he wasn't looking forward to the night in the way he had before, if only because at night so much more was concealed, and he wasn't in the mood for anything that was concealed. He had a book, too, of names, and he spent a minute or two looking through it, trying to come up with something large and yet without pretension. What was that? He liked the name Roman, but he wasn't sure. Zofia probably wouldn't like it, but then she would probably like Peter or Jack. Delilah or Virginia? As he sat there, thinking this over, a car came out of the dusk.

At this hour, everything appeared in shades of blue, and Russell looked at the tinted snow, the clouds that were fading to night, the tires on the aqua blush of the concrete of the highway, and the air itself, which was perme-

ated with a hue that was the color of a new bruise. The car was a blue
Chevrolet, about ten years old, and as it came up from the south, the windshield was filled with that film of reflected sky, at once shiny and impenetrable. The radar showed it was going close to eighty, and when it came by,
Russell could see the interior: two men, both with gray hair and pale skin,
as though they never saw the sun and lived on potato chips and Twinkies,
candy bars and Coke. And yet the color of their skin wasn't only unhealthy,
but a fish-belly or snake-belly white, from which people naturally recoil.
The car went by in a rush and then continued north, trailing away and leaving behind that whine of tires and the momentarily troubled air.

Russell pulled the cruiser into gear, and looked south to see if anyone
was coming. Then, as the car disappeared altogether into the increasing
gloom of the afternoon, he hesitated. He sat back and waited. Now the
silence seeped into the front seat, just the way it had at home. He looked
down at the book of names, and then back at the sky, which was fading in
earnest, the clouds becoming walls and the distance beyond them becoming
opaque. His hands were damp, and he wiped them on his trousers.

The next one was a Toyota, a faded green that was hard to see in the
dusky light. Older, a little rusted. A woman was driving and there was a
man in the passenger seat, looking straight ahead. It was as though the passenger were made out of some hard yet frangible substance, like plaster of
Paris, and he was so rigid that he could be leaned up against a wall like an
ironing board. The woman was going seventy-five miles an hour and she
didn't signal when she went around another car, trying to get into the slow
lane. One brake light was burned out. Still, as Russell sat there, his hand on
the book of names, he hesitated: perhaps it would be better to wait for a jack-
ass from Connecticut in an SUV who was going ninety miles an hour. He
swallowed and then pulled out, smoking it up to catch the car with the
burned-out brake light.

The dispatcher told him the car was registered to a man who lived in
Irasburg, near the border. Kent Wilson. He had a couple of arrests for burglary, possession of stolen property, and assault. Russell came up behind
them and turned on the lights. They pulled over. The man looked straight
ahead, not one way or the other. The woman glanced in the rearview mirror, her eyes lingering there with more than the usual anxiety.

Russell stepped into the bluish air, which moved in sudden pulses as the cars went by. In the cold and the stink of exhaust, in that fading light, Russell thought, Maybe this is a mistake. Maybe I should have waited longer.

"Hi," he said, when he came up to the car. "Do you know why I stopped you?"

"No," said the woman. She had brown hair, cut short, and she was wearing a sweater and a pair of blue jeans. Russell glanced in at the man in the car, who wasn't rigid so much as trembling with effort. Hands on his knees. Looking straight ahead. Russell swallowed. He tried to think of something he could depend upon, and what came to mind was how to manage trouble, or how to talk to people, which was to be friendly, always leaving them the sense that they had a way out, and then, if you found something out, to go after them again later. The idea was to keep the tension expanding and contracting. He looked up at the sky, the layers of clouds with the transparent blue between them, like black paper spread on a tropical sea.

"You were speeding, and you didn't signal back there. The taillight is out," he said.

"Oh," she said. "Sorry. I was just passing that guy back there."

"No big deal," said Russell. "I just want to get you on your way here."

"I told you to fix that light," the woman said to the man.

"I didn't know anything about it," the man said.

"I told you," she said.

"It's no big deal," said Russell.

He took her license and the registration and went back to the cruiser. The dispatcher started checking on the woman, whose name turned out to be Becky Allen. Five feet five inches, a hundred and twenty-five pounds, brown eyes and brown hair. She lived in St. Johnsbury. As he held the license and looked out the window of the cruiser, he couldn't tell if there was any reason to be afraid or not, and so he just watched as the car he had stopped was absorbed into the evening light. The snow faded from a cold-lip blue to a barely luminous gray, the shadows disappearing there as though they had never existed. The chills from the nightmare came back, too.

He got out of the cruiser as the cars passed, the sound of the engines and tires on the concrete tailing away, and he was left with a peculiar sense of being abandoned. Mostly he just wanted to do his work without having to think about other cars, but tonight he wished there had been more traffic.

Up here it came in discrete collections of cars and trucks with long moments between them.

He walked back up to the window and said to the man in the passenger seat, "Are you the owner of this car?"

The man swallowed. He still looked forward, not wanting to swing his eyes toward Russell.

"Do you have any identification?" Russell said.

"No," he said. "I wasn't driving, so I left my license at home." The man hesitated. "It's mine."

"So you're Kent Wilson?" said Russell.

The man nodded.

"Yeah," he said.

"O.K.," said Russell. He tried to watch the stiffness, or to see what was causing it. "No big deal. I want to get you on your way."

He looked into the backseat, but the only things there were a take-out bag that hamburgers had come in, and a woman's jacket. He didn't see anything else out there in the open, like a syringe or a plastic bag. Nothing that he could put his finger on.

"Would you mind stepping back to my car," said Russell to Becky Allen, "so I can write the ticket and then get you on your way?"

The man in the front of the car looked straight ahead, although for one instant he glanced at her. Then he went back to staring.

"Sure," she said. "That's all right."

She got out of the car. Russell said, "You aren't armed, are you?"

She shook her head.

"No," she said. "Nothing like that."

They walked back to his car and she got in on the passenger's side and he got in behind the wheel. She looked a little tired, but it only added to her tension, as though she had to do something and yet as she tried to do it, she had to use more and more energy, so that when she was only halfway done, she had only a quarter of the energy she needed. She put a hand to her hair and pushed her bangs back, and then turned to him. The difficult thing was that every time he got things going the way they should, he didn't feel that he was proceeding in the right direction. Instead, he thought that he was just getting in deeper. At least he could say clearly to himself that he didn't like this sense of being swept along.

Up ahead, Kent Wilson sat in the car and stared straight ahead.

"Kent isn't armed, is he?" said Russell.

She shook her head, although there was something about her movement that said this wasn't an unreasonable question to ask.

"No," she said.

"You're sure?" said Russell.

"Yeah," she said. "As far as I know."

"Where were you coming from?" said Russell.

"Oh," she said. "We just went down to Springfield, Mass., you know."

"What were you doing down there?"

"We went to look for a sofa," she said. "There's a big discount place down there?"

"What's it called?" he said.

"Cost Busters," she said.

"Find anything?" he said.

"No," she said.

"Well," he said. "Everyone likes a bargain, I guess. Do me a favor, will you? Just wait here while I talk to your friend. O.K.?"

"Sure," she said.

Russell got out of the car and went up to Kent Wilson's. It was getting cold, but he didn't want to get into the car with him. Instead he went around to the passenger's side and said through the window, which was rolled down a little, "I'm almost done here. Just going to write this up. Can you tell me where you are coming from?"

"I don't know," he said.

"I mean," Russell said. "Just now. Didn't you go down to Massachusetts?"

"Oh, yeah," he said. "We went down there."

"Where did you go?" said Russell.

"A tire store," said the guy.

"I guess you've got to have tires," said Russell.

The man then looked back up the road, his eyes almost lazy, as though when he was scared, his heart slowed down. The car faded into the night, and Russell noticed that the lights of cars, on the other side of the highway, were on now. Reassuring, but distant.

Then he started walking back toward the cruiser in the keening sound of a truck. Perhaps he should just write the ticket and let it go, but instead he got back into the cruiser and said, "How long have you been using heroin?"

"What?" said Becky Allen.

"Look," said Russell. "I'd like to help."

The girl looked straight ahead.

"Did he say anything?" she said. She made an angry gesture with her head toward the car where Kent Wilson sat. The perfume she had on, the faintly sweaty odor of the T-shirt she was wearing, a nutty fragrance from her hair, and the sad, total lack of movement of her eyes—all that made her seem like desperation itself. Russell wondered if she was infecting him with it, so that the two of them were in a companionship of fear.

"What do you think?" he said.

"I don't know," she said. "I don't know."

They sat there for a while.

"I just don't know," she said.

Russell started sweating. When he looked on the other side of the road, where the lights were so golden, he was reminded of those long, perfectly straight rays of light on that wood road. Without thinking, he said, "I don't know."

"What?" she said. She looked at him. He was staring straight ahead, watching the first stars up ahead as they appeared in the northern sky. "Are you O.K.?"

He wiped his forehead with his handkerchief and nodded. In the desperation of her glance, Russell felt a sudden, piercing empathy.

"You don't look it," she said.

"It's all right," he said. He put the handkerchief away. "Well, how long?"

"A while," she said.

"Are you carrying anything now?" he said.

"I don't know," she said. "I just don't know."

Russell tried to see how the other car was sitting on its springs: was it canted over more than it should be, or was that just the way it sat on the side of the road?

"Is it O.K. if I look in the car?" said Russell.

"Sure," she said. "Go on."

He picked up the microphone and asked for someone else from the barracks to come out to be there when he did this, since he didn't want to be alone with his head in the car while the woman and the man stood around. The dispatcher said Huntington, number 239, was on the other side of the highway, close by. He'd be there soon.

Becky Allen sat without moving in the lights from the dashboard. As it got darker, the lights gave her skin a greenish cast, and from time to time she glanced at him, her eyes filled with a color like artificial lime. There was something about the vital promise of her, even here, no matter how desperate she was, that made this moment even worse. Russell talked about the weather, the length of the winter, and she just nodded, Yeah, yeah, yeah. Huntington arrived, pulling up behind Russell's cruiser like a shark gliding out of the depths.

"I never thought it would turn out this way," she said.

"I know," said Russell.

"What do you know?" she said.

Russell shrugged. He got out of the car and saw that Huntington had gotten out of his car, too. Russell had the sense of the cars, of the people in them, of himself standing there as a kind of animation, as in a computer game. Then he shook his head and said to Huntington, "I'll be right back."

Russell went up to the other car and told Kent that he was going to take a look in it. Then Russell leaned behind the driver's seat and smelled the stink of the old hamburgers. He put his hand along the rear of the seat, careful about it in case a needle was in there. But, even so, his hands were sweating and he tried to be alert: wasn't that the solution? Then he moved the floor mat aside and saw a small gold ring. The man in the front seat turned back and looked at Russell, then glanced down. When Russell glanced up, they were looking into each other's eyes.

"You know," said Kent Wilson, "this isn't good. I mean somehow or other this is going wrong. Right from the beginning."

"Like how?" said Russell.

"Oh," he said, "like getting stopped. You'd think she'd drive better than that, you know what I mean?"

The man pushed his hair back with both hands.

"I'd like to work this off," the man said. "You know? I'd like to give you something. I'd like to get credit for something. You see what I mean?"

"Sure," said Russell. "Like what?"

"She's carrying it," said Kent.

"Where?" said Russell.

"Just ask her," said the man.

Outside, the highway glowed with the last light. Russell turned back toward his car, but as he did so, he tried to take a deep breath, and to think. The man had given up Becky too easily.

He got into his car and sat behind the wheel.

"I'm going to have to search you," said Russell to Becky. "Or you could just give it to me."

"He said something," she said. She gestured. "Didn't he?"

"I don't know what you mean," said Russell.

"Yes, you do," she said. "Yes, you do. That son of a bitch. And to think . . ."

It was totally dark now, and her face was more tired than ever in the green light. She rocked back and forth.

"I don't know," she said. "I don't know."

"Look," said Russell. "I'm going to have to get a search warrant. And then we're going to have to go to the hospital. That way you can have an internal examination."

"I don't know," she said.

"That's the safest thing," said Russell. "That's where you're carrying it, isn't it?"

She sat there without moving, her eyes set on the distance. Every now and then a car went by, its taillights describing long, curving arcs, like tracer rounds.

"I've never been so alone," she said.

"I know," he said.

"I'm not going to cry," she said. "What good does it do anyway?"

"It might help," said Russell.

But he knew that it wouldn't help, and he guessed that as far as she was concerned, everything around her was chaotic; at least he understood what that was like. In a way that he found hard to describe, the sense of both of them confronting a similar difficulty, although from different ends of the world, was reassuring. It was the sense that something in his heart was connected to something in hers. Usually he was repelled by people who were carrying drugs, but in the moment he had the impulse to show a small, perfect tenderness to her. He wasn't certain how this came out of the lingering sense of terror, but it did, in an upside-down, inside-out kind of way.

"O.K.," she said. "You don't need a warrant. Let's go to the hospital." She shivered. "Just let me get my jacket out of the car. O.K.?"

"Sure," said Russell.

He walked her up to the car while she reached into the backseat, where the jacket was. She reached in from the driver's side, over the floor so she could pick it up, and when she did, Kent Wilson said, "I didn't say anything, Becky. I didn't say a thing. You know that. Don't you?"

She just put on the her jacket and turned to Russell and said, "Let's go."

As Becky got into the passenger's side of Russell's car, Huntington arrested Kent Wilson. And when Wilson walked by Becky, he said, "I didn't say anything. I didn't say a word. Becky . . ." Then his voice trailed away as he was led back into the night, where Huntington had parked. In a minute, Huntington drove off up the road, the car accelerating into the distance.

The hospital was in town, about ten miles away, and as they went, Russell could see just the last bit of light in the south, almost gone. They got off the highway and Becky watched the buildings go by, not saying much, although at the end she said, "I want to say something."

"Sure," said Russell.

"One day you wake up and you're in the dark," she said. "It's that simple."

The emergency room entrance had doors that opened automatically, with an explosive huff, and inside Russell smelled the iodine and bandages and coffee. He sat in the waiting room while a doctor, a man of about sixty with a beard and gray hair, took Becky into an examination room. Russell tried to think of names. Maybe Clara. He had once seen it spelled Klara, which he thought was wonderful. Was there something like that for a boy? And then it occurred to him there was. Sandor. But he wasn't so sure about that. Then the clicking of the computer keys, that smell of iodine, the squeak of a wheeled bed disappeared as he recalled, for an instant, the blood dripping onto ice. Then he thought about Becky's vitality, and of the way the blue light had settled on them all. The doctor came out with a sealed Baggie in which there were twenty bags of heroin, which he passed over.

Becky didn't look at it, but she said to Russell, "Wait. Just wait. I want to talk to you. Can we talk in there?"

She pointed to the waiting room, where the TV was on.

"O.K.," he said. "Would you like some coffee?"

"That's all right," she said. "Let's sit down."

The television advertised auto parts, lawns, cars, and a CD you could buy to learn how to use your computer. Russell and Becky sat under the TV, in the irritating flicker of it. Russell looked around, mystified, knowing he had missed something.

"Kent didn't know that I heard him talking about things," she said. "But I did. That was the worst part. Feeling part of it."

She stood up and turned off the television.

"Of what?" said Russell.

She sat there with him, looking at him, in a way that was a mixture of a sexual invitation and something else, too, which was a variety of plea, although it would be hard to call it that precisely, since she was obviously shaking with rage, too. She looked at him for a while.

"Yeah," she said. "I've never been so lonely."

She reached into her pocket.

"Have you got a girlfriend?"

"Yes," he said.

"That's good," she said. "Here. This was in the back of Kent's car."

She held out her hand and dropped into his a small gold ring, which described an arc, in aureate light, as it fell from her hand to his. It seemed so light as to be almost nonexistent, as he tried to feel the weight of a shooting star. He thought it was a present, a piece of jewelry that he was supposed to give to his girlfriend, but then he looked at it more closely.

"Do you get it?" said Becky.

"Yes," he said. "I do."

"That woman who was found at the side of the road?" said Becky. "Kent did that. I heard him talking about it. That ring was hers." She put her hand to her hair. "See what I mean about the dark?" She swallowed and said, "All right, let's get out of here."

"Just wait for a minute," he said. He got up and went to the triage desk and asked for a Baggie with a sealable top, and when a nurse gave him one, he put the ring in it and ran his fingers along the bag's seal strip, pushing the bead of one side into the groove of the other.

Later, in the parking lot of the barracks, he stood on the cold asphalt and looked at the window of the cruiser, which was covered with ice. He thought about the ring, the way it had glowed in his hand, the light touch balancing the fear he had been trying to face. The best thing, he knew, was to accept fate, but this was hardest, since what was fate and what wasn't? He thought of fighting cocks he had seen once, years before, and the man who bred them and trained them had said the best were those that didn't respond to anything, not to the noise around them in the pit, not to the crowds or even the other birds: these were the ones that caused the greatest terror. Had he learned this? Well, there was a chance.

Now, in the parking lot of the barracks, he thought of that hotel room in Sheffield, the clothes that were hung in the closet, the worn bedspread, and his sense of the woman who had lived there evaporating like a volatile chemical. Well, at least she wouldn't disappear into that realm of the forgotten. That was something. There would have to be evidence on the ring, the smallest fleck of skin, of fluid, a cell of blood. But even if they didn't get something that way, they had Kent. He'd try to throw them some other friends, and then the friends would come up with more about Kent, when they found out that he had given them up. It wouldn't take long even without the tests.

Maybe, he thought, Zofia would still be sleeping when he came in and he could go upstairs and sit there for a while. Everything about the room, the slight rustling noise she made when she slept, the sour odor of sleep, the presence of the child that he could feel in the dim light, all of it delicate and certain. He would wait for a while, but then he would take off his clothes and lie down, too. It was Saturday, and later the two of them could go to the pool, where they could float in the hot sun, which streamed through the glass and smelled of chlorine. They could sit in the sauna, too, and feel the heat. When the rills of moisture ran down his back, she'd smile at him and say, "Tickles, doesn't it?"